Deep River
PROMISE

Jackie
Ashenden

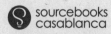

sourcebooks
casablanca

Published by Sourcebooks Casablanca, an imprint of Sourcebooks
P.O. Box 4410, Naperville, Illinois 60567-4410
(630) 961-3900
sourcebooks.com

Printed and bound in Canada.
MBP 10 9 8 7 6 5 4 3 2 1

To Billy Gumboot, the goat. First elected animal.
Don't let anyone tell you that eating other challengers'
ballots in order to win doesn't pay. ;-)

Chapter 1

DAMON FITZGERALD WOKE WITH AN EXCRUCIATING HEADACHE and the sense that he was being stabbed slowly but relentlessly through one eye. The headache was familiar—usually a sign he'd imbibed a little too heavily the night before—but the stabbing sensation not so much.

Cautiously, he raised one hand to touch the eye currently being stabbed only to encounter his own eyelid. So. Not being stabbed then. That was a relief.

He was still a little disoriented though, and his mouth felt like the bottom of a birdcage, so it took him some time to realize that the stabbing sensation was coming from the sunlight shining through a gap in the curtains and straight into one eye.

Sun. He hadn't seen the sun for at least three days, due to the weather being crap, which was strange for LA...

Which was when he remembered that he wasn't in LA. He wasn't even in Juneau, where he'd been for the last couple for weeks.

No, it was worse than that. Way worse.

He was in a room over the Happy Moose bar in a tiny, privately owned town called Deep River, smack bang in the middle of nowhere, Alaska. And he'd been stuck here for three days because the weather had been so bad he hadn't been able to fly out.

Damon lay there for a moment as the realization settled through him, trying to reorient himself, because he'd *definitely* over imbibed the night before and this hangover had teeth. Then with a sudden start, he remembered that sun was a good thing.

Sun meant the weather was better, which in turn meant he could get the hell out of here and back to LA.

Rolling off the bed, he dragged himself over to the french doors that led onto the room's tiny balcony, shoved them open, and stumbled out onto the balcony itself, just to check that the sun was real.

Sure enough, though it must have been early in the morning, the sun was actually shining, the sky a bright, almost painful blue, making the white caps of the mountains looming on all sides look extra white and extra sharp.

Ahead of him was the deep, rushing green of the river the town was named for. Deep River. It had been settled during the gold rush at the end of the nineteenth century by the West family, who'd bought the land Deep River sat on and leased out bits of it to anyone who wanted a place to call home.

A quirky little town, as Damon had spent the last three days finding out.

Deep River consisted of a ramshackle series of buildings clustered on the side of the river, connected by a boardwalk that projected out over the water and a narrow street that ran behind the buildings on the land side. They were old, those buildings, the paint on them faded, the wood cracked and worn through long exposure to rain and sun and snow. Not as picture-postcard as the ones in Ketchikan to the south, but there was definitely a certain vintage charm to them. Like a group of elderly ladies whose beauty was a little faded and careworn, they still possessed the ghost of their stunning youth, a certain timeless magic that tugged at the heartstrings.

Houses very similar to those at the water's edge were scattered up the hill behind the town, and there were a few more buildings along from the boardwalk, huddling against the hill's side.

A set of wooden steps led down from the boardwalk to a dock where several fishing boats and trawlers were tied up, but since it was comparatively empty, most of the boats must have gone up the river to the sea for a day working the nets.

Damon took a deep breath and then another, the fresh bite of the air settling his headache and cooling his skin, waking him up. He wasn't a small-town kind of guy, but there was something quite majestic about the mountains and the forested hills that loomed above him. Especially now the sun was shining.

He'd complained about the rain the night before to one of the locals, who'd then informed him of Deep River's average rainfall, which was some horrendous amount that sounded just wrong to someone from LA.

Still, it did explain the solid three-day downpour and made him feel lucky that it was a beautiful day now.

Movement below him caught his eye, and he glanced down at the boardwalk.

The kid was there again, skulking by the big wooden pole stuck in the boardwalk that had "Middle of Nowhere" painted down the side. A tall, gangly teenager dressed in jeans and a black hoodie.

He always seemed to be in Damon's vicinity, and if Damon didn't know any better, he'd say he was being followed.

Though surely it was a little too early in the morning for teenagers? Weren't they supposed to sleep past twelve or something?

The kid was looking straight at him, though he was too far away for Damon to see what expression was on his face. The fixed way the kid was staring was slightly unnerving.

A woman came suddenly into view. She had shoulder-length blond hair, and it was blowing around in the wind, a bright counterpoint to the plain jeans-and-T-shirt-combo she wore, a parka pulled on over the top, and she moved with great purpose to where the kid stood. She spoke to him a second and then turned her head, and Damon found himself under the intense scrutiny of two people.

His skin prickled, cool air moving across it. Moving everywhere across it.

Aw hell. He'd neglected to dress before stumbling out onto the balcony, and since he always slept naked… Yeah, no wonder both the woman and the kid were staring.

He might have been able to get away with that in LA—people did things on the Sunset Strip in broad daylight that would make a streetwalker blush—but here in small-town Alaska? Not so much.

Cursing, Damon made a reflexive grab for something to cover himself with. His fingers closed around a handful of curtain, pulling it over his groin as he backed hastily through the doors and into his room.

Great. Wonderful. Way to endear himself to the population.

Not that he particularly wanted to endear himself to the population, but standing around naked on a balcony in a tiny town wasn't exactly his finest hour.

Too many beers with Silas in the Moose the night before, that was the problem. And then on top of that, some home-brewed whisky with a kick on it like a mule.

Irritated both with himself and his hangover, Damon sat on the bed and rubbed at his temples, trying to massage away his headache.

He'd come to Deep River mainly to see where the hell his friend Silas Quinn had gotten to and yell at him about how he needed to come back to Juneau because Damon wanted to get rid of his share of Wild Alaska Aviation, the aviation company he'd gone into with Silas, Caleb, and another friend, Zeke, after they'd all gotten out of the military.

But it turned out that Silas wasn't coming back to Juneau, and it was difficult to yell at a man who was blissfully happy, having found love with the owner of the Happy Moose, his erstwhile best friend, Hope Dawson.

And most especially difficult when that happy man had spent three days plying him with whisky, towing him around Deep River, introducing him to all and sundry, and talking about tourism opportunities and investments and how much Damon's financial knowledge was needed.

Damon dropped his hands from his temples and sighed.

Silas had been very persuasive last night, both with his talk of tourism ventures and with the whisky, and if Damon hadn't had urgent responsibilities back in LA, he might have considered sticking around for a while. Caleb, Deep River's former owner, had left the whole place to Damon, Silas, and Zeke in his will, and although none of them had actually wanted to own an entire town, he couldn't exactly leave the rest of them in the lurch. Even if being tied down to Alaska was the last thing Damon needed right now.

Hell, if that had been the only issue, he'd have found someone else to take up the mantle of ownership by now. But that wasn't the only issue.

Deep River was sitting on a huge oil reserve, which had complicated things immeasurably, and not only had Silas decided to stay in his hometown, he'd also decided to take on responsibility for the town himself.

Damon could only commend his friend's decision, even if it wasn't something he'd ever decide for himself. He liked the wilderness—Alaska was a special place, with challenges that he found exciting—but he had responsibilities in the city he couldn't afford to leave hanging for too long.

As if on cue, his phone, which had been just about silent for the past three days due to Deep River's intermittent cell phone coverage, suddenly started vibrating on the nightstand beside the bed.

Damon reached for it immediately, concern twisting in his gut.

A whole lot of notifications on his screen popped up, texts and voicemails and emails that he'd missed. He scrolled through them until a name jumped out at him.

Rachel. The housekeeper he'd hired to come in and help his mother a couple of hours a day. She'd left him a voicemail.

Shit.

Damon called his voicemail immediately, cycling through the messages until he got to Rachel's.

"Damon? You told me to let you know if anything of concern happened with your mother, so I'm calling now to let you know that when I arrived this morning, she was watching her shows, but there was a pot on the stove, cooking away with nothing in it and the kitchen was full of smoke. Of course, Laura swore blind she hadn't put that pot on and that she had no idea who did, but I know she put it on herself and forgot about it. No harm done this time, but…well. Just thought you should know."

Damon's heart sank as the message ended.

Typical of his mother. She was tough and proud, always had been, and she hated getting sick. She hadn't wanted anyone to know about her diagnosis of early onset dementia, had tried to hide it even from him for months before he'd eventually found out.

Yet he'd found out all the same and not too long before the accident that had killed Caleb. And he knew immediately that it would spell the end of his time as a bush pilot. Selling his share of Wild Alaska and moving back to LA to take care of her was going to take time, though, so he'd hired Rachel in the interim. His mother hadn't liked having someone else in the house, but Damon had sold it to her as a way of keeping him off her back, and she'd reluctantly given in.

The decision to leave Alaska hadn't been a hard one. He'd enjoyed his time in the great outdoors, just like he'd enjoyed his time in bomb disposal in the army, but his mother had single-handedly brought him up, and she had no one else to look after her but him.

He had to leave. He just thought he'd have a bit more time up his sleeve with which to tie things up here. But from the sound of Rachel's message, that wasn't going to be the case.

His mom had left an empty pot on the stove to burn, and he'd been out of contact for three days. Hell. Rachel had been fine about keeping an eye on his mom for the past week while he brought to a close his life in Juneau, but he couldn't put that responsibility on her for too much longer. It wouldn't be fair.

It was Damon's responsibility and no one else's.

There was mercifully service, so he hit redial, calling Rachel back. There was no answer, so he left a message saying he'd be leaving Deep River today and that he'd be back in LA within the next couple of days with any luck.

Then he dropped the phone back down on the bed and headed for the shower.

Silas was going to be unhappy his powers of persuasion hadn't worked, but there wasn't much Damon could do about it. It didn't help, either, that he knew he'd been an asshole to Silas the past couple of weeks while Silas had been here and Damon had been back in Juneau. He'd hassled his friend unmercifully to come and deal with Wild Alaska, so he could get to his mom, and it had been an added complication that Damon hadn't been able to tell Silas why he had to return so urgently to LA. His mother had been very clear that she didn't want anyone to know about her condition, not even that she was sick, which meant he'd had to be deliberately vague about why he had to return.

Ah, well, there was nothing to be done about it. Silas would just have to suck it up.

Haven't you forgotten the other thing you were supposed to do here?

Damon shut his eyes as he turned the shower to cold and stepped beneath the icy spray of water.

No. He hadn't forgotten. But he was going to need a whole lot of coffee before he got into that.

———

"See what I mean?" Connor gestured emphatically at the Happy Moose's by now empty balcony. "Who stands around on a balcony without any clothes on?"

Astrid, current mayor of Deep River, surveyed her fifteen-year-old son dispassionately.

They were on the boardwalk by the Nowhere pole—one of the marketing ideas of the tourist information center's manager, Sandy Maclean—and the sun was shining and it was a beautiful blue-sky day, which was a rarity in late spring in Deep River.

She had a lot to do, and what she didn't really have time for was to listen to her son's current theories about Silas's friend. Not to mention that he shouldn't be skulking around outside the Moose, but catching Kevin Anderson's ferry in preparation for getting the school bus.

She unzipped her parka a little way, enjoying the sun's warmth. "You should be on your way to school, Con. Not skulking around spying on people."

"I wasn't spying," Connor said, incensed. "I was watching."

She shouldn't find her son's outrage amusing, but she did.

Connor had been very firmly convinced that Silas Quinn's friend, and one of the new owners of Deep River, was up to no good and had been determinedly following him around, watching him with all the suspicion of a Deep River native.

Which, considering he and Astrid were relative newcomers to the town, having only been here five years, was an impressive feat.

"You don't need to watch him," she said with some patience. "He's just a friend of Silas's." And an impressive specimen if what she'd observed of him on the balcony had been anything to go by. Not that she should have been looking herself, of course.

"Yeah, I know. But he's from the city." Connor scowled up at the balcony on the second story of the cheerfully rundown old building. "And city people are weird."

A fair comment and one Astrid couldn't argue with. But Damon Fitzgerald had been in Deep River for three days now, and while she hadn't met him directly, going by the comments from the people who had he didn't seem especially weird.

Ridiculously handsome, with an easy smile and a charming manner—according to April in the diner at least—but not, fundamentally, weird.

"Just because he's from the city doesn't mean you need to watch him," she said. "Come to think of it, why are you watching him, anyway? What on earth do you think he's going to do?"

"He could be an oilman," Connor said darkly.

Astrid sighed. Ever since the town had found out that oil had been discovered beneath it, it was all anyone ever talked about. Well, that and the new tourism ventures that the town had collectively decided to contemplate.

They'd had to do something to combat the oil company offering people money for their leases and/or drilling rights, something that would return power over the town to the people who lived there and that would enable them to build a more sustainable, reliable income that wasn't dependent on outsiders.

Still, everyone was on edge and even more suspicious than they normally were. Including, apparently, her son.

Ever since the news broke that Caleb West had died and the town had been given new owners, Connor had suddenly become very protective. He'd always been a caring kind of kid, but this protectiveness was new. As if he'd decided all at once that he was now the man he'd one day be and had taken responsibility for the whole of Deep River.

He would disappear on the weekends and sometimes in the evenings too, going God only knew where, and it wasn't until later that she'd discovered he'd either been helping April in her diner, or talking to Mal in Mal's Market, Deep River's general store. Or offering his help to some of the fishermen, or going around to check on various people in the town.

All admirable things for him to do in the normal scheme of things. At least, it would have been admirable if he'd told her why he was doing them. And he wouldn't. All she'd managed to get out of him was that there were things he needed to do and she shouldn't be concerned because he was taking care of it.

Of course, that had only made her even more concerned, since he'd never hidden things from her before. He'd always told her everything.

She had an inkling about the reasons for his new behavior, but since it was something she had no idea how to talk to him about, she hadn't broached it yet.

"He's not an oilman," she said firmly.

Connor's suspicious blue gaze turned on her. "How do you know?"

"Well, oilmen don't generally stand around stark-naked on balconies. Especially not if they want people to take them seriously."

"Maybe." Connor was clearly unconvinced. "But maybe that's what he wants you to think. That you can't take him seriously and you shouldn't be worried."

Astrid gave her son a long, narrow stare.

Connor flushed almost as red as the reddish hints in his dark-blond hair, looking cross and every bit the awkward teenager he actually was. "What?" He kicked at the wooden pole behind him with his heel. "If you say something embarrassing about shaving, I will never speak to you again."

"Just checking to see if you're wearing a tinfoil hat."

He shook his head, as if he were the responsible adult and she the sulky teenager. "Mom, come on. This is serious."

"What's serious is that if you don't get over the river right now, you're going to miss the bus and get another detention."

"Hey, that detention was unfair." Righteous anger burned in her son's gaze. "I was helping out in my community."

Which was just the kind of thing a teenager might say to cover up some minor misdemeanor. Except with Connor it wasn't actually a cover-up. That's what he *had* been doing. He'd been assisting Filthy Phil, the town eccentric, with building fences for the new wildlife sanctuary that the old ex-hunter was setting up on his property.

Difficult to argue that he shouldn't be helping out in his community. But it shouldn't come at the expense of his education.

"It's nearly the end of the school year, Con," Astrid said. "And then you'll have plenty of time to help out in your community. Now get to that bus stop before I have to ground you."

This time Connor rolled his eyes. "Not a great threat, Mom. I never go anywhere anyway."

"It is if you want to keep helping out in your community."

Connor raised a brow. "You're seriously going to stop me from helping people in need?"

Lord, give her strength. Connor would make a great lawyer one day if he ever decided to put to good use his talent for arguing his way out of any situation.

Holding on to her patience by a thread, Astrid jerked her head toward the dock where Kevin Anderson's ferry waited.

"Go on. Get."

"All right, all right. I'll do it." There was a martyred expression on his face. "For you, Mom."

Astrid tried not to smile as she watched him head toward the ferry, already taller than she was and already getting broad across the shoulders. A number of other kids were gathered on the ferry itself, waiting for him. The ferry would take them across the river, to where the main highway was, and from there, they'd catch the bus to school.

He already looks like his father.

Astrid's heart missed a beat as the morning sun caught the red highlights in Connor's hair.

Yes, she was horribly afraid that he did. And soon the rest of the town would see it too.

And they'd all start to wonder why Connor James looked so much like Caleb West.

Chapter 2

FEELING MARGINALLY MORE HUMAN AFTER HIS SHOWER, Damon dressed in a clean T-shirt and jeans, then headed downstairs to find Silas and hopefully some coffee.

The Happy Moose ranked up there with some of the weirder bars he'd been to. It had low ceilings with heavy, smoke-blackened beams, a big wooden bar, and ratty old tables and chairs scattered around the place. There was a pool table down one end and an old jukebox, which was pretty standard. But the thing that made the place really odd was the fact that the walls were covered with the taxidermied heads of different kinds of animals. According to Silas, hunters and trappers used to pay for their drinks with whatever they'd hunted or trapped back in the day, and the prizes were then displayed on the walls.

It made for a disturbing place to walk into early in the morning, when you were suffering from a major hangover and needing caffeine and met the glassy-eyed stares of dozens of different animals instead.

Especially when the place was empty.

Understandable given that if *he* had a hangover, then Silas was likely to have one too and was probably still holed up in bed with his girlfriend, Hope.

Damon sighed, sparing a wistful thought about his last hookup, a fabulous artist in Juneau who'd worked the same creative magic with her hands and mouth as she did with oil and canvas. Initially neither of them had wanted more than the odd weekend now and then, but then she'd decided she wanted a baby, and he wasn't up for anything that serious, so they'd parted amiably enough.

He'd liked her, though. In fact, he liked women a hell of a lot in general, and not just as bed partners. He liked the way they thought, the way they talked, their opinions and their feelings. Everything about them had always been endlessly fascinating to him, and they were pretty much his favorite people to be around.

Hope, owner of the Moose and Silas's girlfriend, had proved to be just the kind of woman he particularly liked: strong and snarky and took no bullshit. Giving back as good as she got. And he had to say, if he had a woman like Hope in his bed, he certainly wouldn't be downstairs at this ungodly hour looking for coffee.

But since he didn't, he'd have to find caffeine on his own.

Damon moved through the empty bar to the exit and pushed open the door, stepping out onto the boardwalk that ran in front of the little collection of buildings.

The morning sun felt like a benediction after all the rain, and the whole town shone and sparkled like it had just been newly washed. A sharp breeze that carried with it the last remains of winter helped with some of the cobwebs in his head, but for the rest, nothing but coffee would do.

Next door to the Moose was Deep River's general store. It was the only building that had a freshly painted sign, the name *Mal's Market* painted a bright and glaring pink. Beside the market was the tiny tourist information center, where the big Nowhere pole stood. The kid and the woman had long gone, but Sandy Maclean, who ran the center, had put out her postcard stands, the breeze ruffling the edges of the cards.

There was a hotel—the Gold Pan—next to the tourist center. It was just as ramshackle as all the other buildings, though some attempt at brightening the frontage had been made with a few flower baskets hanging from the awning overhead, along with a giant replica gold pan tacked to the wall beside the door.

Last in line was April's, the diner. It had big windows that gave a great view out over the boardwalk and the river and was famous for serving coffee so strong it took the lining of your throat out.

Given the epic level of Damon's headache, strong coffee was exactly what he needed, so that's where he headed.

There were only a few people in April's when he walked in; most of her usual customers—fishermen on their way to their trawlers—would have had their breakfasts a couple of hours earlier.

April was behind the counter—a small, elderly woman in a pink nineteen-fifties-style waitress uniform—and she gave Damon a big smile in greeting. "Well, if it isn't Mr. Handsome. A cup of your usual?"

Damon grinned.

His mother was from Texas and despite spending a good deal of her life in LA, she'd always been a great believer in a few old-fashioned values. She'd brought Damon up to believe the same, and so far he'd seen no reason to change that belief.

His mom's rules were simple: Be polite to the elderly. Don't cuss in front of women and kids. Never mistreat an animal. There had been times in his life when he hadn't exactly obeyed those rules, but he'd at least never mistreated an animal.

April had been suspicious of him initially, the way most Deep River folks had been, but over the past couple of days, Damon had worn her down with a combination of politeness, old-fashioned charm, and the ability to listen.

It helped that she clearly enjoyed a bit of flirting too.

"Morning, April," he said. "You look particularly fetching today."

"You're a charmer, mister." She flicked the dishcloth she was holding at him playfully, flushing with pleasure. It suited her, making her eyes look even bluer and bringing a youthful glow to her lined face. "And if you're wanting a free donut, then you're going the right way about it."

Damon was good with people, and it was a skill that had come in useful during his army days. He and Cal had been the ones who'd talked to the locals, reassuring them, making friends, and earning their trust. Mainly because Silas wasn't an effusive type and Zeke made Silas look like a motormouth.

However, though Damon had managed to win April over, her son, Jack, was another story.

Jack gave him a narrow stare from the kitchen area behind April.

Damon couldn't blame him; he respected a man who looked out for his mother.

He gave Jack a nod, then turned his attention back to April, because for all that Jack was protective of his mother, his mother also wasn't stupid. In fact, Damon wouldn't have been at all surprised if April had been an accomplished flirt back in the day, because it was a game she clearly knew and enjoyed.

"Perfect," Damon said. "Because you know if there's a donut in there, I'll be your slave for life."

April's blue eyes danced. "There's a name for men like you, you know."

He grinned. "And what's that?"

"A tease."

"And you love it."

"Oh, if I was thirty years younger…"

Damon leaned his hip against the counter. "Surely it must only be five."

"Right, that's it." She turned her head. "Two donuts please, Jack."

Behind her, Jack's suspicious gaze became even narrower. He lifted a couple of donuts out of the fryer, put them in a paper bag, and came over to the counter, dumping the bag down without a word.

April gave him a disapproving glance. "Manners, Jack."

"Not a problem," Damon said easily, heading this one off at the pass. "He's just looking out for you."

"Is that so, hmm?" April's disapproving stare became slightly less disapproving.

Her son merely looked annoyed. "Don't want you getting taken advantage of."

April rolled her eyes. "I'm seventy-five, Jack. And if a handsome young man wants to humor an old lady, then I'm not going to stop him, okay?"

"I'm not humoring you," Damon felt compelled to point out. "You're an interesting woman."

"There, you see?" April raised her brows at her son. "How am I supposed to resist that?"

Jack shook his head and went back to the kitchen area without another word.

"Don't you mind him," April said. "He's always grumpy in the mornings. Now, where's that coffee?"

As April bustled off to get the coffee, Damon tried not to think of the other thing that had been pressing in on him. The real reason he was here in Deep River, which hadn't been just to yell at Silas, though yelling at Silas had been a pleasant byproduct. It was an important reason and one he'd been trying to figure out what to do with for the past three days.

He still hadn't come to any definite conclusions, despite running a few different scenarios in his head. Not that he'd really put his mind to it; he'd been subconsciously counting on the fact that he had a bit more time to get something in place. Though now, after Rachel's call, that time was running out.

Come on, be honest. You didn't put your mind to it. You've been putting it off.

Yeah, that was fair enough. He *had* been putting it off, and for a whole host of reasons, none of which he wanted to think about right now. However, he couldn't put it off any longer. Today, he was going to have to do something and then he would leave for LA.

April came back with a takeout cup and began fussing about with fitting the lid on it.

Damon folded his arms. He'd need to be careful here. Caleb had been very clear about the need to keep this particular secret, and since the townspeople seemed to love gossip more than they loved just about anything else, he had to be circumspect.

Silas had introduced him to a fair number of people in the town while he'd been here, but he hadn't introduced him to Astrid, the town's mayor. She was very busy, Silas had said. Pinning her down could be difficult, Silas had said. Wait until she's in her office, Silas had said.

Except there hadn't been a moment when Astrid wasn't busy, able to be pinned down, or in her office, and Damon had begun to think that Silas was deliberately keeping him from meeting her.

An issue, when the reason he was in Deep River involved her. And her son.

And he was going to have to talk to her whether he wanted to or not.

"So, April," he said casually. "Where can I find Astrid James?"

April's gaze sharpened, the flirty girlishness falling away, Deep River suspicion written all over her face. "Astrid?" She pushed the cup across the counter to him. "What do you want with Astrid?"

It wasn't unexpected that April would want to know, and luckily he did have a reasonable excuse, largely based on yet something else Silas had been doing his best to convince him of for the last three days.

Deep River had decided to make up for lost oil income by starting up various tourist ventures, and Silas had asked Damon to stay for a while in order to give financial advice, since money was a talent of his. Damon hadn't minded—except now it seemed as if he wouldn't have the time for that either.

"Silas's been trying to get me to look over the new tourism ventures some people here are starting," he said, keeping it offhand. "Told me the mayor's the one I need to speak to about it."

April's gaze turned shrewd. "Oh?"

"I'm not bad with money, so I offered to check out the financials for free."

"Well, well, well. More than just a pretty face, huh?"

Damon grinned. "Hidden depths, you might say."

She laughed. "It's always the charming ones that are the most surprising. Well, the town could surely use someone with financial know-how looking over those ideas. Especially seeing as how most folk here keep their cash under a mattress and wouldn't know compound interest if it bit them in the butt."

"You do, I take it?"

April tapped the side of her nose. "Oh, I know my way around a greenback, don't you worry."

"Perhaps you should be the one looking them over," Damon said, amused.

"No, better for that kind of thing to come from a neutral party." April nodded sagely. "People get twitchy otherwise. Think you have ulterior motives, that kind of thing."

Yeah, he could see that happening in a small place like this.

"Fair enough. So, I need to speak with her this morning because I'm taking off this afternoon."

April's face fell. "You're leaving? But you only just got here."

Disappointing a lady was never Damon's favorite thing. Especially an elderly lady.

"My mom is in LA," he said, giving her a little bit of truth. His mom wouldn't mind that. "Have to get back to her."

April's expression softened. "Well, can't argue with that, though it's a real shame."

Damon became aware of a constriction in his chest, as if part of him agreed that yes, it was a shame. But it was only slight. He'd never planned on staying here for longer than a few days, and now he couldn't anyway.

"Don't worry," he said. "I'll come say goodbye before I go."

April waved a finger at him. "You'd better. Now, if you want to find Astrid, start with the mayor's office above the tourism information center. But if you want to catch her, you'd better get there quick because she doesn't stay for long."

———————————

Astrid sat behind her desk in the mayoral office and ticked off another task on her considerable to-do list with some satisfaction.

It had been a productive morning.

She'd chatted to Gwen, Harry the survivalist's hippie girlfriend, about the success of the hot yoga classes that they'd started up as a way of getting the townspeople more involved in fitness, and then Astrid had suggested running some nutrition classes at the community center in the evenings. Gwen was, as expected, very receptive and had also wanted to talk to Astrid about her eco-resort tourism idea, though Astrid had been a little too pressed for time to get into it in any detail.

She'd had to go and talk to Mal about the fruit and vegetable co-op she'd been trying to organize. Fresh produce was expensive in Deep River, mainly because the bulk of it was airfreighted in, and so Astrid had been looking at ways to get the prices down. There were a couple of growers in the area, including Clive Henderson who had a greenhouse, so she'd decided to put together a co-op, where people could pay a flat fee and get a box of fresh, in-season produce each week. Mal had agreed to organize and stock the boxes in the market, and because Mal was a good guy, he hadn't wanted a cut, since people generally bought things from him whenever they went in there anyway.

It undercut his own products, but he'd told Astrid that airfreighting was a pain in the butt and he'd prefer it if people bought locally.

With the co-op now certain to happen, Astrid needed to visit

Clive and a couple of the other growers and have a chat with them, which was going to take a bit of time.

Then she had to go over the ideas that people had been presenting for generating tourism in Deep River, not to mention go through the boxes that were waiting in the library for processing, since she also managed Deep River's library.

She was busy. Which was just the way she preferred it.

Astrid had never wanted to be mayor, but it was an old Deep River tradition to elect someone who didn't want the position. Sometimes, when the populace didn't like the selection of candidates, they voted for someone totally random in protest. Jesse, the goat, was mayor for a month before he was ousted in a cunning coup that involved a carrot and a very annoyed Kevin Anderson, who reluctantly took the position for the remainder of Jesse's term.

The idea behind electing reluctant mayors was that the mayor concerned would be so irritated at being mayor that they wouldn't do anything, leaving everyone alone to do their own thing, which was what the people of Deep River preferred.

Unfortunately, the opposite had happened with Astrid.

It was true that she never wanted to be mayor, but not only did she have a very strong sense of social responsibility, but she was also driven to make sure Deep River stayed a safe and stable environment for her and her son.

So, since she liked to be organized and in control of things, almost from the moment she was elected she embraced the role of mayor wholeheartedly, much to the initial annoyance of the town.

They'd mostly gotten over their annoyance—a fair few of them had even told her how much they'd been enjoying Gwen's hot yoga for example—and were very tolerant of the initiatives she'd begun.

She appreciated that. While she'd been in Deep River five years, that was still not enough time for some people, and they regarded her with misgiving as a veritable newcomer. Though she'd been working to change that.

The oil business had naturally thrown a wrench in most of her plans, but it wasn't anything she couldn't work through.

Certainly it was better working through that than it was thinking about certain other things that had been an issue since Caleb's death.

Things such as how Connor was his son and no one including Connor himself knew. Yes, that was a problem. She was going to have to deal with that soon because it wasn't fair that he didn't know.

She'd always been going to tell him; it was just the timing had never been right.

And now it never will be.

Guilt snaked through her, along with a thread of old grief, disturbing her concentration. But now wasn't the time to be thinking of that, so she put her pen down beside the big stack of papers on the desk and took a slow, deep breath.

There now, that was better. She was calm. Calm and in control.

A knock came on her office door.

Great, that was all she needed. Another distraction. Briefly she debated pretending not to be here.

The knock came again, louder this time.

She sighed. Ah well, she was distracted now anyway. Might as well see whoever it was. "Come in."

The door opened and a man sauntered in, and for a second, all Astrid could do was stare at him, every single thought vanishing from her head. Mainly because the last time she'd seen him, he'd been standing on a balcony stark-naked.

Not that she'd looked. At all. He'd been too far away to see properly as it was.

She definitely hadn't noticed that he'd been nothing but golden skin and hard, defined muscle, just like she definitely *didn't* notice how all that golden skin and muscle was now covered up by a sky-blue T-shirt that had *Wild Alaska Aviation* written on the front and a pair of worn-looking jeans sitting low on narrow hips.

Not that the clothing detracted at all from his looks. The color of his T-shirt only served to draw attention to the dense blue of his eyes and highlight strands of caramel and gold in his dark-brown hair. His jaw was almost impossibly square and strong, his nose straight as a blade, and his mouth...his mouth was sin incarnate, curling as it did in the corners, as if he had the most delicious secret to share but only if you were very lucky.

Astrid stared because he was magnificent and she couldn't help herself, and even though she'd caught glimpses of him around the town since he'd been here, those glimpses didn't do justice to the reality right in front of her.

Damon Fitzgerald was possibly the handsomest man Astrid had ever seen.

Then he smiled, slow and charming, and it was devastating. Helen of Troy might have launched a thousand ships with her face, but this man could launch a million more with that smile.

He came into the office, moving with an easy, loose, and oddly graceful stride, like he wasn't in any particular hurry but was nevertheless certain about where he was going and how he was going to get there.

"You Astrid James?" He came to a stop in front of her desk, his voice as deep and rich as she thought it would be.

He was ridiculously tall, his shoulders broad. She felt like she was sitting at the foot of a skyscraper.

"Yes," she said with what she hoped was some degree of cool, leaning back in her chair and giving him a dose of Deep River suspicion. It wouldn't hurt to let him know that though he might have charmed other people in the town, he wouldn't necessarily charm her. "And I know who you are already," she added. "You're the guy I saw standing bare-ass naked on the balcony of the Moose this morning."

Probably wasn't the greatest thing to have said, but he'd put her off balance a little and she didn't like it. Charming men, in her experience, were usually covering for something, and she didn't trust them as far as she could throw them.

He at least had the decency to look slightly shamefaced, raising a hand and rubbing at the back of his neck. "Yeah, sorry about that. Had a hangover and kind of forgot I wasn't wearing clothes."

Which would have mollified her if that smile hadn't still been playing around his mouth, making him look like a boy who knew he'd done something he should be ashamed of and yet was quite pleased about it all the same.

It was ridiculously charming.

"Uh-huh." Astrid did her best to resist that smile. "Well, my son was definitely not impressed."

"No, nor should he be." Damon's hand dropped from the back of his neck, his blue eyes sparking with something that made her breath catch. "Believe it or not, I actually do have some manners." He took a step toward the desk and leaned over it, extending his hand, his smile now slightly rueful. "If you could forget about me being the naked guy on the balcony, I'd appreciate it. I'm actually Damon Fitzgerald. Silas's friend."

Astrid eyed the extended hand. Some old and unfamiliar instinct was telling her that taking it would be a bad idea. However, not taking it would be rude, and she didn't want to be rude either.

Then again, if she didn't, she'd be admitting that he got to her, and since she didn't let men get to her these days, she leaned forward and took it.

His fingers were warm as they closed around hers, his grip strong but not painfully so. Her skin prickled with an unexpected heat and her heart beat oddly fast.

Oh, she did not want that. Not at all.

She pulled her hand away, covering the abruptness of the motion by gesturing at the scuffed wooden chair that sat on the other side of her desk. "Take a seat, Mr. Fitzgerald," she said, ignoring her stupid physical reaction. "Tell me what I can do for you."

His blue gaze regarded her speculatively for another moment. Then he reached for the chair, pulled it back, and sat with an easy, lazy grace. He leaned back, long, powerful legs stretched out in front of him, and folded his arms across his broad chest.

He somehow reminded her of an old-time cowboy, the ones that ambled and moseyed, unhurried and measured, all slow smiles and syrupy drawls. In no rush. Patient.

"Call me Damon," he said in that deep, rich voice. "And as to what you can for me…well, I'm here to talk about Connor."

Chapter 3

ASTRID JAMES'S COOL GRAY EYES WIDENED IN SURPRISE, which he was expecting. And then just as quickly narrowed into thin slits of quartz. Which he was also expecting.

A mother was never going to simply take some stranger wandering into her office and asking her about her son at face value. In fact, he'd be surprised if she wasn't deeply suspicious on some level and most especially when she'd seen that stranger with his junk flapping in the breeze barely an hour before.

No, it wasn't Astrid's suspicion that bothered him.

It was the fact that she was gorgeous that did.

She was built delicate, with the kind of precise, elegant features that belonged in elegant society, rather than a tiny backwater like Deep River. Her skin was creamy, her hair pale gold, and her eyes were the color of mountain mist; she looked like she'd been carved from sharp, clear ice. A snow queen…

But no, she wasn't a snow queen. Not when the warmth from her hand was lingering against his palm like he'd brushed it over a living flame.

He ignored it. She might be pretty, but he wasn't here for a pickup. He was here to talk to her about her son and then get back to LA. ASAP.

"What about Connor?" The look of cool welcome she'd given him just before had disappeared to be replaced by something much more wary.

Damon allowed his smile to fade, since it was clear she wasn't going to be moved by it.

A superstitious man might have said it was fate that the pretty blond he'd seen from the Moose's balcony had turned out to be

Astrid and that the kid who'd been following him around the past couple of days was her son, Connor.

But Damon was not a superstitious man. And there was a reason Connor might have been following him around.

He was Caleb West's son after all.

Damon regarded the woman sitting on the other side of the desk steadily.

How to go about this? How to break it to her that he was here to fulfill Caleb's last wish, to make sure that the son he'd sired fifteen years earlier, the son who no one else in the world knew about except the boy's mother and Damon, was "looked after"?

There were so many things to consider. Did she mourn Caleb's death? It had only happened a few weeks ago, and hell, he, Zeke, and Silas were still dealing with his loss, let alone the woman who'd had his kid. And things were made even more tricky by the fact that no one knew Cal even had a kid, or that said kid was living in Deep River. Not even Cal's sister, Morgan, knew.

The easiest thing would have been to ignore the letter the lawyer had handed to him as the will reading had ended and Silas and Morgan had walked out. The letter was for Damon only, the lawyer had said. Mr. West was most clear that no one else should know about it.

Already Damon had had a suspicion about what was in that letter, and he'd been proved right. *Look after my boy*, Caleb had instructed him. *See to his future.*

Being responsible for another child was pretty much the last thing on earth Damon wanted, and walking away would have been a hell of a lot easier. But he'd never walk away from a friend, especially one who'd fought beside him.

He still wasn't sure how he was going to "look out" for Connor, not when he had to be back in LA, but maybe he and Astrid could come to some kind of arrangement.

She was regarding him with that same cool look, yet a subtle tension had gathered around her. Those exquisitely carved fea-tures had hardened, her gray eyes solidifying from mist into solid steel. Her irises had a rim of dark charcoal and a dark charcoal center too, the color highlighted by the silver-gold of her lashes. She wore a plain white T-shirt, which somehow enhanced her snow-queen vibe.

"Okay," Damon said at last. "Here's the deal. Personally, I don't want anything to do with your son. But you should know I have an obligation to fulfill."

A whole host of emotions flickered over the mayor's face, but they were gone so fast, Damon couldn't tell what they were.

She leaned back in her old, creaky wooden chair. "A personal obligation," she echoed. "Don't tell me. You're here on behalf of Caleb."

Smart woman. But then it wasn't all that difficult to work out. He was one of Cal's buddies and now Cal was dead; it was logical for her to assume some provision had been made for his son.

"I didn't do the right thing, Damon," Cal had said that night when they were both on watch, the moonlight bright over the rocky desert that surrounded them. *"When Astrid got pregnant, I told her I didn't want anything to do with a kid."* His friend's face had been shadowed, his voice quiet. *"I know I was only seventeen, but it was a cowardly thing to do, and I regretted it. So when she called me out of the blue, wanting a place to stay, I couldn't say no. She's in Deep River with him now, and I've spent the last couple of years trying to make it up to them."*

The memory was an uncomfortable one, bringing with it other things that Damon didn't want to remember, so he pushed it away, concentrating instead on the woman sitting behind the desk.

"I am," he said simply, because in the end, simple was best. "I got a letter after Cal died. It went just to me, none of the other guys know about it. And all it said was that I had to make sure Connor was looked after and his future was taken care of. So that's why I'm here."

Astrid was silent, her expression unreadable.

Abruptly, she shoved back the chair with a screech and stood up, moving over to the window that looked out over the board-walk and the river. She stood there with her back to him, the sun-light falling over her blond hair, turning it brilliant gold. Tension rolled off her in waves, as well as a bristly kind of energy. Like a cat sensing a threat to its territory and raising its fur.

He had the oddest urge to lift his hand and stroke her to soothe her.

Hell, why had Cal chosen him to handle this? Silas would have been the better choice. Silas was a man of few words, but he knew how to do serious. Plus, he was also from Deep River and knew how the place worked. He knew Astrid too.

You know why Cal chose you. Because you were once a father.

Once. Not now.

The dull ache that he always felt when he remembered Ella shifted behind his breastbone, but he ignored it. He didn't have time for old memories.

"I'm sorry," he said into the silence. "I know this is a—"

"Shock?" she finished for him without turning around. "Yes, you could say that."

Damon studied her tense back. Cal hadn't offered much in the way of information about her, only that she'd lived in Ketchikan and they'd both gone to the same high school, getting together at a party when they'd both been seventeen. He'd refused to take responsibility for the pregnancy, telling not a single soul about it, hiding it from everyone, including his parents. Then years later Astrid had contacted him again in dire straits and he'd given her and Connor a place to stay. Cal hadn't mentioned what those dire straits were, only that Astrid had never forgiven him for abandon-ing her and his son. Which meant that trying to make up for his mistake had been difficult.

Given her reaction just now, Damon had a suspicion that it was still going to be difficult and he hoped it wouldn't end up becoming a problem. He really couldn't stay here any longer.

Come on, what did you think was going to happen? Did you really think this would be easy? You should have tackled this days ago.

His jaw tightened. Yeah, he should have, but he hadn't. And actually, what he'd hoped was that Astrid would smile, tell him she and Connor were fine, and send him on his way. That would have been the best outcome all around, especially given what was happening with his mom.

Except it didn't look like that would be the case.

He stayed silent, giving her a couple of moments to process what he'd said and trying to quell his own impatience. To pass the time, he took a look around the cluttered little office, noting the ramshackle wooden bookcases pushed up against the walls and the old-fashioned metal filing cabinets, the photos of previous mayors on the walls. One of them appeared to be a goat. There were also a few Alaska tourism posters featuring the usual moose, bears, mountains, whales, and the odd dog sled. One was slightly different. It looked hand drawn and encouraged people to "find love in the middle of nowhere!"

Everything was very, very tidy. Even the pen discarded on the desktop was straight.

Was that her? Did she like to keep things neat? She certainly seemed to be the kind of cool, precise woman who liked to make sure everything was in its place.

Why do you care what she's like?

He didn't care. He was simply passing the time.

"Why do you know about Connor?" she asked eventually, still looking out the window. "I mean, why did Cal tell you about him?"

A fair question. But he wasn't going to get into details, so all he said was, "He told me while we were on deployment, just before a big operation, and I think it was just in case he didn't come back."

She didn't reply, staying very still, her attention remaining on the river outside.

Then suddenly, as if a switch had been flicked, the prickly aura around her vanished, the tension bleeding out of her posture. She looked at him, her pretty face composed, gray eyes cool mist once more. "Well, it's nice that he thought of me and Connor, but help isn't necessary. We're doing just fine on our own. My son's future is well taken care of, thank you very much."

It was exactly what Damon had hoped she'd say and yet... something tugged at him. The smallest thread. The tiniest of doubts. He wasn't sure where it came from; whether it had been her moment of prickliness or something more, he didn't know. And he really should have gotten up, thanked her, and left.

But he didn't.

"Your son's been following me around," he said. "You know that, right?"

Astrid let out a breath and turned from the window, leaning her elbows on the back of her chair. "Yes, I'm aware. He thinks you're up to no good."

The posture pulled the fabric of her T-shirt tight across the soft curves of her breasts, making Damon suddenly more aware of them than he wanted to be.

Damn. And here was an even better reason for him to get out of Deep River: he did *not* want to be attracted to the mayor.

"Why would he think that?" Damon asked instead, concentrating very hard on her face.

"I have absolutely no idea. He told me this morning that he thought you might be an oilman."

A thread of reluctant amusement wound through Damon. "An oilman? Seriously?" He grinned, almost enjoying the thought of some kid thinking he was a hard-bitten oil executive. "Do I look like an oilman?"

"To be honest, no." She gave him a leisurely survey. "You look like..." Her gaze caught his and she trailed off, and for a second, something electric hovered in the space between them.

Her cheeks went pink.

Uh-oh.

He knew that look, just as he knew that electricity. It was familiar. Intimate. And most of the time, very welcome.

Except not right now. Out of all the women in the entire world to have physical chemistry with, the last woman he wanted to feel that way about was the woman whose child he was supposed to be looking out for. That had complicated written all over it, and Damon didn't do complicated anymore.

Then again, because he was a man who liked women, and she was a very fine-looking woman, he couldn't resist holding her gaze a little longer than he should have. "I look like what?"

A soft and pretty deep-rose color swept over her pale skin, but she didn't look away. Her gray eyes were almost crystalline, charcoal and silver and quartz. Beautiful eyes…

"You look like a city boy out of his depth." Her voice was still cool, the slight hint of challenge edging it.

And he could feel something inside him respond, the part of him that loved a challenge, that liked risk, the competitor looking for the next opponent.

Yeah, time for him to leave.

He grinned and pushed himself out of the chair, breaking the tension. "In that case, it's time for this city boy to get back to his city."

Surprise rippled across her face. "So, what? That's it? You're not even going to insist?"

He raised an eyebrow. "Why would you think I'd insist?"

"You seem like the type of man who would." She'd straightened up, folding her arms, the remains of her blush still staining her cheeks.

"Sometimes," he agreed. "But not today."

"But…" She stopped, clearly nonplussed.

And he had to admit to liking that just a little bit. She seemed so very cool and in control, and he did enjoy ruffling a woman.

Damon shoved his hands in his pockets. "What? Or did you want my help after all?"

"No," she said far too quickly. "No, we definitely don't."

"Good." He gave her one last smile, slightly regretful since if things had been different, he might have asked for her number. "I'll see myself out."

He was almost to the door when she said suddenly, "One more thing."

He paused but didn't turn back. "Yes?"

"Please don't tell anyone who Connor's father is."

Interesting. Cal hadn't wanted anyone to know either.

For a second, Damon wondered why that was, and then realized that since he was leaving, it wouldn't be his problem.

"Sure," he said easily. "Your secret's safe with me."

———————

Astrid watched from the window as Damon Fitzgerald stepped out of the building and onto the boardwalk below, moving with that fluid, athletic grace to the door of the Moose, then disappearing back inside.

Almost as soon as the door banged closed behind him, a shadow detached itself from the Nowhere pole and moved over to one of the Moose's windows. Connor put a hand over his eyes as he peered through the glass.

Astrid muttered a curse. She could have sworn Connor had gotten on the damn ferry. What on earth was he doing? After he'd promised her that he'd go to school! The idiot. Didn't he know she could see him from here? Clearly he either didn't, or he didn't care. She was thinking the latter.

Annoyance rippled through her, not helped by the interaction she'd just had with Damon.

Thank God, he'd taken himself off. Almost as soon as he'd

gone, all the air in the room that had escaped when he'd entered it had rushed back in and she'd been able to breathe again.

Shock, of course. Nothing to do with the moment when his gaze had held hers and something hot had sparked to life in those sky-blue depths. And she'd felt herself blush in a way she hadn't blushed in a very long time.

No, absolutely not.

It was shock that after so many years of secrecy, someone else knew who Connor's father was.

You're not entirely alone with it, then.

Astrid ignored the thought. It didn't matter that she was alone with it. That's what she'd wanted because she couldn't tell everyone when she hadn't even told her son, after all. And as to that, well…

She'd thought she'd have more time. She hadn't thought Caleb would be killed in a plane crash. No one had seen that coming, least of all her, so she couldn't blame herself for that.

But the fact that her boy hadn't even had the opportunity to get to know the father he'd now lost, the father he hadn't even known he'd had, yes, that was absolutely her fault.

Turning from the window, she moved over to the desk and picked up her pen, glancing down at her to-do list. But then she put the pen down again.

No. Busy was good and it was a nice distraction, but what she should be doing was going down and taking her recalcitrant son by the scruff and giving him a good lesson in the consequences of lying to her, since it was too late to send him to school. The high school was an hour and a half away by bus, and now that he'd missed that bus, there wasn't another. She didn't have a car either, so she couldn't take him. And he knew it, the little ass.

The problem with Connor was that there wasn't much she could use in the way of consequences. Forbid him to help people? That wouldn't work, and it would only end up rebounding on the people who liked him helping. There was forbidding him internet time, but since—unlike seemingly every teenager on the planet—he didn't spend much time online, that wasn't likely to work either. Not helped by the fact that Deep River's internet connection was patchy at best, nonexistent at worst.

She reached down and straightened the pen, then adjusted the paper stack of people's various ideas for tourism ventures for Deep River.

Well, whatever. She needed to go down and give him a piece of her mind.

Astrid strode out of the mayor's office and went downstairs, going through the little hall that led out onto the boardwalk. The door through to the tourist information center stood open as she went past, and Sandy Maclean, who ran it, lifted a hand in greeting from behind the counter, peering from over the tops of her very round glasses.

Astrid waved a hand in return but didn't pause. Sandy was almost as bad as April in the diner when it came to gossip, and she wasn't about to give her any ammunition. Instead she stepped outside and headed to the Moose a couple of doors down.

Connor hadn't noticed her approach, still pressed up against one of the windows, trying to see inside through the dim glass.

"Hey," Astrid said coolly as she stopped right behind him. "Weren't you supposed to get on the ferry? At least that's what I thought you were doing. Or did you somehow fail to find Kevin's boat that you've successfully managed to find every day for the past three years?"

Her son started guiltily, then turned around to face her. The knuckles of his hand clutching the strap of the backpack he had slung over one shoulder whitened, but his bright-blue gaze was very direct. He didn't look one whit ashamed of being caught.

"Mom, look," he said very seriously. "I'm sorry. Yeah, I know I lied to you about going to school. But you weren't going to let me stay, and someone needs to keep an eye on that guy." He jerked his thumb in the direction of the Moose. "Everyone else has jobs to go do, but I don't. And I don't mind sticking around to make sure everything's okay."

Seriously? He'd stayed home because of Damon? This had gone too far.

"You do have a job, Con," she said flatly. "School is your job, and I have a legal obligation to make sure you go. Do you really want me to get Morgan to make you go?"

Morgan West, Caleb's sister, was Deep River's state trooper rural equivalent, a village public safety officer. Which meant she was the law in these parts.

"Morgan isn't here," Connor pointed out, not without some smugness. "She's still on that training course."

That was, sadly, true.

Sandy was fussing around ostentatiously with the postcard stand just outside the information center, but Astrid knew she was only out here to see what the kerfuffle was about.

Connor noticed too. "Oh, I think Ms. Maclean needs some help with—"

"No," Astrid interrupted, feeling like she needed to lay down the law in some way. "No more help today. You're officially grounded. Which means you need to go home and stay there."

Connor's chin came up at a belligerent angle. "Mom, really? Come on. I'm just trying to look out for the town."

"Yeah, and I get that. But I don't want you skipping school. That's a hard no, Con."

"School isn't that important. It's nearly done for the year anyway. All the things I need to learn, I can learn from Mal. Or Mr. Anderson. Or Joe at the—"

"You are not learning from Joe!" Astrid interrupted, horrified.

Joe was an old trapper who spent most of his time with his friend Lloyd getting drunk in the Moose and fighting, and she most definitely did not want Connor learning anything from him.

"Mom, I know you're worried." Connor hitched his backpack higher at the same time as he made a calming motion with his free hand. "But you don't need to be. I'll be fine. I'll keep an eye on that guy so that—"

"What guy?" a deep male voice said from the doorway of the Moose.

Astrid's stomach dropped as both she and Connor turned toward the doorway.

Sure enough, Damon Fitzgerald, tall and ridiculously gorgeous, the strap of a duffel bag slung over one shoulder, was standing there staring at them.

Connor flushed scarlet. Then he straightened up, squared his shoulders, and much to Astrid's annoyance, he stepped in front of her, putting himself between her and Damon.

"You," Connor said, scowling. "I'm keeping an eye on you."

Chapter 4

DAMON HAD TO HAND IT TO THE KID; HE LOOKED FEROCIOUS standing there protectively in front of his mother. He had Cal's height and was starting to get his breadth too, not to mention Cal's mile-wide streak of pure mule.

But the cool challenge in his bright-blue eyes was all Astrid.

Damon had just been saying his goodbyes to Silas and taking his friend's disappointment that he wasn't staying as best he could when they'd been interrupted by raised voices from outside the Moose. Damon, who didn't get mad easily, had found himself on edge and irritated, so he'd slammed open the Moose's door to find out just who the hell was interrupting his goodbye to his friend.

A family argument between the kid and his mother, apparently.

And now they'd turned on him. Or at least Connor had.

He was staring hard at Damon, all squared up and ready to fight.

Unfortunately for the kid, Damon didn't fight teenage boys.

"Oh?" He kept his tone very casual. "And why is that?"

"Connor," Astrid said warningly from behind her son.

"It's okay, Mom." Connor didn't take his eyes off Damon. "I got this."

Damon nearly smiled, reminded of himself at that age. He'd been a little bit like Connor: protective of his mother, wanting to be taken seriously—desperate to be a man, take on a man's responsibilities.

But smiling would have been the wrong thing to do; the kid would think he was being laughed at and that would only make the situation worse.

Damon held the boy's gaze. "I'm not here to cause trouble."

"Is that right?" Connor's chin rose. "How do we know that?"

"Connor," Astrid repeated, sounding exasperated. She tried to step sideways, but Connor angled his body so he was in front of her again.

Yeah, he really was protective. A young wolf defending his turf. Damon could only respect that.

"You've got my word," he said neutrally. "And if you won't take mine, you can take Silas's."

Connor's jaw worked as if he were chewing something over. He had his backpack strap in a white-knuckled grip, while his other hand was in his pocket. Mirroring Damon's stance—probably unconsciously.

There was something a little bit hungry about the way he stared at Damon. A little bit desperate. As if Damon had something he really wanted but didn't know how to ask for.

"Are you an oilman?" Connor demanded all of a sudden. "You better not lie to me."

Luckily, Astrid had mentioned earlier her son's suspicions, or else Damon might have lost the battle against a smile. Not that he was laughing at the boy, definitely not. It was just that the poor kid must not know what the hell an oilman looked like if he thought Damon was one.

Fighting amusement, Damon didn't move and he didn't smile. Only held the boy's belligerent blue gaze, not challenging him but not backing down either. It was a fine line, but he'd learned how to walk it while on deployment with trigger-happy, nervous villagers.

"No," he said. "I'm not an oilman. I'm a bush pilot. Or at least I was one. I'm not now. I'm heading back to LA. Right now, in fact."

Instantly, the belligerent look disappeared off Connor's face to be replaced by shock. "What?"

Just for a second, he looked very young and a little lost, and the ache behind Damon's breastbone, the one that never went away, shifted.

Weird. He hadn't felt that in response to anyone, let alone a kid, not for years. Not since Ella had died. It was almost as if he cared, which was strange since he didn't care much about anything except his mom these days. His life was all about drifting along on the surface of things, never delving too deeply, and that's how he preferred it.

Clearly the sensation was an aberration.

Then Astrid, who hadn't seen the change of expression on her son's face, muttered, "Connor, for God's sake. Don't be so rude."

The lost look slid away abruptly, as if it had never been.

"I'm not being rude, Mom," Connor said, continuing to glare darkly at Damon. "Just looking out for Deep River and making sure strangers are on the level."

Interesting. It was clear that Connor wanted something from him—why else would he be following Damon around?—but he didn't know how to get it, and it was also clear that he didn't want his mother to know that he wanted it.

So what was it? Damon was a stranger, yet for some reason, Connor had fixated on him.

There could be a reason for that.

Well, yeah. Damon was the only stranger in Deep River, so it wasn't any wonder. Or...perhaps it was because Damon had a connection to Cal. Sure, Silas also had that connection, but then Silas was a known quantity. And talking to Silas about Cal would reveal Cal's secret...

No one here knew who Connor's father was, and Astrid had told him she wanted to keep it that way. But...did the kid know?

Astrid, losing patience and clearly annoyed, stepped out of the way of her son. "Get up to the house, Connor James," she said flatly. "You and I need to have a little chat about manners."

Connor hid his feelings well, but Damon could see the flickers of desperation in the boy's eyes. "But, Mom..." he began.

"It's not a problem," Damon said before he could stop himself, instinctively responding to the look on Connor's face. "He's just making sure his people are okay."

Astrid stared at him in surprise, though why she should be surprised he had no idea. Did she really think he'd turn this into an issue? Connor was fifteen and still figuring out what it meant to be a man, while Damon was thirty-two and already knew what being a man meant.

Being a man did *not* mean picking a fight with a kid.

Connor glowered even harder, which Damon understood. He'd probably been hoping for a fight and Damon had just denied him one.

Conscious that Sandy at the tourist information bureau was still fussing around with postcard stands and glancing their way, Damon decided it was time to draw this little scene to a close.

"Want to see me to the city limits?" He looked at Connor. "Make sure I'm gone?"

Didn't you not want to get into anything complicated?

He wasn't getting into anything complicated. All he was going to do was give the kid a chance to say his piece to Damon without his mother around, which he clearly wanted to do.

Connor grasped the lifeline Damon had extended like it was the last life preserver on the *Titanic*. "Yeah," he said, his belligerence now more slightly forced, as if he was playing it up for his mother's benefit. "I think I'll do that."

Astrid frowned at her son, then glanced back at Damon, as if she'd sensed something was going on between them but didn't know what to make of it.

"It's all right, Ms. Mayor." Damon kept his voice casual. "If he wants to see me off the premises, I'm okay with it."

Astrid opened her mouth, shut it again. There was something up with her, Damon could sense it. Her misty-gray eyes had sharpened into steel again, and that bristly energy was sparking around her once more.

Was it her son's behavior? Or was it something else?

"A word, Mr. Fitzgerald," she said crisply.

It was obvious she meant without Connor hanging around.

Damon glanced at the teenager. "Can I have a minute with your mother?"

Astrid rolled her eyes, clearly irritated. "Really?"

But Connor, after a second's obvious shock at being asked, glanced at Astrid, then back at Damon. The look he gave Damon was very much of the *touch a hair on her head and I'll kill you* variety. "Yes, you may," he said magnanimously.

Damon nodded, acknowledging and accepting the unspoken threat.

Connor gave him one last narrow look, then turned and strode off over the boardwalk toward the stairs that led to the dock.

"How nice that someone around here has some authority," Astrid said dryly.

The expression on her precise, lovely features was calm, but that bristly energy snapped and crackled around her. She was agitated, that much was obvious.

"What's up?" He gave her a reassuring smile. "I'm really not bothered about Connor's manners if that's what you're worried about."

"That's not what I'm worried about." She glanced in the direction of the dock, where her son had just gone down the steps, then looked back at Damon. Something glittered in her gray eyes that seemed awfully like a plea. "He doesn't know. He doesn't know about…" She stopped and glanced around again, as if looking for eavesdroppers. "His father."

Well, that cleared up a few questions, even if it generated a few more. Though they were questions he wouldn't be finding answers to, since he'd be leaving. In about half an hour tops.

"Noted." He hitched his bag higher on his shoulder. "And don't worry, I won't mention a word of it to him."

Astrid's gray gaze was unreadable. "Why are you getting him to follow you?"

"Because it seems like he needs to say something, so I might as well give him a chance to say it."

"Why?" The question sounded a little sharp. "What does it matter to you?"

Damon eyed her in silence for a moment. She sure was protective on her boy's behalf. Not unexpected given that she was his mother, but there was something else there that he couldn't put his finger on. An edge to it that seemed slightly out of proportion.

You can't get interested. You're leaving, remember?

Yeah, he was.

"Because Cal asked me to check on him," Damon said mildly. "You said you didn't need my help, and fair enough. But I think I need to at least give him an opportunity to speak to me if he wants to. Got to at least give me an effort when it's an old friend's last wish, right?"

Her gaze was very direct and very cool as she studied him, though what she was looking for he had no idea. But he didn't miss the crease that appeared between her fair brows. Perhaps she didn't know what she was looking for either.

"Okay," she said at last. "But please don't say anything to him. I…" She stopped again, her mouth compressing as if to hold something back.

"You what?"

But Astrid only shook her head. "It doesn't matter. Just…" She waved a hand. "Be careful with him. He's a good kid."

Of course he'd be careful with him. And he found himself wanting to hear what she'd been going to say. Except he didn't know her well enough to push, and besides, he was leaving. Now.

"I will," he said. "Don't worry."

She didn't say anything, only nodded, turning her gaze back on her son who was lounging on the dock. His posture was casual, but he was looking steadily Damon's way, keeping a beady eye on him.

The bristly tension in her had eased, but he could still feel it radiating from her. She was worried for her son.

It made him want to reassure her—he didn't like it when a woman was distressed—but he wasn't sure what to say since he didn't know what she was worried about in the first place.

So all he said was, "Take care of yourself, Ms. Mayor. Like I said, don't worry. I'll try not to corrupt him with my shocking city ways."

She gave him a sideways glance. "You mean like standing naked on a balcony?" Whatever worry had been in her eyes before had gone. Now, he caught the very distinct glitter of a tease, not to mention a hint of challenge.

Interest stirred inside him yet again. He did like a challenging woman.

Don't be a fool. It's time to go.

Yeah, it really was.

He smiled. "Something like that."

Then he walked away, heading over the boardwalk to the stairs, his boots ringing on the worn wooden boards. And he didn't feel the slightest pang of regret at an opportunity missed. Not at all.

He went down the stairs to the dock and walked along it toward where Connor stood. The boy watched him approach, determined not to take his eyes off him even for a second.

"So," Damon said casually as he came closer to the kid. "Want to show me how people in this town get over the river?"

Connor eyed him warily. "The ferry." He jerked his head toward the battered red fishing boat that was moored at the end of the dock. "But you already know that."

Didn't miss a trick, did he?

"Sure," Damon said. "Just looking for an icebreaker."

Connor's blue eyes narrowed. "I'm not talking to you. All I'm doing is making sure you leave Deep River without trying any-thing funny."

Damon lifted a shoulder, as if he didn't care one way or the other. "You don't have to talk to me if you don't want to. No one's forcing you."

Keeping things easy and casual was probably going to be the best approach, walking that line between not being a threat and yet not being a pushover either—the immovable object to the unstoppable force. He was good at that.

Except for that one time the unstoppable force had run right over the top of him, and no amount of being immovable had stopped it from crushing him flat.

Yeah, he wasn't going to think of that time.

Damon turned toward the ferry. "Come on, then." He didn't wait, heading on down the dock, hearing the boy's footsteps clat-tering after him.

The guy who handled the ferry crossing—Kevin Anderson, a big man, burly and laconic, whom Damon had had a long chat with in the Moose a night or two ago—gave Damon a nod and grunted when Damon told him he wanted to go across.

The man couldn't have been called effusive by any stretch, but Damon noticed the pointed look he gave Connor as the kid climbed on board after Damon.

"Bit late for the bus, Connor," Kevin commented. "Your mom know you skipped school?"

"Yeah." Connor didn't look away from the other man's stare. "Don't worry, she grounded me. But I'm just making sure this guy"—he nodded at Damon—"gets out of Deep River okay."

"Huh." Kevin glanced at Damon too. "Is that right?"

"I thought it would be best," Damon replied, meeting Anderson's suspicious stare with his own. Letting the other guy know that he had it in hand.

"We can't be too careful of strangers," Connor said. "Mom said it was okay. Not that I need her permission," he added quickly. "I just want to protect our town."

A puzzled look crossed Anderson's face, but he didn't question it, only nodded. "Sure, sure. Best you keep an eye on him, then."

"Oh, don't you worry," Connor assured him. "I will."

Damon hid a smile and turned to go stand in the prow and wait.

The boat turned toward the far side and began to motor across, and sure enough, a couple of seconds later, he felt Connor's presence at his side, along with a good healthy dose of eau de sweaty teenage boy.

"I'm not going to jump in and swim back." Damon gazed at the far bank where the road was and the Deep River airstrip, the mountains towering beyond. "If that's what you're worried about."

Connor snorted as if that was the most ridiculous thing he'd ever heard. "As if."

A silence fell and Damon let it sit there a moment, the only sounds the rumble of the ferry's motor, the rush of the river, and the occasional cry of the gulls.

Then he asked, "Want to tell me what's got you all riled up?"

"No."

"Why not?"

"Cos it's none of your business, that's why."

"Considering it's me you're pissed with, that makes it very much my business. I'm also not here to do anything to the town and I think you know that."

"I don't know that." Connor began kicking the side of the boat with one scuffed sneaker. "All I know about you is that you turned up randomly, suddenly owning the whole town."

Ah, so that was part of the issue, was it?

"If it helps, I don't actually want to own the whole town." Damon watched as the boat approached the far bank. "I have responsibilities elsewhere, so Silas is more than welcome to my share."

"Sure, that's what people say when they don't want other people to know what's going on."

Damon glanced at him. "So what do you think's going on?"

The boy's face was very set and he met Damon's gaze challengingly. "I don't know. You tell me."

Okay, this wasn't getting him anywhere. Connor was obviously determined to be as prickly as his mother.

Damon glanced back over the river again. "I get that you don't like me, and I get that you don't trust me. And you've made it very clear you don't want to talk to me. But we're nearly here, so if you've got a question, now's the time to ask it."

"I don't have a question," Connor muttered. "Why would you think I had a question?"

"I don't know," Damon said dryly. "You tell me."

Connor reddened. "I don't have a question," he repeated, though this time it sounded like it was more to himself than anything else.

Damon said nothing, letting the silence occupy another couple of moments. The kid would have to come to it in his own time. The only thing Damon could do was let him have some space to realize that.

The other side of the river loomed, the mountains pressing in. Flying into Deep River had been a bitch, and it was a good thing that the rain had eased up, because the last thing Damon needed was to run into difficulties flying out.

"Need a hand tying up?" Damon called back to Kevin, who'd come out of the wheelhouse.

Kevin nodded.

But Connor was already moving, going over to where the rope was coiled neatly on the deck, picking it up, and getting himself ready to leap onto the dock.

Damon watched him. *A good kid*, Astrid had said, and Damon could see that. The boy's protectiveness suggested a care for his mother and for his town that went deep. Kevin's reaction to him too, playing along with Connor's earnestness without making fun of him, spoke of affection and tolerance.

And really, for all Connor's belligerence, who couldn't warm to a boy looking out for his town? Especially a boy looking out for his mom. Yeah, Damon knew all about that.

Pity he couldn't ask the kid about Cal, cut through all the bullshit, but he'd promised Astrid he wouldn't and he was a man who kept his promises.

Except the one you made to Cal.

Technically, he hadn't promised. Technically, he was just following an instruction.

Technically, you're being a dick about not wanting to get involved.

Damon didn't like that thought one bit, so he watched Connor instead as the boy grabbed the rope, then leapt with all the agility of a mountain goat onto the dock and tied it around one of the metal moorings with casual competence. It looked like he'd done it a thousand times before.

A kid whose father had been killed and who may not even know, if what Astrid had said was true. And there was no reason to doubt her. She was the kid's mother after all.

Yet Damon had a sneaking suspicion that she was wrong… Perhaps the boy did know.

Connor stood on the dock, staring at Damon, one blond eyebrow raised in disdainful teenage inquiry.

Damon sighed, then went over to Kevin, making some attempt to pay the guy. But Kevin simply shook his head, so Damon put his money away, said goodbye, then got off the boat and onto the dock.

He strode along it in the direction of the tiny airstrip and the small hangar that currently housed Wild Alaska's two Cessnas.

Connor clattered along behind him, catching up.

"Just so you know," Damon commented without turning, "I'm

going to be getting out of here in pretty much the next ten minutes, so your window is limited."

"What responsibilities do you have?" Connor asked.

Ah, so he had been listening, hadn't he?

Damon quickly debated how much of the truth to give him.
Not all of it, but he could give him something. "I have to go home
to take care of my mom. She's sick."

"Oh," Connor said. "That's, uh… I'm sorry."

"You can't tell anyone, though, okay? She doesn't like anyone
to know she's ill."

A secret for a secret might help, though there were no guaran-
tees. Wouldn't hurt for Connor to know that he felt the same way
about his mother as Connor felt about Astrid anyway.

"Yeah, okay." Connor sounded less belligerent and a bit more
subdued. "I mean, I promise."

They went up the wooden stairs from the dock and then along
the gravel path that led to the airstrip. Connor didn't say anything, though a brief glance at him told Damon that there must
have been a lot going on inside his head, because he was frowning
ferociously.

There wasn't much time left. The ball was in the kid's court and
he was going to have to make a play now if he wanted something
from Damon.

A tricky moment. Damon could have put pressure on him, but
he sensed that would be the wrong approach. Connor had to make
his own mind up.

"You were in the army, weren't you?" Connor asked. "With
Silas?"

"That's right."

"And you live in LA."

"More or less. I've been in Juneau the last few months."

"So are you going straight back to LA?"

"Have to head to Juneau to drop the plane off first."

They were approaching the hangar now, the doors standing open. The little Cessna he'd flown from Juneau was waiting for him, the Wild Alaska Aviation logo emblazoned on the side.

He was going to miss flying when he was back in LA, that was for sure. He'd miss the wide-open blue of the Alaskan skies, its unforgiving mountains, and the deep green of the bush too. Even though he was a city boy, he couldn't deny that the wilderness up here had a magic all its own—a magic he hadn't expected when he'd first arrived in Juneau with Silas, Caleb, and Zeke.

A magic he suspected he wouldn't find anywhere else and certainly not in LA.

He walked into the hangar, approaching the plane, then stopped and looked at Connor. "Time's nearly up, kid."

Connor stared at him, chewing on his bottom lip, a whole host of emotions flickering in his blue eyes.

Come on, Damon said silently. *You want to ask me. I know you do.*

The boy said nothing.

Damon sighed. If Connor didn't want to ask him anything, then he didn't want to ask. Couldn't force him.

You could stay, give him some more time.

No. He couldn't. Time was the one thing he didn't have.

Damon looked away, doing a visual check of the Cessna in preparation for flight.

Then Connor said, "You knew my dad, didn't you?"

———————————

Astrid sat on one of the barstools in the Moose, leaning her elbow on the bar, a cup of coffee slowly cooling beside her.

Silas stood next to her, having pulled her into the Moose after Damon had left, to talk her through Kevin Anderson's fishing charter plan, but she wasn't paying attention. She was too busy thinking about Damon and his treatment of her son.

Connor definitely had a bee in his bonnet about Damon—for whatever reason; Astrid had no idea—and he'd been incredibly rude. Acting as though Damon was going to pull out a knife or something and challenging him head-on.

Come on, you know.

Guilt settled in her stomach, heavy as lead. Yeah, okay. Maybe she did.

It had been five years since she'd escaped the verbally abusive relationship she'd been in before coming to Deep River, but the scars were still there.

Connor had liked her ex, Aiden, very much. He'd been young, too young to know what the barbed comments and put-downs Aiden had directed at Astrid meant. All he'd known was that Aiden was nice to him, had given him male attention, and since he'd been starved for that attention, he'd lapped it up.

Astrid had tried to hide Aiden's emotional manipulation and abuse from her son, wanting to protect him since Aiden had shown Connor nothing but his good side. But eventually she'd had to leave. She'd been alone then, with no one to call on for help. Her parents had kicked her out when they'd found out she was pregnant, so she couldn't even go home.

There had been only one person she could call: Cal.

He'd told her to come to Deep River, that she could find a place for herself here, and so she had. The town had felt like a haven, a sanctuary. It represented safety and stability, and she felt more at home here than she had anywhere else.

But Connor had been gutted at leaving Aiden. And then when he'd found out that Aiden hadn't been the heroic father figure he'd been searching for, he'd felt terribly, terribly guilty.

He didn't trust men now, especially men who were nice to him, which Astrid could relate to. But his protectiveness over her was… problematic.

And part of her had been expecting Damon to be as manipulative as Aiden had been in response to Connor's aggression, building it up while at the same time tearing strips off her for Connor's rudeness, that she should have taught him better.

Yet Damon had been nothing like that. He hadn't been manipulative and he hadn't criticized her. He'd been calm in the face of Connor's rudeness. Patient too, taking him seriously, which she knew for a fact Connor desperately wanted, no matter how hard he tried to hide it.

Her poor boy, who didn't even know he'd lost his father…

The guilt settled more heavily in her, weighing her down.

"Hey." Silas's deep, rough voice rumbled in her ear. "Are you listening?"

Astrid started, then pulled her thoughts away from her son. "Yes," she said, hoping she sounded as cool as she normally did. "Of course I'm listening."

Silas, big and broad and muscular, leaned one hip against the bar and folded his arms, green eyes sharp and assessing. "You want to do this later?"

"No." She reached for her lukewarm coffee. "Why would I want that?"

"Heard you and your boy arguing outside just as Damon left. Things okay?"

Silas was a good guy, if a little too "white knight" for her liking, but she didn't know him well enough to talk with him about her worries for her son. Besides, she'd always preferred to deal with her own problems herself. It was easier that way.

So all she said was "Perfect." And took a sip of her coffee, forgetting it was tepid. Ugh. She put the cup down again. "Now, back to Kev's plan—"

"Because I've seen him around quite a bit."

What was it with men who couldn't take a hint?

"Yes, I know." Astrid gave him a steady look. "He had a little issue with Damon and don't ask me why because I don't know. But now Damon's gone, it won't be a problem, I'm sure."

Silas said nothing, the expression on his handsome face concerned, which was not encouraging. "Sonny told me that he'd seen Con up at Phil's place helping out with building fences when he should have been in school. And Harry mentioned that the kid had approached him to tell him that he could help if Harry needed anyone to test out his survival skills workshop." Silas paused, then added, "Also when he should have been in school."

There was a sinking sensation in Astrid's gut. She'd known about Phil. Not about Harry.

"I see," she said. "And Harry didn't think to come and talk to me about it?"

"I suspect he thinks it's not such a big deal." Silas's mouth quirked. "You know Harry."

Astrid did know Harry. He was a survivalist, a homesteader, and a prepper. He had a good heart, but he was also slightly paranoid and had a healthy disregard for authority of any kind. Of course he wouldn't think skipping school was a big deal. In fact, he might even encourage it.

She gritted her teeth. She'd tried to talk to Connor about where this sudden need to help people had come from, because although he'd always been the caring type, he hadn't ever skipped school because of it before, but he wouldn't tell her.

In fact, for the past month, he hadn't told her much of anything at all. It was unlike him.

"Well, if you hear of Connor doing any of those things again, can you let me know?" She tried to sound calm, because she didn't like the feeling that things were slipping out of control, especially things like her son. "I'll have to have a talk with him."

"Hey, at least he's not stealing beer from Mal's."

Astrid forced a smile at Silas's attempt at humor that she hoped was convincing. "No, true."

Apparently it didn't convince Silas.

"You know, we look after each other in this town, Astrid," he said, his sharp gaze unwavering. "And everyone needs help at some point in their lives. Even the mayor. There's no shame in asking for it."

Oh, Astrid knew that very well. It was just…complicated. Especially when it involved secrets. Secrets that had gotten way too big already and that the longer she stayed quiet about, the bigger and more unwieldy they got. And who knew what would happen if they got out? If everyone found out that Caleb West's son had been here all this time and Astrid hadn't told them? People would not be impressed. At all. Perhaps they'd make it unpleasant, and she'd end up having to leave…

No. No way.

"Thank you, Silas. I'll keep that in mind." She grabbed the paper with Kevin's fishing charter idea on it and slipped off the barstool. "I'll go over this in the afternoon. I've got to see some growers this morning, and I was hoping to get to the library before lunchtime."

"Okay, well, don't say I didn't offer." Silas pushed himself away from the bar. "We're going to have to decide which ideas are the most workable and bring them to a town meeting, you know that, right?"

Of course she knew that. It was how everything in Deep River was decided. A town meeting where town business was discussed, and if a decision needed to be made, it was put to a town ballot.

Everyone had a say and everyone had a voice, and it had been that way for nearly a century.

"Yes, obviously. We can sort through this stuff tomorrow if you like and make a decision about which ideas to bring to a meeting the day after."

He shook his head. "No. Need to run them by Damon and Zeke first."

"Seriously?" Astrid frowned. "Damon? Who just left?"

Silas sighed. "Yeah, I tried to make him stay. He's good with money and we could use someone with financial skills to help with business plans. But he's got other things to do. He said he'd give me a call about it once he was back in LA."

It didn't surprise her that Damon had left and so quickly. He hadn't struck her as the type of man who hung around a tiny town like Deep River.

"What about your other friend? Zeke?"

Silas's expression turned cagey. "Yeah, he's a little more difficult to get ahold of."

"Why? He owns part of your aviation company, yes?"

"Yeah."

"So he's in Juneau, right?"

"Not at present."

Astrid gave Silas an irritated look. "You're being awfully mysterious about this. If we can't get hold of him, then we can't get a decision."

"I know that." He turned toward the back of the bar. "Don't worry about it. It's my problem. I'll handle it."

"Or we could just not ask him," Astrid muttered, but not loud enough for Silas to hear. Mainly because it wouldn't make any difference. Silas Quinn might have carefully navigated the difficult business of the oil, not to mention been successful in spearheading the current effort to get into tourism to make up for the lack of oil dollars, but he was also, like most men of her acquaintance, a stubborn ass.

She was just turning toward the exit herself when the Moose's doors were pushed open and a familiar tall, muscular figure strode in.

Apparently, Damon hadn't flown off to LA like he'd told everyone he was going to.

Astrid stopped dead, a strange fluttering starting in the pit of her stomach. It felt a little like excitement, which didn't make any sense, so she ignored it. "Weren't you supposed to be leaving?" she said, trying for her usual cool tone.

"Yeah," Silas added from behind her. "Didn't you have pressing business you absolutely couldn't wait another day to handle back in LA?"

Damon's mouth curved in a smile that didn't quite reach his eyes. "Strangely enough, that business wasn't as pressing as I thought."

"Really?" Silas came up to stand next to Astrid, sounding deeply suspicious. "What brought this on, then?"

She didn't care why Damon was staying. She didn't care that he'd apparently changed his mind. She had things to do and she should leave.

Yet she didn't.

Then Damon's gaze unexpectedly settled on her, making that flutter in the pit of her stomach flutter even harder.

She crushed it. Flat.

"I thought more about these tourism ideas you've got going on and I've decided I can spare a couple more days." But Damon wasn't looking at Silas as he said it; he was looking at her.

There was an expression in his sky-blue eyes, a glitter of something serious that made the fluttering sensation in her gut close into a fist, clenching tight.

Connor.

"Need to talk to you if you have a moment," Damon said.

Astrid swallowed, her mouth dry. "Sure."

Silas was frowning. "Everything okay?"

"Yeah." Damon gave his friend an easy grin. "Would Hope mind if I stayed on another few days?"

Silas didn't reply immediately, glancing first at Astrid and then back at Damon, making Astrid's gut clench even tighter.

Oh great, what was Silas thinking? It had better not be about her and Damon, wondering what was going on between them. Because there was no reason for them to talk together alone about anything.

"No," Silas said, his gaze turning speculative. "I don't think she'll mind."

Okay, she needed to take control of this and stat.

"I presume this is about the financial information you requested from me earlier?" she asked Damon coolly, making it up as she went along and hoping he'd take the hint.

"It is," he replied, much to her relief. "I can come to your office if you'd like, or you can come upstairs while I drop my bag off."

Better to get this over and done with, right? Like ripping off a Band-Aid, etc.

"Perhaps I'll come upstairs." She held out a hand toward the door. "After you."

"Damon," Silas began, giving Astrid a sidelong glance.

But Damon was already heading toward the exit. "You and I can talk later. Over a beer, okay?"

He didn't wait for a response, disappearing through the door near the bar that led to the stairs.

Silas turned his attention on Astrid. "What's going on?"

"Financial stuff," she lied, already beginning to follow Damon since she really didn't want to be left down here having to deal with Silas. "We'll talk later too."

Damon's room was one of the bigger ones, at the end of the upstairs hall, with its own bathroom and, of course, the balcony that looked out over the river.

It contained an old but sturdy wooden bed pushed up against the wall facing the french doors, an old dresser, a desk near one of the other windows, and a brown leather armchair that stood near the desk.

A clean, tidy room, but nothing fancy.

Astrid looked around, her brain automatically cataloguing what could possibly be improved on in order to attract more tourists here. The views over the river and the mountains beyond were spectacular, but there was definitely a shabby, worn air to the room.

Damon dumped his bag carelessly on the bed and then turned to face her, his arms crossed over his broad chest. He wasn't smiling now, the lines of his face stark in their beauty.

He looked like a very serious angel.

"Better shut the door," he said. "That is if you want some privacy."

She did, so she shut it, turning back to him and getting straight to the point. "This is about Connor, isn't it?"

Damon's gaze was very direct. "He knows, Astrid."

"What? What are you talking about?"

Damon hesitated a moment, and for a second, she thought she saw a hint of compassion in his gaze. "He knows who his father is."

Chapter 5

ASTRID WENT WHITE AS A SHEET, HER PRETTY EYES DARKENING. "No," she said in a shocked voice. "He doesn't know. He can't."

All the unflappable capability she'd been radiating this morning in her office had disappeared, and even that taut, bristling energy was gone.

For a moment, she looked as lost as her son.

Sympathy shifted inside him, though perhaps, given that she'd kept a vital piece of information from her very hurt and worried son, it shouldn't have.

Then again, Astrid hadn't given him the impression that she was a cruel or mean woman. Certainly in the past few days he'd been in Deep River, he'd heard nothing but good things about her. That she was a touch reserved maybe, but also that she was calm and cool and she got things done.

He suspected that there was more to her than that, though. He'd seen little flashes of dry humor, little sparks of temper too. That snow-queen cool was a front, he was sure of it, but what lay beneath it, he didn't know.

What he did know was that if she'd kept something from Connor, then presumably it had been for a good reason.

Connor himself, when he'd told Damon that he knew Cal was his father, had shrugged it off. The kid had muttered something about how he wasn't angry with Astrid for not telling him and that she was probably trying to protect him, though from what he didn't say. Damon had the sense that he was trying to convince himself as much as he was trying to convince Damon.

Whatever, the kid's confession had made it clear to Damon that he couldn't leave Deep River quite yet.

Cal had wanted Damon to make sure Connor was okay, but it had soon become evident, as Damon had talked to him, that the kid wasn't okay.

He hadn't let slip much, and Damon hadn't pushed him, but it was obvious that Connor was upset and angry and hurt, and was desperately trying to hide it.

Damon couldn't go off and leave the kid like that—he just couldn't. It wouldn't be right. And most especially not when he'd made a promise to Cal.

Sure, it was going to mean involving himself in something far too complicated for his liking, not to mention dealing with messy things like emotions and whatnot, but perhaps that would be okay.

He could be a neutral party, the peacemaker, like he'd been in the army. It was easy to be laidback and calm when the ability to feel about anything in any depth had been burned right out of you.

So he'd called Rachel right there and then—mercifully, there was service at the airstrip—to let her know that he'd be a few more days, just enough to give him some time to deal with the Connor situation.

"He does know." Damon kept his voice measured. "He's been following me around because I'm a friend of Cal's and he knew it."

The lost expression on Astrid's face lingered, then abruptly vanished, her mouth hardening into a line, her jawline tight. "How?" she demanded. "How did he find out?"

"The same way I did, apparently. He got a letter after Cal died. Seemed Cal had written one before he was deployed and got the lawyer to hold on to it and send it in case of his death."

Astrid shut her eyes and put a hand to her forehead, rubbing at it as if she had a headache. She looked even paler than she had in her office.

The thread of sympathy inside him pulled harder and he let it. He might not feel things deeply these days, but he wasn't without compassion.

Going over to the small desk pushed up against the wall near the balcony, he pulled out the chair.

"Sit," he ordered calmly.

Astrid opened her eyes, shooting him an irritated look.

He ignored it. "Come on, sit down before you fall down."

She let out a breath and dropped her hands from her forehead. She looked like she wanted to argue, but then thought better of it, moving over to the chair he'd pulled out and sitting down instead.

"There." She gave him a look that was every bit as challenging as her son's. "Happy?"

"Ecstatic." He folded his arms. "Want to tell me why you didn't tell him about Caleb?"

"A lot of reasons." She leaned back, resting her head against the back of the chair and closing her eyes again. "God, what a mess."

"Want to share?"

"Not particularly." She opened her eyes again. "Look, it's nothing personal, Damon. You might have been a friend of Cal's, but I don't know you from a bar of soap, and it's really none of your business."

She wasn't wrong. It wasn't his business. And normally he wouldn't have argued with her about it. In fact, if he'd had his way, he'd be flying the Cessna the hell back to Juneau right now.

But this was kind of important and he'd never been able to turn his back on someone who needed help, most especially not when that person was a kid.

"Sure," he said mildly. "But sadly Caleb West made it my business. And I can't ignore the last request of a good friend. Cal told me to take care of Connor, so that's what I'm going to do."

Irritation rippled over Astrid's finely carved face. "He doesn't need taking care of. That's my job. And anyway, you were perfectly happy to leave us to it before."

"Yeah, but that was before he told me that he knew Cal was his father."

Astrid let out another long breath as if striving for patience. "Well, I appreciate your concern for him, but honestly, it's not needed. He'll be fine. I can tell him about Cal if he wants—"

"If you'd wanted to tell him about Cal," Damon interrupted, not without gentleness, "you would have done so by now."

She glanced away. Her mouth had a vulnerable cast to it, a tight expression on her face.

Yeah, there was something about Cal and her relationship with him that hurt. Something that she'd been protecting her son from too, which was presumably why she hadn't told him.

Cal had told him he hadn't done the right thing by her. That he'd run. He'd been scared, he'd said, and hell, Damon knew the feeling. He hadn't been much older than Cal when Rebecca had had Ella. That terror of knowing you were responsible for the life of another human being, and such a small human being too… Worse than any other fear he'd ever experienced and he'd experienced quite a few.

But he hadn't run, because his mother had taught him to take responsibility for his actions. And besides, he and Rebecca had both wanted Ella very much, even though they'd been young.

Except he wasn't going to think about Ella. This wasn't about him, thank God. It was about Astrid and Connor and Caleb. And it seemed very clear that Astrid had complicated feelings about Cal, as well she should considering what he'd done.

Perhaps you shouldn't be getting interested in her?

Perhaps not. Then again, if he wanted to help Connor, he needed to find out what was going on with Astrid.

She leaned forward in the chair, her elbows resting on her knees, gazing at the ground. Her summer-gold hair fell forward over her shoulders, leaving her nape bare. Her skin was pale and very soft-looking.

"Is he angry with me?" she asked into the silence.

He could have fed her some reassuring lies. But she didn't strike him as the kind of woman who'd want empty assurances.

"He told me he wasn't, but I think he was lying."

Her pretty, golden lashes fell, veiling her gaze.

A beam of sunlight came through the window, falling over her, and she seemed very fragile all of a sudden, as if she was made of spun glass and the slightest of touches would shatter her.

He could feel that sympathy tugging at him even stronger, insistent even. It must have been such a burden to keep Cal's name secret. She wouldn't have been able to talk to anyone about it, not here, where Caleb West had been almost a prince.

Which kind of makes Connor his heir, right?

The realization came slowly, like the gradual onset of dawn. Was that why Connor had been so protective? And so suspicious of him? Because he viewed this town as his? Which made Damon a usurper in a way. Silas too, though Silas might be given a pass because Deep River was his hometown.

Yeah, that was logical. It was certainly what Damon himself would feel if he'd been Connor. Poor kid. No wonder he'd been so aggressive and suspicious. He considered this patch his and Damon was trespassing. No, worse than that—Damon now owned it.

Hell, if this didn't constitute an excuse for a drink, he didn't know what did.

He turned and went over to where he'd dumped his bag on the bed. Unzipping it, he hunted around inside among the tangle of clothing and various other things until he'd unearthed the bottle of the very good whisky he'd brought with him. He pulled it out, went over to the desk where a couple of glasses sat, uncorked the bottle, and poured a couple of measures into both glasses. Then he picked up one glass and held it out toward Astrid where she sat in the chair near the desk.

"Here," he said. "You could use this."

She lifted her attention from the floor, looked at him and then the glass in his hand. Her gray eyes were dark. "No, thank you. It's still morning."

"My mother used to say that there was no problem that whisky couldn't fix." He raised a brow. "You wouldn't want to prove my mother wrong, now would you?"

Astrid narrowed her gaze.

"Come on." He shook the glass a little. "You're so pale you look like you should be haunting some deserted mansion."

She let out a breath and shook her head. Then grabbed the glass from his hand, put her head back, and drained the whole lot.

Interesting. He'd thought he'd have to insist more.

"Still morning, huh?" He gave her an inquiring look. "Need another?"

"Why not?" She held out the glass, her gaze not without challenge. "I've got nothing but an angry fifteen-year-old, a food co-op to organize, a library to manage, and a pile of suggestions from people who think their beer coaster collection would be a good tourist draw. Got plenty of time to drink whisky with a complete stranger."

Color had returned to her cheeks and that fragile look was dissipating, those pretty eyes of hers turning back into steel.

Good. That was better than that lost expression she'd given him.

He smiled. "Hey, I'm not a complete stranger, remember? I introduced myself and you shook my hand. But now that I remember, you never introduced yourself to me."

She frowned. "What?"

"I said, 'Are you Astrid?' and you said, 'Yes.' You never actually introduced yourself formally."

"That's ridiculous."

"Is it? Not sure I want to have too many more 'complete stranger' accusations leveled at me." He was teasing her, which probably wasn't a good idea all things considered, but he couldn't resist. Especially when she frowned at him like that. "Come on, Ms. Mayor. Introduce yourself."

She raised an eyebrow, getting slightly haughty. "You can't be serious."

Her cool tone and that expression shouldn't have rippled through him the way it did, a silent dog whistle to the rogue inside him. The one that very much enjoyed teasing a pretty woman and much to their mutual satisfaction.

"I am," he said. "Deadly. You really want me to keep calling you Ms. Mayor? Or should I try 'Your Honor' instead?"

"Don't be silly." She shook her empty glass at him, refusing to give in. "Just fill it up, please."

"Nope. You want more whisky, you have to give me some manners."

She rolled her eyes, doing a good impression of her teenage son. "Oh, fine." Sitting up, she arranged her expression into one of polite, professional welcome. "Hello. I'm Astrid James, town librarian and current mayor of Deep River. Pleased to meet you." And she extended her hand again.

Damon knew he shouldn't take it; given that faint crackle of electricity he'd gotten off her when he'd shaken her hand earlier, it wouldn't be good idea. But like he couldn't resist a tease, he couldn't resist a touch either.

She was pretty and cool and strong, and there was a spark in her that he liked. All in all, a combination that was pretty much his catnip.

So he took her hand, giving her his long, slow smile as he did so. "Pleased to meet you, Astrid."

A faint wash of pink stained her cheekbones, and for a second, her eyes glittered like stars. Her hand felt small in his, her skin warm, and he experienced the oddest urge to stroke his thumb against her palm just to see what she would do.

Abruptly, she pulled her hand away, but the pink in her cheeks remained. "There," she said. "Now you're not a complete stranger and neither am I. Can we get to the whisky, please?"

He grinned and reached for the bottle, pushing away the warmth of her skin lingering on his palm and the delicious crackle of electricity that whispered through him.

Because he couldn't take this any further, even though he was tempted. A tease, sure. A couple of smiles here and there, but nothing more. They both had more than enough on their plates without making this even more complicated.

Picking up the whisky bottle, he leaned over and topped up her glass.

"So where's Connor now?" she asked, sitting back in the chair and taking another sip of the alcohol. "Did you send him home?"

Damon put the bottle back on the desk, then leaned against it. He picked up his glass, cradling it in one hand, swirling the liquid. A good Scottish single malt, his mother's favorite.

"That's where he said he was headed."

Connor had clammed up pretty quickly after he'd asked Damon about Cal. As if he'd regretted telling him. Damon probably shouldn't have pushed him with the questions—it had been too much, too fast—because the boy had turned away, flinging "I'm going home" behind him as he'd stalked off back toward the ferry.

That's when Damon had made the decision to stay, watching the boy's tall, gangly figure leave, trailing hurt and anger behind him like a cloud.

Astrid shook her head and took another sip of her whisky. "He won't be there. He'll have gone off to do something else, like helping Phil build fences and Harry build his bunker, no doubt."

There was a note of resignation in her voice, a trace of weariness. He could see it in the slight smudges beneath her eyes too.

She was worried for her son.

"Has he been doing this a lot?" Damon asked. "Helping people out?"

"Yes." She sighed. "It feels ridiculous to complain about it, but he's been skipping school to do it."

That made sense if Damon's theory about Connor viewing himself as the town's heir held true. Of course he'd want to help. Especially given the oil situation hitting the town. He'd be worried about people, worried about what was going to happen, and he no doubt viewed the entire town as his responsibility now that his father was dead.

He wouldn't want that responsibility given to a bunch of people he didn't know, even if one of them had been born here. He'd come to Deep River after Silas had already left, after all.

Hell, the responsibility that kid must feel he had to shoulder had to be crushing.

Probably a good idea to tell her that?

Yeah, it was never a great situation to have to tell a parent your theories about their child who you'd only just met. Then again, Damon had once been a teenage boy himself, with a single mom who'd worked very hard and whom he felt responsible for.

He didn't want to interfere with Astrid and her son, but Cal had given him a mission and he wasn't going to walk away from it. Not yet at least.

"I have a theory about that," he said. "Want to hear it?"

———————

The whisky sitting in Astrid's stomach was giving her a nice glow and her hand was still tingling from the warm, firm grip of Damon's fingers.

And he was leaning against the desk, cradling his own glass, the sun falling across his dark brown hair, striking sparks of gold and caramel from it. His sky-blue eyes were fixed on her, and there was a heat in them that made something quiver deep down inside her.

A faint smile curved his beautifully carved mouth, warm and sympathetic, making her want to wrap herself up in it like she would a cozy blanket when it was cold.

He was so ridiculously attractive, and she shouldn't even be noticing, not when all of this Connor stuff was happening. Aiden had been attractive too, and charming to boot, and look how that had turned out.

Beneath the glow of the whisky sat guilt and the edge of a familiar bitterness. She'd made a lot of mistakes over the years, but she'd thought she'd done better since she'd come to Deep River. Yet clearly not. She should have said something to Connor about Cal. Connor clearly hadn't trusted her enough to tell her about the letter he'd received, and maybe that was her fault.

You knew this would come back to bite you at some stage.

Yeah, she had. She'd just hoped it would have happened when the timing was better. Not that the timing with this particular secret was ever going to be better.

"Your theory based on what?" She didn't bother to hide her sarcasm, letting her anger at herself get the better of her. "Your twenty minutes of being alone with my son?"

He irritatingly refused the bait, merely shrugging one powerful shoulder, making the blue cotton of his T-shirt pull tight across it in a distracting way. "Fair call. But I was a teenage boy once. And my mother was a single parent. And I was what you'd call overly responsible, so I have a bit of insight."

He was so calm and measured. It irritated the crap out of her. "You don't have to placate me. I'm not a horse you need to soothe."

"When I start offering you carrots and sugar cubes, then you can start to worry about me placating you." Damon's smile deepened, amusement lighting his eyes. "Anyway, so far I haven't offered any of my horses whisky."

Damn him. She didn't want to be jollied out of her temper. She didn't want him being nice to her. What she wanted was a fight, which was never a good sign.

She kept her temper on a tight rein these days, ever since Aiden. Getting angry and hurt about the things he'd said to her only made him worse, so she'd gotten very good at ignoring them. Cool and calm had been the way to handle him, and cool and calm she'd ended up being.

And she'd stayed that way even in Deep River, because though the people here had never intimidated her or been cruel the way Aiden had been, it always paid to be careful. Especially with men, because men were unpredictable at the best of times, and most especially when they were being nice. When Aiden had been nice to her, it was always because he was building up to some cruelty he was going to dump on her later or because he'd needed something from her for Connor.

Damon probably wasn't like Aiden, but who could tell? You could never judge a book by its cover, no matter how pretty that cover was.

"I'll bear that in mind," she said, pushing the irritation away and trying to find her usual cool manner.

She didn't want to ask him about his theory. She didn't want to acknowledge that he might have an insight into Connor that she, as his mother, didn't. But it would be stupid not to even listen to him just because she was feeling irritated. Especially when that irritation was more about herself and the way she'd handled things with Connor than it was about Damon. Or Aiden for that matter.

Best not to give in to her temper. Treat this the way she treated most issues that cropped up as mayor: be objective and don't let her personal feelings get in the way.

"Okay." She took another sip of the whisky. It really was very good. "Tell me then."

"Well," he said without a hint of smugness, "it's like this. Your boy's helping people and being protective of the town because I'm pretty sure he feels it's his responsibility. Caleb used to own Deep River, but he's gone now, and so Connor's trying to fill his father's shoes. And he's got even more pressure on him because Deep River has been given to a bunch of strangers who don't know the town or its people." Damon's blue gaze was very steady. "That's got to hurt. He's Cal's son, but Cal didn't leave him Deep River. Cal left Deep River to Silas and me and Zeke."

Astrid frowned, turning the words over in her head, thinking.

As much as she hated to admit it, what he said did make a certain amount of sense. Connor had started all this behavior pretty much straight after Cal had been killed, and she hadn't really thought much about why, at least not immediately. She'd been too shocked and not a little bit grief-stricken. She and Cal didn't have any kind of close relationship, but she'd been upset for Connor's sake, as well as battling her own guilt.

Connor had always loved this place, even before Cal died. Once he'd gotten over the heartache of being parted from Aiden, he'd fallen in love with it right from the very first moment they'd motored across the river on Kev's ferry.

It was as if he'd come home.

The dual spikes of grief and guilt stuck inside her, Damon's words sinking in. Oh hell, he was right, wasn't he? Connor viewed this place as his and he was afraid for it. Afraid about the oil. Afraid it had been given to a bunch of strange men he didn't know and didn't trust.

Afraid he wouldn't be able to protect it.

Like he wasn't able to protect you.

Astrid's heart clenched tight in her chest. She was conscious of Damon's gaze resting on her, a flood of warm blue surrounding her. And maybe it should have felt like an extra pressure, but it didn't. His was a very calm presence, projecting steadiness, reassuring in a way she couldn't put her finger on.

Was that why she'd already told him far more than she'd meant to about Connor?

She wasn't used to it, not from a man, and it made her feel edgy and resistant. Men weren't to be trusted. Her father, who'd been the most appalled by her pregnancy, had insisted she leave. Cal had abandoned her. Aiden had manipulated and hurt her.

They'd all betrayed her in one way or another, and though over the five years she'd been in Deep River she'd gradually come to trust the people here, it hadn't been easy.

So why she should feel that she could trust a guy she'd only just met, and a stupidly attractive guy at that, she had no idea. But she resented it.

She'd made some bad choices in the past; she didn't want to make any more.

"I guess it makes sense," she said reluctantly. "And I can see Connor feeling like that."

Again, there was no hint of smugness on Damon's face that she'd agreed with him, not like Aiden had gotten on his sometimes when he'd scored a point off her.

He only nodded. "It's a lot of responsibility on his shoulders. The kid must feel he has to look out for everyone in the entire place, so no wonder he's skipping school. He won't have time for that if he's busy making sure everyone's okay."

The guilt inside Astrid bit deep. She lifted her glass and drained the rest of the whisky, trying to ease the feeling.

Her poor boy. All of this was her fault, wasn't it?

"Hey." Damon's deep voice was soft. "Don't beat yourself up about any of this. Nothing you can do about the past. It's what you do now that matters."

Damn the man. Could he read minds or something? Her ability to hide her feelings must be slipping. Either that or she'd had too many whiskies.

"I'm not beating myself up," she lied smoothly. "I'm only feeling sorry for him."

"Sure." He tilted his head, watching her, that reassuring smile still curving his beautiful mouth. The sun in his hair made it seem more deep amber than brown, his eyes that astonishing blue; he looked like a fallen angel, all sexy and wicked and ready to sin. "But if you are, don't."

Astrid had to look away. He was like the sun: blinding if one looked too long at him. "I'll take that under advisement, thank you."

A brief silence fell.

Then Damon said, "So the real reason I decided to stick around for another couple of days is to give Connor some time to come and talk to me about Cal if he wants. Or I can talk to him, it doesn't bother me which. He doesn't know I changed my mind, so if you could tell him I'm staying, I'd appreciate it."

She'd already gathered that he wasn't leaving and his decision to stay...well, she wasn't exactly thrilled by it. Him hanging around here, involving himself with her son...

It's only a couple of days.

That was true. But she didn't trust him—or rather, she didn't trust her own gut instinct that was urging her to trust him. He might have been Cal's friend, and Cal had clearly trusted him enough to look out for Connor, but Astrid didn't. She knew nothing about him other than he was from LA, had a beautiful smile, and was as handsome as the Devil himself.

She'd made a bad choice in hoping Aiden would be a good father figure for Connor and instead had put him at risk. She'd never willingly make that mistake again.

"Like I said." Astrid kept her voice cool. "I'll take that under advisement."

If Damon was annoyed by her tone, he didn't show it. He merely studied her with those warm blue eyes.

"You don't trust me," he said eventually, and it wasn't a question.

There was no point in pretending otherwise. "Would you? In my place?"

"No." His smile turned rueful. "Not sure I'd trust anyone I first saw hanging out on a balcony stark naked."

She didn't want to smile back, but it was almost impossible with him looking at her like that, so she glanced at the floor instead and bit her lip. "Not a great start, no."

"So what can I do to help the process along? More whisky maybe?"

The thought of sitting here in the sun sipping whisky with a charming man was all too attractive, which meant that she shouldn't. No, it was more important to get out of here and get on with the stuff on her to-do list. Number one being figuring out what to do about her son.

"I'll think about it," she said shortly, getting to her feet and moving to the desk where he stood, placing the glass back on the desk next to his hip. Then she looked up at him. "Though don't hold your breath it's going to happen anytime soon."

A mistake to get near him. A mistake to look at him too, she knew that immediately.

He was very tall, and the way he lounged against the side of the desk seemed designed to highlight the masculine perfection of his long, lean body. Wide shoulders and narrow hips, powerful chest. Flat stomach. The sleeves of his T-shirt stretched over sharply defined biceps, the deep blue contrasting with the deep gold of his skin. He smelled of something warm and a little spicy, like sandalwood or cloves.

He didn't seem at all angry or even mildly annoyed at her response. "Fair enough. If you don't want to trust me, I'm not going to force you." He paused, his smile fading, though warmth still lingered in his eyes. "But if Connor comes to me wanting to talk, I'm not going to send him away."

His voice was the same, rich and deep. Yet there was something in it she hadn't heard before: a note of iron.

And it came to her in a sudden rush that although he might on the surface be calm and easygoing, laid back and unbothered, that didn't mean he was any of those things. There was something hard in him; she could sense it. A core of strength that wouldn't bend and wouldn't break. That would remain immovable, no matter what she did or what she said.

It should have irritated her immensely, and it did—yet another part of her found it deeply reassuring, and she had no idea why.

Time to go.

Oh yes, it most certainly was.

"Is that a warning?" she asked, staying right where she was, because apparently she was also an idiot.

"It can be." His gaze searched her face, heat curling through his melted-honey voice. "If you want it to be."

She didn't want it to be. No, most definitely not.

Are you sure? You'd love a challenge like him.

"I don't think so," she said, both to him and the voice in her head. "Thank you for the drink, Mr. Fitzgerald."

He inclined his head. "Anytime, Ms. Mayor."

Astrid had to force herself to turn and walk out the door, and she could feel his gaze on her the whole way.

Chapter 6

LATER THAT EVENING, DAMON PUSHED OPEN THE DOOR TO the Moose's back office to find Silas sitting on a chair behind the old desk shoved up against one wall, his lap full of toned, athletic legs and the lean curves of a pretty woman with long, dark auburn hair and dark eyes: Hope, Silas's girlfriend, who ran the Happy Moose.

"I turn my back and look what happens." Damon leaned against the doorframe and grinned at the pair of them. "Can you not keep your hands off each other even for two seconds?"

Silas held up a hand with one finger raised—not the middle finger, surprisingly enough—finished the kiss he was laying on Hope, then lifted his head.

Hope leaned back in Silas's arms, dark eyes gleaming. "No," she said. "What do you want, pretty?"

Hope hadn't been impressed with him initially because he'd been a bit of a dick when he'd gotten here—too worried about his mom, and getting his share of Wild Alaska sold so he could get back to LA, for his usual manners. But they'd reached an understanding over the past few days: she allowed him to call her pretty if she got to call him the same in return.

He'd been called a pretty boy enough in his life that he was tired of it, but he didn't mind it with Hope. Especially since she made a mean Long Island iced tea despite telling him the Moose didn't do cocktails.

"Don't you want to know why I came back?" he asked, raising an eyebrow.

Hope rolled her eyes. "We're not all interested in your every move, Damon. No matter what you'd like to think."

"I'd like to think that you lie awake at night wondering when would be a good time to throw this asshole over for me but, you know, I wouldn't want to assume."

She laughed, then lifted a hand, touching Silas's face with a tenderness that made Damon's chest feel unexpectedly tight. "I wouldn't assume," she said. "You know what they say: 'assume makes an ass out of you and me.'"

At that moment, the volume of conversation coming from the bar rose, a couple of distinct male voices rising above the rest of it.

"What?" Silas said. "It's seven o'clock already?"

Damon looked toward the bar. Apparently at seven o'clock every Friday night, two old trappers, Joe and Lloyd, would have an argument that sometimes involved blows, but which mostly involved them being thrown out.

It was so regular you could set your watch by them. Or at least that's what Silas had told him. He'd never seen it before himself and he wouldn't have minded watching, but he had other things to do.

Such as talking to Silas about how he'd be staying on for another few nights.

Such as wondering what to do about one overly responsible teenage boy and his lovely, cool, and fascinating mother.

Flirting upstairs that morning with Astrid had been an indulgence, especially when there were more important issues to talk about. But he hadn't been able to help himself.

In the army, he'd gotten good at bomb disposal. There was something about the combination of risk, precision, and keeping a cool head that he'd enjoyed. Plus the added attraction of solving how to disarm various devices. They were puzzles and he liked puzzles.

Astrid was just such a puzzle. Or no, maybe given that bristly, prickly energy she sometimes radiated, she was more like an unexploded device. Cool metal on the outside, but packed full of explosive material on the inside, not to mention difficult to disarm and maybe lethal if set off by mistake.

He was going to have to proceed carefully, treat her gently and with caution. Because dealing with Connor meant dealing with her, and everything would go a lot easier if he could maybe get her to trust him even just a little. She was very wary, that was for sure.

Was that because of Cal? Because of the way he'd hurt her all those years ago? Or was there something more going on behind those misty gray eyes?

Yeah, there was more, he'd lay money on it, and he needed to find out what more. Certainly if he was going to help Connor he'd need to.

Hope was in the process of pushing herself out of Silas's lap before heading toward the door. "Axel's having the night off," she said to him as he protested, mentioning the bouncer and some-time barman who usually handled Joe's and Lloyd's antics. "I'll deal with it." She paused beside Damon and gave him a warning look. "Don't start drinking now, please. He was quite useless to me last night and I was not happy."

"Hey," Silas called after her, looking annoyed, but she'd vanished into the bar.

Damon stepped into the small office cluttered with book-shelves, a battered filing cabinet, and the desk pushed beneath the window that looked out over the main street. He didn't bother shutting the door.

"How's married life?" He gave Silas an amused look as he came over to the desk.

"I'm not married yet, you know." Silas leaned back in the chair, stretching his long, denim-clad legs out in front of him. "Though I've been thinking about it."

Damon was unsurprised; Silas barely said a sentence without the word *Hope* in it. "Congratulations. When can we expect the happy event?"

"When I ask her. And when she says yes." Silas gave him a direct look. "So? Spit it out, then. Why did you change your mind about leaving and this financial stuff?"

Damon sat on the edge of the desk. He'd been thinking most of the afternoon about what he was going to tell Silas without giving away the fact that his change of heart had been Connor, which meant he was going to have to lie.

He didn't like that, but there wasn't any way around it, not without giving away Cal's secret, and since it didn't only concern him, it wasn't his place to reveal it.

"I found out I could spare a couple of days after all," he said casually. "So I figured I might as well stick around and have a look at these tourism ideas, check out the financials, help with business plans, that kind of thing."

Silas gave him a narrow look. "So nothing at all to do with the mayor, then."

Shit. Was that what Silas thought? That he was here for Astrid? *And you're not?*

Hell no. This was all about Connor and Damon's promise to Cal. An inconvenient attraction to Astrid was something he could easily ignore.

"No," Damon said firmly. "Nothing at all."

Silas's suspicion in no way lessened. "Be careful, Damon. She's a woman with a difficult past, and she really doesn't need a difficult future, okay?"

Interesting. What did Silas know?

"Difficult past, you say?" he asked, ignoring Silas's suspicion for the moment.

Silas shook his head. "I don't know anything for certain, but even if I did, it's not my story to tell. Hope's mentioned a couple of things about her is all, and it sounds to me like she's had enough bad crap in her life without anyone else adding to it."

Damon didn't take offense. He liked women and that was well-known. Silas was only looking out for a fellow townsperson. Still, he didn't need to worry. Damon wasn't in the market for anything more than casual, and that ruled Astrid out completely.

"Hey." He raised his hands. "I hear you. No dick moves, I promise." And he meant it, yet his brain kept circling around the words *difficult past* as he remembered that lost look on her face and that air of fragility…

He wanted to know what had happened to her, because something had. Something that would have had an effect on Connor, that perhaps had prompted the kind of behavior the kid was displaying now.

Silas eyed him. "Damon…"

Damon met his friend's gaze squarely. Silas had a white-knight streak in him and that was commendable, but sometimes the guy went tilting at the wrong windmills.

"Give me some credit," he said without heat. "The mayor's attractive, sure, but I'm not here to hook up. She's not interested anyway, she made that clear."

His friend let out a slow breath, his harsh features relaxing. "Okay, fine. Well, I can't say I'm disappointed you're offering advice. Like I've been trying to tell you, Deep River could use it. We need to make sure everything's rock-solid when it comes to taking on these oil assholes."

Silas had already told him about the oil company executives who'd been calling people in town, trying to get them to sell their leases and/or hand over their mineral rights. The town had voted not to sell, but the money had been a strong draw. People in the town didn't have much, and everyone had families to support. Having alternative sources of income would strengthen people's resolve against the oil companies and hopefully keep them out of Deep River for good.

A little arrow of guilt pierced him. He'd been difficult over the past few weeks and he knew it, complaining about being stuck in Juneau and hassling Silas about staying in Deep River, wanting to walk away from his responsibility to the town. And it had been made even harder by his mother's insistence on no one knowing about her illness.

Yeah, but you told Connor.

That was true, he had. And Silas was owed some truth, especially considering what a dick Damon had made of himself. Silas didn't know his mom and Damon didn't have to be specific about what kind of illness she had.

"About the past few weeks," Damon said slowly. "I wasn't deliberately trying to be an asshole about selling up and going back to LA. I do actually have some good reasons for it."

"I figured." Silas's gaze was measuring. "But if you didn't want to tell me about them, then I wasn't going to force you."

"Okay, so the truth is that my mom isn't well and she needs some help. I've got a housekeeper coming in a couple of hours a day to keep an eye on her, but she doesn't like having a stranger in the house, so it's not a great permanent solution."

Silas's expression turned sympathetic. "Ah. Well, that's crappy."

"Yeah, it is." Damon shoved away the inevitable tight feeling that filled his chest whenever he thought about the situation with his mother. She didn't like Rachel being around but never liked it when he looked after her either, which was going to make the future difficult. "What about Zeke?" he went on, changing the subject. "I presume you've told him about all of this?"

Silas shifted uncomfortably in his chair. "I haven't been able to get ahold of him since Cal's funeral."

That was weird. Then again, given Zeke's whole "wild man" schtick, not completely out of character. The guy would take off into the bush for a few days, sometimes a few weeks, before turning up and acting like nothing had happened. He'd been the same way in the military, though with less disappearing.

He wasn't a man who explained himself, so Cal, Damon, and Silas never knew why he kept leaving, despite having asked him on numerous occasions. However, he was always around when he was needed, so while his disappearance wasn't out of character, the fact that he was needed right now and wasn't around made Damon wonder.

He'd been the one meant to do the cargo run that had ended in Cal's death and hadn't been able to go at the last minute for reasons he wouldn't disclose to anyone else. He hadn't said anything, but Damon and Silas both knew the accident had hit him hard because he'd up and left the minute Cal's funeral had ended.

Damon frowned. "Any idea where he went?"

"Nope. I've left a ton of messages on his phone. I texted him, emailed him, and got nothing back, so who knows?"

Worry turned over inside Damon's gut, but that was another feeling he didn't let take root. Vague concern was fine, but nothing deeper, not these days. Anyway, sometimes a man just needed to go somewhere else for a time to clear his head, so perhaps that's what Zeke was doing right now.

"He'll turn up," he said, partly for Silas's benefit and partly for his own. "He always does."

"True. But no harm in seeing what I can dig up about where he might have gotten to." Silas abruptly spun his chair around to face the computer. "I don't like the idea of him being in some sort of trouble and not having any help."

Damon pushed himself off the edge of the desk. "Yeah, I agree. Let me know if there's anything you need." He glanced down at a folder that was sitting on the edge of the desk, helpfully labeled *Deep River Potential Tourism Ideas*. "Can I take this?" he asked. If he was going to offer advice, he'd better have a look at what was being suggested.

"Sure," Silas said absently. "Oh, and, Damon? I wouldn't mention Zeke to anyone. At least not until he turns up. The town is already unsettled enough with this oil crap. They don't need to know that one of the new owners has disappeared."

The new owners…of which he was one.

Damon took a breath, thinking about Connor and the responsibility the kid was carrying around on his shoulders. Bad enough for an adult man, let alone for a fifteen-year-old. And now he was skipping school… Yeah, he didn't like that. Not good for the kid and it was worrying his mom too. The mayor didn't need that on top of everything else she was managing, which from the sound of it was quite a bit…

He needed a plan to help, that was clear. He wasn't going to be here long, but hopefully it would be enough time to make good on his promise to Cal and help his son.

"No problem," he said to Silas as he turned to leave. "If anyone asks, I'll tell them Zeke's on a spiritual quest or something."

But as he left, it wasn't Zeke that he was thinking about.

And it wasn't Connor either.

It was Astrid James's cool gray eyes.

———————

Sweat ran into Astrid's eyes as she put her hands down on her yoga mat and straightened her legs into downward dog.

"Breathe," Gwen said softly. "Concentrate on where your energy is going."

The community center hot yoga class was halfway through, the little stove in one corner of the large open space throwing out a tremendous amount of heat.

It wasn't a large crowd, but enough people turned up every morning to make it worth Gwen's while. Every class she attended made Astrid proud. Everyone had been resistant when she'd first initiated the classes, but Gwen's positivity, plus the offer of free coffee and a donut from April's for every attendee, soon helped things along.

Of course, the coffee and donut didn't really go with the whole yoga vibe—Gwen's words—but Astrid wasn't going to be picky. If it got people off their butts and doing some exercise, getting joints mobile and muscles stretched, then it was all good.

She enjoyed the classes herself, leading by example. There was something meditative about them, which was helpful, especially when she had too many other things on her mind.

Things such as a very handsome, exceedingly charming man, whose warm blue eyes and slow, sexy smile seemed hell-bent on disturbing her peace of mind.

"Hold," Gwen said, and began to count.

The muscles in Astrid's legs burned and began to shake, but she didn't move, testing herself. Trying not to think of the tension in her own house the day before.

She'd dashed home at lunchtime to see if Connor had come home, but he hadn't. Not for the first time, she'd wished the cell phone reception was more reliable so she could text him or maybe even track him, but he never responded to her texts anyway.

He'd returned later that day and refused to talk to her about anything, merely taking one look at her stricken face before saying, "I don't want to talk about it, Mom."

She'd known that stubborn cast to his chin, recognized it well; he wouldn't be pushed. So all she'd said was, "At least tell me you're okay."

He'd sighed and nodded his head. "Yeah. I'm okay." But there had been a guarded look in his bright blue eyes. As if he didn't quite trust her anymore.

That had hurt. But then she supposed she deserved it.

"Damon is staying in town for a few more days," she'd told him, not sure what else to say.

Something had shifted in her son's gaze and maybe for the first time in her life, she hadn't been able to read it. Hadn't been able to tell what was going on in his head at all. Which had scared her. She'd wanted to ask at least a dozen more questions, but he'd only muttered, "Thanks," before shuffling off to his bedroom and closing the door very firmly.

"And come down into child's pose," Gwen said, dragging Astrid back into the present. "Breathe deep."

Her muscles screamed with relief as she came down onto her knees, leaning forward so her forehead was pressed to her mat. Her T-shirt was sticking to her skin, the hot, humid atmosphere in the room embracing her like a warm, sweaty hug.

"And that's the end of the class," Gwen murmured. "Thank you all for coming. Namaste."

People shifted slowly, coming to their feet and picking up their mats, the sound of conversation rising.

Astrid did the same, noticing out of the corner of her eye that Debbie Long, whose husband Carl worked on the trawlers, was preparing to come over, no doubt to talk to her yet again about Carl's unique collection of beer coasters and did Astrid think that could be something tourists might like.

Gwen, too, was casting hopeful glances her way as Clare Owen, who ran the local B&B, engaged her in conversation.

Since a casual conversation with Clare usually lasted a good half hour—the woman couldn't be direct if her life depended on it—and it didn't look like she was going to stop talking anytime soon, Astrid walked quickly past to the community center's doors.

She didn't have time to talk to either Debbie or Gwen this morning, not when she still had to look at Kevin's fishing charter idea, plus the details of Phil's wildlife sanctuary.

She was busy. Too busy. And that was good, especially with Connor weighing on her mind.

Outside, it was a crisp and beautiful morning. With all those mountains around, Deep River got a lot of rain, so it was extra nice when the sun decided to show itself, the deep, intense blue of the sky contrasting sharply with the year-round snow on the peaks that surrounded the town. Almost the same blue, in fact, as the eyes of the man lounging in the gravel area just in front of the community center's doors.

Damon.

He looked tall and broad and delicious dressed in those

battered and worn jeans. Today, instead of a T-shirt, he wore a casual black button-down shirt made out of some kind of textured and soft-looking, touchable fabric. The sleeves were rolled up, exposing muscled forearms and strong wrists, and somehow the dark color made his skin look even more golden, his hair a deep shade of caramel, and his eyes...

Yes, she needed to stop looking now.

What on earth was he doing here?

Her heart was beating much faster than it had been during class, her palms sweaty where they clutched at her mat.

"Good morning, Ms. Mayor." His voice rolled over her, rich and deep as he approached, his hands in his pockets, his smile slow and sexy. "How was your class?"

His outrageous good looks made Astrid very conscious of how sweaty and red-faced she was, and that her hair was sticking to the back of her neck. And no doubt her T-shirt to her body, and not in a sexy way.

Aiden hadn't liked her appearance to be anything less than perfectly groomed and had always had something to say about it if she wasn't wearing makeup or a pretty dress. So when she'd come to Deep River, she'd worn nothing but jeans and T-shirts and had defiantly thrown all her makeup away. She never thought about her appearance these days.

But she was excruciatingly aware of it now, and the same old feelings of discomfort and shame she'd used to feel around Aiden were coming back, winding through her like ivy, clinging to her. She hated it.

Resisting the urge to touch her hair, she forced the feelings away, holding on to her temper as she came down the wooden steps from the community center's porch.

"Good morning, Mr. Fitzgerald," she said coolly. "To what do I owe the pleasure so bright and early?"

He gave her a leisurely survey, and she braced herself for the distaste that would no doubt soon show in his expression. Yet it wasn't distaste that flickered in his eyes but something hotter and far more...appreciative.

A little jolt of shock pulsed through her. Since when had a man looked at her with appreciation? With heat? The way a man looks at a woman and likes what he sees?

A long time. She couldn't remember how long.

That fluttering feeling in the pit of her stomach that she'd felt the day before in the Moose was back, a feminine kind of excitement. A reminder that though she might be done with men, her body was not and it liked this particular man. It liked the heat and appreciation that burned in his eyes.

She could feel a similar heat in her cheeks and knew she was blushing like a teenager. How intensely annoying. With luck he wouldn't notice, since she was red as a beet already.

"I'm here to offer you some help," he said in that unhurried way he had. "With some of these tourist ideas that the town wants to get off the ground."

Astrid blinked in surprise. "How can you help with that?"

"I know a thing or two about money, and I'm good with investments." He shrugged those broad shoulders. "Silas thought I could look over them and offer advice."

People were starting to come out behind her, the conversation lowering to a startled buzz as the mostly female attendees caught a glimpse of Damon standing like a Hollywood movie star in the middle of the gravel parking area.

He must have noticed, because he glanced behind her, his smile widening in that warm, genuine way. As if he really was pleased to see them all. "Morning, ladies."

A scattering of "mornings" echoed back, including a couple of giggles that were very reminiscent of a pack of teenage girls mooning over the star quarterback.

And that annoyed her too. Unreasonably.

"In that case, you really should go to the mayor's office." She tried to keep the irritation from her voice. "My office hours are from nine onward."

"It's a Saturday," he said. "I wasn't sure if you'd be in the office."

God, he was so reasonable. He made it impossible for her to sustain any kind of annoyance. Which naturally made her even more irritable.

It's not him you're annoyed at. It's yourself.

Oh yes, she was well aware. But knowing that didn't help one bit, especially when he smiled at her like that, watching her with that warm, steady gaze.

Trying to get ahold of herself, she pasted on a cool smile. "I can be. But I need to go home and have a shower first." She started walking past him, determinedly keeping her attention forward. "Meet me at the mayor's office in fifteen minutes."

Much to her intense aggravation, he fell into step beside her. "Not a problem. Though we can just as easily meet at your place. Then you won't have to—"

"The mayor's office." Astrid stopped walking and gave him a steady look, the thought of him in her actual house alarming for reasons she couldn't have articulated even to herself. "Fifteen minutes."

He studied her for a moment, making her feel even hotter than she already was. "Sure. I'll get us coffee from April's. And maybe a couple of donuts too."

"I don't want a donut. I have perfectly good granola at home."

"But we're not meeting at your home. Which means I'll provide the breakfast." He lifted a hand and then, quite casually, hooked a lock of her hair behind her ear. "You'll eat a donut and you'll like it. And then we'll discuss Deep River's tourism possibilities." His hand dropped, his expression becoming serious. "Don't worry. We won't talk about Connor if you don't want to."

"Oh, but I—"

"See you in fifteen, Ms. Mayor."

And before she could say a word, he turned and strolled off in the direction of the town center, his hands in his pockets.

"What is going on with *that man*?" Debbie murmured from behind her. "He seems sweet on you."

Great. The last thing she needed was people thinking *that* about her and Damon. What the hell had he been thinking, touching her the way he had? In full view of the others?

Her skin felt tingly and tight where his fingertips had brushed the side of her ear and her heartbeat was racing.

You liked it.

Argh. No, she had *not* liked it. Not in any way. And she was going to have words with him about doing that kind of thing in future. Strong words.

"No, he's not," she said crisply, not looking at Debbie. "He was just…brushing something off of my ear." Then before Debbie could say anything else, she strode away determinedly.

Astrid went up the winding gravel road that led to the small scattering of homes sitting on the hillside above the town. Hers was white and wooden and had been built into the side of a rocky bluff, with wooden stairs constructed against the rock face leading up to her front door.

It wasn't a big house—none of the houses in Deep River were—but it had an amazing view from the small deck that had been built around the front of it, and that was worth the aggravation of getting groceries up the steps.

Shutting the front door behind her, she went down the tiny hallway to the large living area with its views over the town and the river beyond.

Dumping her yoga mat on the old couch that had been pushed up against the wall facing the windows, she went back into the hallway, then stopped in front of Connor's door. Childish wooden letters spelling his name had been stuck on the wood, but the first *O* had fallen off.

She lifted her hand to knock, then dropped it again. Was there any point trying to force a conversation with him? He'd been very clear that he didn't want to talk to her and he'd always been a kid who didn't like to be pushed into anything. He had to come to it in his own time. She didn't know how to broach the topic anyway, and apart from anything else, he was likely still asleep.

Muttering a curse under her breath, she eventually stepped away and went to have her shower instead.

Ten minutes later, she found herself debating over clothing choices, which was ridiculous and never normally an issue. She didn't dress for anyone but herself. Yet she couldn't stop thinking about the appreciative look in Damon's sky-blue eyes, or about how much she'd actually liked it, no matter what she told herself.

Would it really be too bad if she wore something nice? Before she'd had Connor, she used to enjoy dressing up. Putting on some makeup and pretty clothes. Going dancing and having fun with her friends. Then he'd arrived, and there was no time for fun, no money for pretty dresses, and all her friends had disappeared. Being with Aiden had been great initially, until his preference for her being pretty and feminine at all times had become pressure and a stick he used to beat her with, and eventually she'd ended up hating that side of herself.

It had been that feminine and passionate side that had gotten her pregnant in the first place too, and so even now, she tried to keep it in check wherever possible.

Still…it wouldn't be wrong to wear something nice. They would be in her office, so no one else would see and gossip about it. And she wasn't going to be doing anything ridiculous like going on a date. It would only be…letting herself enjoy a handsome man's appreciation. That was allowable, surely?

Astrid went to her dresser and pulled out a drawer, looking through her T-shirts and tops. She wouldn't go all out—she'd thrown away all her sexy clothing anyway—but she could put something on that she liked, that she knew suited her.

Pulling out one of her favorites, a light blue T-shirt in a silky fabric that did nice things to her eyes and skin, she put it on, then followed it up with a pair of close-fitting jeans. She brushed her hair until it hung in a straight, glossy, golden fall to her shoulders, then surveyed the meager store of makeup she'd allowed herself a couple of years after she'd come to Deep River. Most of it had dried up or flaked away since she never wore it, but now she regretted not asking Mal to order her some more. Ah well, she'd just have to settle for lip gloss.

Still, makeup or not, she felt good as she stepped out of the house and made her way back down toward the town center again, better than she'd felt in a while in fact. And that fizzing excitement gathering in the pit of her stomach only added to it, an excitement she couldn't pretend wasn't to do with Damon Fitzgerald.

She needed to get a handle on herself.

He was waiting by the entrance to her building when she arrived, holding two coffees and a paper bag in his hands, a folder under one arm. He smiled as she appeared, slow and sexy, making the excitement spread out, effervescent and light.

"Nice T-shirt," he murmured. "That color is pretty on you."

She flushed and looked away, trying to hide her pleasure that he'd noticed. "Thank you."

"I hope you left room for at least one donut." He waved the bag he was carrying. "In among all that worthy granola."

"Well, seeing as I forgot about my worthy granola, I'll probably take you up on that donut offer." Fighting the stupid urge to smile at him, she busied herself opening the door, then tried to gesture him up the stairs first. But he only shook his head.

"My mom was very clear on the rules. Ladies before gentlemen."

Astrid couldn't resist. "And are you, in fact, a gentleman?"

"Sometimes." His smile took on a wicked edge, a hot blue spark in his eyes making her breath catch. "And sometimes not."

Oh boy…

Astrid turned away quickly, before she did something very silly like ask him what happened when he wasn't a gentleman, and went up the stairs to her office.

Is this really such a good idea? To be alone with him?

She ignored the thought. Being alone with him was fine. They were going to talk about business and nothing more. It wasn't as if she was going to throw herself into his arms or anything, not when she barely knew him.

Stepping into the mayor's office, she moved over to her desk and sat down, feeling more restrained now that there was a large expanse of wood between them.

Damon sat in the old wooden chair on the other side of the desk, putting the coffee and donuts down on the desktop. He ripped open the donut bag and took one out, handing it to her. "Here. Quality brain food."

"Did you tell April some of that was for me?" she asked as she took the donut from him. It was still warm from the fryer and covered in sugar. "You get free coffee and donuts if you take the hot yoga class."

"Ah, I wondered why April suddenly had a long queue. And no, I didn't mention it. I was happy to pay anyway."

"Is this you being a gentleman?"

Damon's blue gaze sparked. "Careful, Ms. Mayor. I could start to like you if you keep that up."

"Well, we can't have that now, can we?" She bit into the donut, a reckless feeling spiraling through her, probably fueled by the aftereffects of yoga. Definitely *nothing* to do with the hot look in his eyes.

You need to be careful.

Oh, she was being careful. Nothing would happen. But what was wrong with enjoying this reckless, excited feeling? It had been so long since she'd felt it, and he would be leaving soon anyway. So why not enjoy it while she could?

He looked good enough to eat sitting there with his long legs stretched out, the worn blue denim of his jeans pulling across his powerful thighs. The soft, black fabric of his shirt lay open at the neck, exposing the golden skin of his throat, and she could see the beat of his pulse, steady and strong.

It made something ache right down deep inside her.

Damon reached for one of the coffee cups on the desk and pushed it in her direction. "Here. Milk, no sugar. I hope that's okay. Should have asked April how you liked your coffee. Maybe next time."

Milk, no sugar was perfect. Just the way she liked it.

"You're assuming there will be a next time." She took the cup, the cardboard warm between her hands.

"Good point." His gaze glinted from beneath his long, dark lashes. "Do you want there to be a next time?"

Oh, he'd be dangerous to her if she let him. So very dangerous. But then she'd once loved living dangerously. Before a succession of men had ground her down. Her father. Cal. Aiden…

A sliver of cold cut through the heat inside her and she had to take a sip of her coffee to warm herself up.

Perhaps it would be best if she stopped playing and nipped this in the bud. Before it got out of hand.

"Hey, I know you didn't mean anything by it, but you probably shouldn't touch me in public the way you did at the community center." She hoped she sounded measured. "People will talk."

He picked up the other cup, holding it in his big, capable hands. The look on his handsome face was enigmatic. "How do you know I didn't mean anything by it?"

Ah.

Astrid shifted. She knew she should look away from him, but she couldn't quite bring herself to do it. "Why did you do it, then?"

"You had a curl stuck to your cheek." He smiled again, that slightly rueful, boyish one that she found so utterly irresistible. "I couldn't help myself."

"That smile works on everyone you turn it on, doesn't it?"

"Not everyone. Though I'm kinda hoping it works on you."

There was no mistaking the blue fire in the depths of his eyes. Heat spread through her, the breath catching in her throat as the air between them became dense and thick, like the moment just before a summer storm breaks.

"What do you want, Damon?" she asked, her voice slightly husky. "We're here to talk about these tourism ideas. Or at least that's what you told me."

Chapter 7

DAMON HAD TOLD HER THAT, IT WAS TRUE. IT WAS ONLY THAT it was difficult to think of tourism or money when she was in the room. When she was wearing that silky blue T-shirt that turned her gray eyes luminous and made her skin look like fresh cream. When her hair glimmered like spun gold in the light coming from the window behind her.

When she flirted with him a bit hesitantly yet with the sort of cool challenge that he found the most exciting. The most fascinating.

He liked melting snow queens. He wanted to melt her.

Waking up early this morning, he'd read through the papers he'd taken from Silas's desk the night before. Then, because he only had a few days after all, he'd gone in search of Astrid ASAP.

Investigations about where she was soon yielded the fact that she took a hot yoga class every morning in the community center.

Intrigued, he'd made a beeline for the center and had watched her come out, her yoga mat tucked under her arm, blond hair sticking to her skin, her cheeks flushed, and her eyes brilliant. And he hadn't been prepared for his reaction to her. An intensely physical, almost visceral reaction.

She'd looked beautiful, as if she'd spent a couple of hours in his bed rather than in a yoga class. And he hadn't been able to think.

Then she'd come closer, pink-faced and sweet, one golden curl stuck to her cheek, and so very different from the cool, collected woman she'd been the day before. He'd reached out to tuck that curl back behind her ear before he could stop himself, her skin so warm and silky…

No. He had to exercise his control. She was off-limits in every way, and flirting with her like this was stupid in the extreme.

"You really want to know what I want?" He gripped the thin cardboard of his cup, ignoring how it burned against his fingertips. "I want to take you to dinner. I want to talk to you. I want to get to know you. And then I want to take you home and spend the night with you." It was far too blunt, but for some reason, all his charm had suddenly deserted him and all he had left was honesty. "But you're the mayor of Deep River and you're Connor's mom. And I'm leaving in a couple of days. And so what I want isn't a good idea, not given those other things."

He shouldn't have said anything in the first place. He should have kept it to himself. But she'd asked him, and he'd wanted to give her the truth. Maybe if she hadn't responded the way she had to him, it would have been different, but she had. And so he wanted her to know that he found her attractive in a lot of different ways.

"I see." The flush in her cheeks deepened and she looked away, sipping on her coffee and taking another bite of her donut. Trying to be casual, no doubt, but he could see through her. She'd liked what he'd said, that was clear.

"Serves me right for asking, I suppose," she added.

He wasn't going to ask her if she felt the same way about him. He suspected she did, but since it wasn't going to change things, there wasn't much point.

"So," he said into the heavy silence, changing the subject and pushing away the way she made his heart beat faster, "how was Connor this morning?"

She dusted the sugar off her fingers. "You said you weren't going to talk about Connor."

"I'm not. I just wanted to know if he gave you a hard time about Cal."

She shook her head, but the expression on her face shuttered, the pretty blush dying away, the glitter in her eyes dimming.

Helpless concern rippled through him. He wanted to reach out and put a hand over hers, ease that look on her face, but he stayed where he was. Touching her was not a good idea.

"What happened?" He leaned forward. "Was there a problem?"

"It's nothing. He just…didn't want to talk about it. And I was going to try and have a conversation with him about it this morning, but he was still asleep."

Ah, kid… This was tough, no doubt about it. And if he was angry with his mom but didn't want to talk to her about it, it was probably because he was trying to protect her.

"Did you tell him I was staying on?" he asked.

"Yes. He didn't say anything."

No, he probably wouldn't. One thing, though, was clear: Connor needed someone to talk to. Damon had told Astrid yesterday that he'd wait for the kid to come to him, which would be the ideal scenario. But if Connor didn't, and if Damon ran out of time, he might have to search the kid out himself.

Tough call.

"Do you want to talk about it?" he asked carefully.

"No." There was no denying the firmness in her tone. "I don't. I think we should discuss the tourism ideas for Deep River instead." She swallowed more coffee, then put the cup down on the desktop, obviously now in business-mode. "Shall I run by you some of the ideas we've collated?"

Damon leaned back in his chair. She didn't want to talk about Connor and that was fine. He'd muse on what he was going to do about it later. In the meantime, he could help with this.

"Sounds good." He nodded to the folder he'd put down on the desk with the coffee and donuts. "This morning I went over some of the suggestions Silas received, and there were a couple that looked like they could be interesting. Why don't you take a look at those, then show me what you have?"

"Okay, good." She pulled open a drawer in the desk, took out a similar-looking folder, and put it down. Then picked up the one Silas had given Damon.

The suggestions for possible tourism options were mostly

good ones, and he'd been intrigued in spite of himself. Kevin Anderson's potential fishing charter business was a solid idea, as was Harry's wilderness skills and guided hikes along some of the game trails that looped through the bush surrounding Deep River. With Silas taking people on scenic flights, there was a good base from which to build other options that centered on Deep River's natural beauty and didn't require a whole lot of capital up front.

"My take on this," he said as Astrid leafed through the folder, "is that if you start small and invest a little here and there before gradually building, it'll be less risky in the long run. Because there'll be other things the town will need to invest in that aren't only tourism projects."

Astrid leaned back in her chair, sipping on her coffee. "Such as?"

"Infrastructure, mainly. This place isn't built to cater to a lot of tourists, and if you're going to be chasing those dollars, you're going to need some amenities, like public bathrooms. Then you'll need businesses that will cater to them. More stores, for example. Entertainment. Places to eat. Places to sleep."

She pulled a face and he laughed. "Yeah, I know. You're thinking it's going to turn into some kind of tourist hellhole, but it won't if you do it right. Because what you don't want is a whole lot of tourists milling around with nothing to do and nowhere to go and leaving you crap reviews online."

She snorted. "Reviews? Really?"

"Yes, people write reviews on Tripadvisor and on their Facebook pages and the various Deep River businesses' Facebook pages—which if they don't have yet, they're going to have to get—or they post pictures on Instagram. What you don't want is people saying what a terrible time they had in Deep River. You want them to have a whole experience. The magic of the wilderness. The pristine scenery. The amazing wildlife. Getting away from the rat race, et cetera et cetera."

Her gaze narrowed. "And 'entertainment' is going to help with that?"

"Well, let me put it to you this way. Are you really going to want a bunch of tourists cluttering up the Moose every night?"

"Hmmm." She reached forward for another donut. "I suppose not."

He grinned. "It's okay. You can have my donut."

In the process of taking a bite, Astrid stilled, her forehead creasing. "Oh. Sorry. I wasn't thinking." She held out the donut to him. "Here. It's yours."

He wondered what she'd do if he leaned forward and took a bite out of the donut, brushing her fingertips with his mouth. Would she blush again? Would she let him take another bite? Lick sugar from the tips of her fingers?

Not helpful.

No, it wasn't. At all.

"It's okay. Eat it. I can get another." He shoved away the flare of interest from the more disreputable parts of himself situated below his belt. "So, back to the tourists. Where are they all going to sleep? You think the ones with money are going to be happy with the Moose's rooms?"

Astrid bit into the donut and chewed. "Nate has the Gold Pan. And there's Clare's B&B."

"Who do they cater to? Hunters and trappers? Fishermen?"

Astrid glanced down at the paper sitting in the folder in front of her and groaned. "Oh, not Mike's luxury motel idea again."

Damon lifted an eyebrow. "Again?"

"Yes. He tried to make something of it last year and people weren't happy about it. There were arguments."

"I think it's a good idea. Done well, places like this can cater to a higher-end tourist. And it doesn't have to be casinos and roller coasters. Ecotourism is a whole thing, so why not go that route?" He shifted in his seat, his legs out in front of him, crossing his ankles. "Of course, that's a long term plan since it'll require more serious investment."

She frowned, her attention still on the paper in front of her, the donut finished. A dusting of sugar sparkled on the side of her cheek and he wanted to put his hand to it, brush it away. He could also see the marks of a sleepless night in the dark smudges beneath her eyes.

His thoughts wandered yet again. Why had she ended up here? Cal had mentioned that he'd given her a place to stay here, but why? What had happened to her that she'd left wherever she was and turned up in Deep River?

"There's kids too," he went on, trying to get back on track. "If you want the family dollar, there's got be some options for them."

"Phil's," she murmured. "His wildlife sanctuary."

"Phil's?"

Astrid took another sip of her coffee. "Filthy Phil. Old guy who lives up the hill behind the town. Bit of an eccentric. He was a trapper back in the day, but he rescues animals now and he's got quite a collection."

An old eccentric with a house full of animals? Could be quite the tourist draw. "Might work," he said. "Go hard with the quirky small-town stuff. People love that."

She looked up, her expression thoughtful. "You should take a tour around the town, talk to people. Get a feel for the place."

"Not a bad idea." He took a swallow of his own coffee. "I've already done a bit of chatting to the locals over the past three days."

"So I hear," she said dryly.

He grinned, meeting her misty gray gaze. "That bad, huh?"

Unexpectedly, she smiled back, slow-blooming and sweet, a rare treasure that hit him somewhere near his heart. "Oh, come on. You must know you've charmed half the population."

You should probably stop this.

He ignored the thought. "Only half? Does that include you?"

Her gaze met his and held, and he could feel the familiar, dense crackling energy of sexual tension fill the space between them.

He very badly wanted to taste her, reach across the desk, thread his fingers through her pretty gold hair, and bring her mouth to his. Would she taste as soft and as sweet as the sugar on her cheeks? Or would there be a cool bite to her, a hint of citrus?

"Damon." His name sounded husky and there was the ghost of a plea in it, though for what he didn't know. To stop or to…

No. Bad idea. If you can't control yourself, then get the hell out.

"Think I might go and get myself another donut after all." He pushed himself sharply out of his chair and stood. "Need anything?"

She blinked in surprise. "I…"

"Good," he said and, without waiting for a response, turned and walked out.

———

Astrid sat back in her chair and took a long breath. What had just happened? Because she was pretty sure something had.

One minute Damon had been lounging across the desk, all long and lean and muscular, blue eyes glinting at her from beneath thick, dark gold lashes. His smile had vanished and he'd looked… hungry. Starved even.

The next minute he'd gotten to his feet and walked out, muttering something about a donut.

You know what happened. Come on.

Astrid closed her eyes, feeling that moment of attraction that had shimmered between them. Different from before, more intense. The hungry look in his eyes had been for her and she knew it, and a part of her had recognized the same hunger in herself too.

Men had never starved for her. It had always been the other way around. She'd been a lonely child growing up, the later-in-life baby that neither of her parents had either expected or wanted, and the requirements placed on her were simple: she wasn't to disrupt their lives in any way. Hungry for any kind of attention, she'd played around as a teenager, gone to the wrong parties, associated with the wrong people. She'd put out a desperate vibe and that had frightened boys off. Wanting someone more than they wanted you had never been a good thing.

But there had been no denying the want in Damon's eyes.

Warmth uncurled inside her at the memory, flowing through her veins and spreading out. It had been so long since she'd been anything more than "the mayor" or "Connor's mom" that she barely remembered what it felt like to be just Astrid. To be a woman.

Because that's what he made her feel like.

You don't want to go there, not with him.

No, she didn't. Yes, she did. Maybe, just once…

Astrid shoved her chair back and stood up, not sure what she was doing, only that she needed to move and get some distance between her and her thoughts. Because thinking *maybe* could lead her to…

Nothing. There was nothing it would lead her to.

She scanned around for something to tidy up that hadn't already been tidied, desperate for some distraction.

It was all looking pretty neat, so she picked up a cloth from a drawer in her desk and went over to one of the old wooden bookshelves, dusting some nonexistent dust before moving on to the series of photos on the wall of previous mayors.

Sonny Clarke, her predecessor, grinned at her from beneath the greasy, black-knitted beanie he never took off, while in the next photo Jesse, the goat who'd been elected in a protest vote, watched her with yellow eyes.

She dusted the glass and goaty face beneath it, her brain returning stubbornly to the brilliant glitter in Damon's eyes and the way he'd been looking at her, as if she was something good to eat. A dangerous thing to fixate on when pretty much every interaction she'd ever had with men had ended badly. At least for her.

It might not end badly this time. After all, he'll be leaving, right?

"No," Astrid muttered to herself. "No way."

"No?" a voice said from the doorway. "No way what?"

Astrid turned.

A small, curvaceous woman in a beautifully tailored blue linen dress stood in the doorway. Her strawberry-blond hair was coiled at the nape of her neck, her face heart-shaped and pretty. She projected an aura of delicate femininity, yet there was nothing overtly feminine about her direct blue stare.

Morgan West. Caleb's sister and Deep River's Village Public Safety Officer, a.k.a. the law, was earnest, principled, honest, and completely committed to her job as town protector.

Astrid liked her very much, though there was always a certain amount of guilt attached when it came to Morgan, because she was another person that Astrid hadn't told about Connor. And considering that Morgan was his aunt…

"Morgan," Astrid said, forcing the guilt away and smiling. "You're back."

"Hi, Astrid." Morgan grinned and came into the office, while Astrid put down her dusting cloth in order to give her a brief hug.

"How are you?" Astrid asked, giving her a concerned look.

Morgan hadn't returned to Deep River immediately after Cal's funeral, and rumor was that she'd been at some kind of police training course. But there had been a few whispers questioning that and even more so after Silas had appeared with the news about the oil and how he was the new co-owner of the town. Speculation had been rife about why Morgan hadn't been named in the will, and then once they'd discovered that Silas had offered the town to her and she'd refused, people were full of questions about why she hadn't wanted Deep River.

Certain factions within the town—traditional factions—had been disapproving. The town belonged to the Wests and should stay with the Wests. They were slightly mollified by the fact that Silas was Deep River born and bred, but they still hadn't been very happy that Morgan had refused. She would come in for a bit of flak for that.

"I'm doing okay." Morgan had a very determined look on her face. "Tell me. How bad is it?"

That was Morgan: direct and to the point. She didn't beat around the bush. And Astrid knew exactly what she was asking.

"The town is in an uproar," she answered, just as blunt. "People are worried. They want to know why the sole remaining West didn't contest the will or accept when the town was offered to her. And that's not even going into this oil stuff."

An expression that Astrid couldn't read flickered over Morgan's pretty face. "Right. So, kind of what I expected. Silas came to the party though, didn't he?"

Astrid let out a breath. "Yeah, he did. In fact, he's been great—pulled the town together, got everyone to make a decision about how they were going to tackle it."

Morgan nodded, as if this was what she'd expected. "Good. I knew Silas could handle it."

Astrid debated whether to just come out and ask or whether to let it lie. But then it was something Morgan wouldn't shy away from, so she decided not to either.

"Silas said that he offered you the town and you refused it," she said carefully. "I don't mean to pry, Morgan, but people were asking. They were shocked about the oil too. I mean, did you even know Caleb had been prospecting? That there were reserves under the ground?"

"Can we not talk about it now?" Steel shone in her blue-gray eyes, yet there was no mistaking the note of pain in her voice. "It's private family business."

Well, if Morgan didn't want to talk, then she didn't want to talk.

"Okay, no drama." Astrid kept her tone mild. "People will just have to suck it up."

Morgan's mouth worked as if she'd been going to say something, then it firmed, Officer West firmly in control. "I'd like a rundown on the situation if you've got time."

"Of course." Astrid gestured at the chair that Damon had vacated. "Take a seat and I'll walk you through it."

"Astrid." The steel in Morgan's gaze had eased. "I'm not trying to be difficult, okay? At the moment, all I want is some normality."

That was something Astrid could get on board with. She could use some normality right now herself and it was a pity there wasn't much of it to go around.

"Hate to say it, but normality pretty much disappeared when Cal died," she said.

Grief flickered across Morgan's face. "I suppose so." She turned abruptly and went over to the chair near the desk and sat down. "Tell me anyway, then."

Chapter 8

COMING OUT OF THE MAYOR'S OFFICE, HIS HEAD STILL FULL OF the glitter of heat in Astrid's eyes, it took Damon a moment or two to notice a familiar figure.

Connor was once again lounging near the Nowhere pole, his hands in the pockets of his jeans, his strawberry-blond hair gleaming the sun.

Hell, that was another thing to think about. Were people going to notice the resemblance at some stage? He'd met Morgan West at the funeral, and her hair was exactly the same color. It wasn't common either.

Connor came to attention instantly and started toward him in a very determined manner. Clearly the kid had something to say, which was good. Damon had been hoping Connor would seek him out rather than the other way around.

"I'm going to April's to get donuts," he said casually as Connor approached. "Want one?"

"You were supposed to be leaving." Connor sounded personally offended by this, his blue eyes snapping with anger. "You weren't supposed to be hanging around."

Damon didn't react. "Nice to see you too, Connor."

"What were you doing in Mom's office?" The kid was bristling with the same prickly energy he'd noticed around Astrid. "You don't need to talk to her."

Damon studied his face. There was something more going on than simple anger that Damon hadn't left and that he'd been talking to Astrid. Naturally it would be complicated by Caleb's death, but that wasn't the only thing at work here.

"I like that you're looking out for your mom." Damon kept his voice uninflected, holding the kid's gaze so Connor could see the truth in his eyes. "But you don't need to protect her from me. I'm not going to hurt her. I've just been talking to her about tourism opportunities for Deep River. That's all."

"That would sound good if I trusted you. But I don't."

"Fair enough. I wouldn't trust me either. Have you been waiting for me?"

Connor looked disdainful. "No."

"Do you want to talk?"

"Absolutely not."

"Shall I get us a donut and hot chocolate?"

The kid's jaw worked, every line of him in denial.

Damon gave him a minute.

"Coffee," Connor said, the very essence of grudging. "I like coffee." And then, as an afterthought, "Please."

Damon nodded, keeping his grin to himself as he pushed open the door to April's and went inside. He'd take grudging. That was progress.

A couple of minutes later, he came out again, carrying coffees for himself and Connor, plus another bag containing the donuts.

"I'm not talking to you," Connor warned. "But thank you for the donuts."

Damon decided not to respond to that, jerking his head toward the dock, then starting toward it, the boy trailing along behind him.

A couple of boats were still moored, but most of them had gone downriver to the sea. Kevin Anderson's was on the other side of the river, though whether he was picking someone up or dropping them off, Damon couldn't tell.

He went down the wooden stairs and along the dock a ways, then putting down the food and drink, sat down on the side, his legs dangling over the edge.

Connor came up to him, hovered there a minute as if uncertain what to do, then finally, reluctantly, sat down beside him.

Damon handed him his coffee and a donut.

"Thank you," Connor said politely, taking them.

Good manners even when annoyed. That was an excellent start.

Silence fell and Damon let it sit there, broken only by the rushing of the river beneath the dock, the sound of the odd conversation drifting from the town nearby, and the call of a bird somewhere overhead.

The sun was still shining, settling warmly on his back and doing a good job of convincing him that it was summer. Though it wouldn't actually be summer for another few weeks yet.

It was peaceful in this place. More peaceful than Juneau. He'd thought the day before about the magic of Alaska, but this town had a magic all its own. In the mountains that surrounded the town and in the deep green of the river it was named for.

He liked it very much.

"You like her, don't you?" Connor asked after a moment.

Ah, hell. Damon knew what he was talking about and he did not want to get into it. "You really want to talk about me and your mom when you could be asking me about your father?"

But the kid didn't back down. "It's just a question."

Damon glanced at him.

Connor looked back, challenging.

"Yeah, I do like her," Damon said, giving him the truth because he wasn't going to lie. Connor deserved the truth and so did Astrid. "But just so you know, nothing's going to happen. I'm leaving the day after tomorrow."

Connor's gaze was full of distrust and suspicion, but there was something more swimming in the depths. Something that Damon thought looked an awful lot like fear.

His heart shifted in his chest, the feeling unexpectedly sharp. At another time, he might have been worried by that, because his feelings were always muted, the sharp edges blunted long ago. But there were too many questions in his head to be concerned about that now.

Why was this boy afraid? And about what? Was it him, Damon himself? Connor had been mad about Damon talking to Astrid, which mean the kid was worried for his mother.

Someone has hurt these two and badly.

The thought sat in his head, the edge keen as a razor blade. The kid's protectiveness and worry, his fear—they were all giveaways. Astrid was more guarded and reserved, and there was a wariness to her. She radiated "only so far and no farther." Yet there were hints of a more passionate nature underneath all that cool, little flickers of fire and electricity.

People hid stuff all the time, and he knew that better than most.

These two were hiding something. And if he wanted to know what it was, he would have to go carefully.

Why do you want to know?

A redundant question. He had a promise to keep and if that involved finding out what had hurt a boy and his mother, then he would. And maybe he'd hurt the son of a bitch responsible in turn, because he had no problem with that. No problem with that whatsoever.

"You said you'd leave yesterday," Connor said. "And you didn't."

"No. I didn't," Damon agreed. "Thought I'd stay in case you wanted to talk to me about your dad."

"You mean you stayed for me?" Connor looked frankly disbelieving. "Why?"

"The truth? Because your father asked me to."

Connor's face went blank. "What?"

"You got a letter from your dad and so did I. He wanted me to look out for you, make sure you were okay. So that's why I'm here."

Connor stared at him for a moment longer, then glanced away, out over the water, holding his coffee in his hands. "I didn't ask to be looked out for."

"I know."

"He could have looked out for me himself." Connor's voice deepened with hurt. "He knew where I was."

Caleb, you asshole.

Damon had the strangest urge to put a hand on Connor's back, a comfort and a support, just to let him know he was there. But he knew the kid wouldn't welcome it, so instead he said, "You know why he didn't, don't you?"

Connor shook his head, his jaw tense, his attention still out over the water.

"He was ashamed," Damon said. "He was ashamed of the way he treated your mom when she got pregnant. He…ran away. He was only two years older than you are now, so he was very young. Over the years, he came to realize what an awful thing he'd done, and so when Astrid needed some help, he gave it to her. And to you too."

"But he didn't want to see me. He knew where I was and he didn't come."

"Like I said, he was ashamed. You know what Caleb West was to this town. I think he was afraid of what people might think of him."

Connor looked down, saying nothing.

"He was wrong," Damon went on softly. "He should have said something to you. He could have done that at least."

"Yeah, well, he didn't." Connor took an angry bite of his donut.

Well, the kid might be angry, but at least he wasn't going to waste a good donut.

Damon let the silence hang for another couple of moments, trying to think about how he could help, what he could do. It seemed as if all the adults in Connor's life—and some of them for good reasons, no doubt—hadn't been very clear with him. They'd kept information back. Which mean that right now what the kid really needed was to be told what was going on.

It wasn't his place to do that, but he had a duty to Cal. And who else did Connor have to talk to who already knew his secret and who knew his father? No one. And Damon was neutral ground too, which helped. Kid wouldn't have to worry about getting angry with him because he had no horse in this race.

"Your mom was protecting you, I think," Damon murmured. "By not telling you who he was."

"How is that protecting me?"

"Cal didn't want anyone knowing he had a kid. And I guess your mom wanted to protect you from that." Damon paused. "Every boy wants their father to be a hero, right? Running away from responsibility and denying that you have a kid isn't exactly heroic. I suspect your mom wanted better for you than that."

Connor stared out over the water. He finished the donut, then sipped at his coffee, his posture stiff, his jaw tight. "Mom told me once that my dad was a soldier and he was fighting a lot. And that one day she'd tell me all about him. When I was old enough."

Damon thought about the wariness in Astrid, that prickling energy when he'd talked to her about Connor. Complicated. All of this was complicated.

"Your father was a flawed guy," he said, sipping at his coffee too, keeping things neutral. "But at heart, he was a good one. And he was trying to make up for mistakes he'd made when he was very young." Caleb's haunted face from that night on watch drifted in his memory, full of regret and grief yet also determination. "I think he knew he'd left it too late, but he still wanted to do the right thing by you."

"If he'd wanted to do the right thing, he could have left the town to me instead of you assholes."

"Ah." Damon tried not to grin at the boy's aggrieved tone, something in him easing slightly since being aggrieved was better than hurt. "Is that why you're running around helping people? Throwing yourself between the town and me? You trying to protect this place?"

Connor glanced at him, a fierce expression on his face. "Of course. My dad might not have left it to me, but it's still my responsibility. You're a stranger. You're all strangers. I don't know what you're going to do, so someone has to make sure that Deep River stays safe."

Sympathy gripped him. Connor was an intense, determined kid with a highly developed sense of what was right and wrong. A good kid, as Astrid had told him.

Damon met his gaze, giving him honesty, taking him seriously. "I get it. And that's a legit concern. Any stranger that comes into your town, you're going to want to check them out, see if they're on the level."

Connor's jaw jutted, his gaze narrowing, obviously searching for signs that Damon was laughing at him. He didn't find any. "Yeah. That's right."

"That's good. Protecting those you care about is important. It's what separates a good man from a crappy one."

"Well, I—"

"But you can't protect a whole town on your own, kid," Damon interrupted gently. "That's a hell of a responsibility for a grown man, let alone a teenager."

"So? I can take it."

"Sure you can." Damon sipped on his coffee peaceably. "But you know, Cal left it to three of us. Not just Silas. Or me. Or Zeke. He spread the responsibility around 'cause that's tough for one person to carry."

"Yeah, but he did it," Connor pointed out. "He was on his own."

"No, he wasn't. Cal had his sister. And he had the mayor. In fact, he had the whole town with him, helping him and supporting him, because people look out for each other as well. Understand?"

A muscle flicked in Connor's square jaw.

"You're on your own," Damon went on, giving it to him straight. "You don't have any buddies at your side. You don't have a sister.

You can't have the mayor because she's your mom and you have to protect her. And because no one knows who you really are, you don't even have the town."

Connor looked away. He picked up a stone sitting beside him on the dock and threw it hard into the river.

Damon didn't want to hurt him. He only wanted Connor to acknowledge the weight of the burden he was carrying, that it was heavy even for an adult. Responsibilities always were.

"You know I told you that my mom was sick?" Damon said after a moment.

"Yeah."

"I can't look out for her on my own. Because I have responsibilities to Wild Alaska, to Silas and Zeke. So I get a housekeeper to check on her, to make sure she's okay. It's not the best, which is why I have to go home soon. But trusting the housekeeper helps Mom and it helps me handle what I need to up here. Everyone wins."

"Is this some kind of 'everyone support each other' story that old people like to tell?"

This time Damon didn't hide his grin. "Guess I can't get anything past a teenager these days, huh?"

Connor gave him a withering look. "I'm not stupid."

"And I'm not stupid either. Which is why I trust Mom's housekeeper." He let his grin fade. "You've got a weight on your shoulders, kid, and I get it. But if you need someone to help you carry it, you can trust me, okay?"

Something flickered through the boy's eyes, something that looked like longing. Then it was gone, suspicion replacing it, along with a cool wariness that reminded Damon forcibly of Astrid. "What? You're not going to tell me it's none of my business and that I should butt out?"

Damon shook his head. "Why would I do that? Deep River's your town. You're a West, right? All of this is your business."

Connor stared at him for a long moment, his expression unreadable. The kid did a nice line in stoic when he wanted, that was for sure. Then he looked away again. "Why did he tell you about me? Why did he ask you to look out for me?"

The scar on Damon's heart, the one that he'd carry for the rest of his life, ached.

There were lies he could tell Connor. Lies that would stop that scar from aching, that didn't have the potential to tear it or make it bleed. But Connor needed more truth, not less, and besides, that scar was an old one and most of the time it didn't hurt.

"Because I was a father once." He hadn't said those words to anyone else, not for years. "And Cal knew I'd do what he asked."

Connor threw in another stone. "You had a kid?"

"Yeah. A little girl."

"Where is she?"

He could feel the tightness of that scar and the exact shape of it. Strange to feel it again after so many years, when all it used to do was ache. But gradually, time had worked its magic, and these days he could even pretend that scar wasn't there at all.

Except it was.

"She died," he said.

He could feel the kid looking at him. He didn't look back though. Some things you had to keep to yourself and the kid didn't need to see what was no doubt in his eyes.

"I'm sorry," Connor said at last and with feeling. "That sucks."

Bizarrely, the aching tightness eased. Telling someone about Ella was always hard because not only did he have his own grief to bear, he had to bear someone else's. Their sympathy and their pain as they tried to empathize, tried to imagine what it was like to have something similar happen to them and then shy away from it, the reality too awful to contemplate.

Yeah, it had always been complicated telling people. So now he never told anyone.

But Connor was a kid, with a kid's viewpoint. He didn't and couldn't understand a parent's unique hurt. His sympathy was honest and heartfelt, but Damon knew the boy wasn't taking on anything else but that.

And somehow "that sucks" was the best response he'd heard for years.

"Yeah," he said and he didn't have to force the words. "It does."

Connor didn't say anything for long moments after that and neither did he, the pair of them sitting in a silence that bordered on companionable.

The river rushed beneath the dock, the mountains stretching up all around, touching the hazy blue of the sky, the sun lying warm on their shoulders. An eagle soared above them, wings outstretched, drifting on the breeze.

Then finally, Connor shifted. "How long are you staying?" He didn't look at Damon.

"Today and tomorrow."

"Okay." Connor slowly pushed himself to his feet. "Good."

Then he turned and walked away.

Damon watched him go, a complicated kind of emotion sitting in his chest, then his phone suddenly vibrated in his pocket. Clearly some service was back.

He tugged it out, his heart clenching as he saw on the screen that it was his mom.

"Hey, Mom," he said, answering the call. "What's up?"

"There's a stranger in my house," Laura Fitzgerald said without any preliminaries. "I don't like it, Damon."

"It's just Rachel, Mom." He kept his tone patient. "The housekeeper, remember?"

"I don't need a housekeeper. I've been keeping my own damn house for years."

"I know. But she's not there for you. She's there so I don't have to keep calling you and interrupting your shows."

"You don't have to keep calling me." His mother sounded cross. "I'm perfectly fine."

"Of course you are, but I'm a worrier."

"Well, you don't have to worry about me." There was a pause. "When are you coming home?"

Tension gathered inside him. It was the first time she'd asked him that.

"Soon, Mom," he said. "Very soon, I promise."

His mother seemed satisfied with the assurance, though she complained about Rachel for a few more minutes before ending the call with her usual abruptness.

Afterward, Damon sat on the dock and stared at nothing.

Really, the quicker he tied everything up here in Deep River, the better it would be for all concerned.

———————

After she'd given Morgan a rundown of the past couple of weeks, and Morgan had left, Astrid debated waiting in her office for Damon to turn up again, especially since they hadn't finished talking about all the tourism stuff.

But she had other things to do and trailing around the town looking for him was going to take up too much time. Sure, the town wasn't very large and it wouldn't take that long to find out where he was, but it would probably be best if she didn't go looking for him immediately. She needed a break from his distracting presence anyway.

The library needed her attention, but her first stop was Mal's Market, so she could talk to Mal about how her meeting with the growers had gone the day before.

The market was a treasure trove of a place, full of towering shelves piled high with all kinds of things ranging from cereal boxes to complete dinner sets, boxes of nails to bottles of hairspray, tins of sardines and tins of pâté, while in the rafters above were stored fishing rods, skis, ski poles, shovels, and brooms, among other things.

There was also an internet station where reliable web access could be obtained via Mal's satellite connection, plus plenty of DVDs in the DVD library, as well as videos for those who still had VCRs.

A magical place, full of the smell of sawdust, wood polish, wet parkas, and spices. The place people came when they needed anything at all, even if it was just a good gossip with Mal.

Mal was behind the counter now, a tall, burly man in his late fifties with a salt-and-pepper beard, a buzz cut, tattoos up both arms and dressed in jeans and blue flannel. He was chatting with a collection of people all standing around the counter, mostly female Astrid couldn't help but notice.

And then she realized who was at the center of the collection.

Damon Fitzgerald.

He leaned against the counter, smiling that devastating smile and talking easily with the assembled crowd, all of whom appeared to be hanging on his every word. And no wonder. With his caramel-brown hair, sky-blue eyes, and his fallen-angel handsomeness, he looked like a king holding court with his subjects.

Her heart stumbled in her chest, her breath catching.

It wasn't fair. All those things he'd said in her office about wanting to take her to dinner and talk to her, then maybe even take her home afterward, she suddenly wanted too. But he was right. It couldn't happen between them. There were too many complicating factors, especially the ones he didn't know about.

Aiden had seemed to be too good to be true too, exactly like Damon. Handsome and charming, excellent with her son. A man a woman could fall for so easily. A man who'd turned out to be one of the worst choices she'd ever made.

No, she couldn't risk that again. Damon had to remain off-limits.

Stopping in the middle of the aisle, she debated whether to simply turn around and walk out. But then they still had the town's tourist ideas to discuss, and he was only going to be here another day…

Her whirling thoughts stopped in their tracks as Damon looked up, his gaze catching hers, and everything went entirely out of her head.

Everyone turned to look at her.

"Hey, Ms. Mayor." He was all deep-voiced charm and that amazing smile, warmth igniting in his blue eyes that she knew was just for her. "I've been looking for you."

She didn't want to smile back, but not smiling was impossible when he looked at her that way. "Well, you've found me." Somehow, even though she knew turning around and walking out was better, she found herself going up to the counter instead. "Anything I can help you with?"

"We didn't finish our conversation earlier." He raised a brow. "Got a minute now?"

No, she didn't have a minute. And talking to him was a very bad idea.

"Sure," she said, hoping she wasn't blushing like an idiot because he seemed to have that effect on her every time he even looked in her direction, and she didn't need an audience to that right now. "I need to have a word with Mal first."

Amusement glinted in Mal's eyes, as if he knew exactly the kind of effect Damon was having on her.

Curse the man. Both men.

"About the growers," Astrid began.

"Yeah, I already know," Mal said before she could go on. "I thought you'd have a bit much on your plate with all this tourism stuff, so I called them both this morning to find out how your meeting with them went." He grinned. "It's all fixed up. First lot of produce will be boxed up and ready to go tomorrow morning."

"Oh, good. That's great." Her momentary irritation vanished. "Thanks, Mal."

Excellent. Another project safely off the ground. Hopefully it would be viable and end up being good for everyone.

"Phil's wanting more books though," Mal said casually. "I spoke to him this morning on the phone. He got through the last stack quicker than he thought, and he said could you get him some more."

"No problem. I think the title he specifically requested last week has just come in, so I'll get it up the hill to him."

"Phil?" Damon glanced at her. "As in 'animal sanctuary' Phil?"

Ah yes, she'd mentioned that to him, hadn't she?

She nodded.

"I'll take them up if you like." His eyes glinted from beneath his lashes. "Someone told me to go and speak to people in the town, and I haven't had a chance to talk to him yet."

Her. That had been her. A small glow of warmth centered itself in her chest for absolutely no reason at all, because who cared if he took her suggestion? Certainly she didn't.

The women clustered around the counter—Debbie Long, Jenny Anderson, Melissa Evans, and Maria's friend Coco Smith— all murmured admiringly.

"That's a lovely thing to do." Jenny put a hand on one of Damon's powerful shoulders. "Phil would appreciate that so much."

Jenny liked a handsome man—hell, most of those women did, and Astrid couldn't blame them for falling all over Damon. Men like him didn't turn up in Deep River often. No, scratch that. They didn't turn up in Deep River at all.

Still. The way they were looking at him irritated her the way it had after hot yoga this morning.

Jealous maybe?

How stupid. There was nothing for her to be jealous of. Yet the sight of Jenny's hand on his shoulder, touching the textured fabric of his shirt, a fabric she wouldn't mind touching herself, was… annoying.

"He would appreciate it," she agreed coolly. "I was just on my way to the library, so why don't you come with me and I'll give you his books?"

Damon's smile curved his beautiful mouth. "I was hoping you might say that." Pushing himself away from the counter, he stood at his full height, turning that smile on the adoring female crowd. "Ladies, thanks for your time. It's been a pleasure." He glanced at Mal and held out a hand. "Appreciate your time too."

"No problem." Mal took Damon's hand and shook it, smiling back. "Good to talk to you. I like a man who makes an effort to get to know the locals."

The warmth in Astrid's chest glowed hotter. He really had taken on board her suggestion, hadn't he? It made her feel ridiculously pleased, though she had no idea why.

"You do know that Phil's is a good half-hour walk?" she said as Damon turned toward the exit.

"You don't think I can walk a half hour carrying a couple of pounds' worth of books? Maybe I'm falling behind in my workout regimen."

A patently untrue statement given he was built like a Greek god.

"Hmmmm." She made a show of examining him as she followed him out of the market. "Seems like you could maybe handle it. You can never tell with city boys, though."

Wickedness glinted in Damon's eyes. "Are you calling me soft?"

"If the shoe fits," she murmured as they came out onto the boardwalk.

He laughed that distractingly sexy laugh. "Harsh, Ms. Mayor. But maybe you're right. It's been a while since I've gone twenty miles with fifty pounds on my back. Perhaps I should run there to build up my stamina?"

"You should. I'll time you."

There was no reason for her heart to lift as they turned toward the library, her leading the way. But it did. His presence was as warm as the sun on her shoulders and somehow exciting. He could be so reassuring and yet under that reassurance was a sense of danger. The kind of delicious, sensual danger that women loved…

And look how that turned out last time.

Badly. It had turned out badly.

"Want to tell me why you left so abruptly earlier?" she asked, trying not to think about Aiden. Or her past in general. Or how the excitement inside her just didn't know when to quit.

Damon strolled beside her, his hands in his pockets, his attention ahead of him as they walked along the boardwalk to the street. "I think you know why."

A flush crept over her. Stupid question to ask. On the other hand, wasn't it better to know for certain?

"I wouldn't like to assume," she said. "Leads to all kinds of misunderstandings."

He glanced at her. "You want me to say it, then? Fine. I left because it was either that or I reached over your desk, dragged you out of your chair, and kissed you."

Oh. *Oh.*

"That's clear." Her voice had gotten husky, dammit. "Good thing you left, then."

"Isn't it?"

A silence fell between them, crackling and electric.

She was so very aware of him as he walked beside her, long legs, narrow hips, and broad shoulders… There was nothing soft about him in any way.

If she'd been just a woman in a bar that he'd approached, she'd have given him her number the moment he'd asked for it. Or maybe she'd even have approached him and asked him for his.

It wasn't to be, though. More's the pity.

Astrid tried to ignore that as she led the way along the road from the boardwalk, going down the little gravel path that led to the library, Damon following along behind her.

The library was situated in a small, self-contained wooden cabin on the riverbank just along from the Deep River town center. It had a porch out in front that Phil had donated a couple of his hand-carved chairs to, with a few wind chimes that Gwen had made hanging from the eaves. Sparkling crystals dangled from the bottom of the chimes, sending prismatic glitters everywhere, and while Astrid privately thought the crystals were overkill—for good vibes, Gwen had told her—she'd always liked the sound of the chimes.

Perhaps it was wrong to have wind chimes making noise outside a library, but Astrid didn't care. It was a happy, welcoming sound and it soothed her.

She went in—she never locked the place since no one ever locked doors in Deep River—heading over to the sole work desk that stood in one corner, a big box of books sitting next to it.

"This is the nicest damn library I've ever been in," Damon said as he came inside after her, looking around with interest.

The library was only one room, with shelves lining the walls and one long shelf running down the center of the room, books shelved on both sides. There were no couches or places to sit, since the library was small and every square inch had been given over to books.

"Isn't it?" Astrid bent over the box and opened it, going through what was inside until she'd found the book Phil had particularly wanted—a romance, since he loved romances—stuck a bar code on it, then went to enter it into the system.

Damon wandered over to one of the shelves, studying the titles. "So you're the librarian as well as the mayor?" he asked.

"Yes. When I first got here, the town had a library but no one to manage it, so I decided I would."

"And who pays for it?"

"The Wests. There's some money they put aside for town expenses, and my salary is part of that, as is a small allocation for books."

"Seems like a good system."

"It works well, yes."

Astrid put the book through the scanner, issuing it to Phil, and when she looked up, she found Damon had turned from the shelves and was watching her. A shiver of heat whispered over her skin.

"What?" she asked.

"I spoke to Connor after leaving your office this morning." He moved slowly over to the desk. "Kid was hanging around outside as I left, so I bought him a coffee and a donut and we had a conversation." Damon paused. "For the record, he was waiting for me so he could warn me off you."

Astrid's gut lurched. "Oh, God, I'm sorry. I don't know—"

"It's okay. Connor was just worried about you. And he's worried for this town. And it seems I was right: he feels responsible for it and for you too."

Worry hit her and guilt—and grief too. Worry for her son and guilt for what she hadn't told him. Grief for what she'd put him through and what he felt he had to take on, for the fact that he hadn't told her any of this.

She would have given everything in that moment to have not met Aiden that day in the café where she'd been working. To not have had Connor sitting nearby because he'd been sick and she'd had no childcare and had had to bring him to work despite her boss's disapproval. To not have talked to him or for him to notice Connor and ask if he was her son. He'd been so nice to her and she'd been at the end of her rope…

If only she hadn't brought him into their lives, maybe things would have been different…

She lifted a hand to her forehead, half turning away, not sure why it was hitting her so hard now, when she hadn't even thought about Aiden for at least a year or so.

It was Caleb's death and all that had brought with it, that was the issue.

"Hey, what's up?" Damon's voice was warm with concern. "I didn't mean to upset you."

"You didn't," she said. "It's fine."

It wasn't fine, though. Her eyes were prickling with unexpected tears and her throat felt tight. God, what was wrong with her? She usually managed her own emotions much better than this.

It took her a moment to realize that Damon had come around the desk to her, moving even closer. And then his fingers closed around hers, gently pulling her hand away from her forehead. The concern in his voice was there in his eyes too, and she was gripped by the almost overwhelming urge to lean against him, lean into his strength, because he had such a lot to spare and her reserves right now were so low.

But she knew how that went. He'd play nice at the beginning. Get her to trust him, to depend on him. Get her to think that maybe this time would be different. And then he'd turn on her the way men like him always did.

Damon could be different, it was true. But she couldn't risk it.

He frowned, letting go of her hand and searching her face. "If it's about Connor, it's okay. I know he hasn't spoken to you, but he asked me how long I'd be here and when I told him, he said 'good.' I think that means he's okay to talk to me at least."

Yes, that was good. Her poor boy needed someone, especially if he felt he couldn't talk to her, and clearly he did. Strange that he should trust this man though, when after Aiden, he didn't tend to trust men in general.

Or perhaps it's not strange. Perhaps Damon is actually someone you can trust.

She couldn't believe that though, not yet.

"He doesn't want to talk to me, does he?" It sounded so pathetic she wished she hadn't spoken. But it was too late now.

"It's not that," Damon said firmly. "He probably doesn't want to worry you with it. And I say that because I was his age once, and my mom was a single mom too. She worked two jobs, was constantly worrying over money, and so any issue I had, I handled it myself because I didn't want to add to the load."

Her brain latched onto the small morsel of information. "Oh yes, you mentioned your mom was on her own."

"Yeah. My dad up and left when I was barely a toddler, so my mom brought me up herself. I know how it goes, Astrid. And Connor knows too. He's just trying to lighten the load."

Astrid's throat constricted. Of course Connor was. But what Damon didn't realize was just how heavy that load had been, both for her and Connor.

You should tell him. He'd understand.

No, she couldn't. Damon was an unknown quantity, and with this attraction between them, once she told him one thing, she'd find herself telling him everything. And she couldn't do that. She'd been burned and burned badly, and there was no trust left in her.

So all she did was nod, concentrating instead on his gaze, so blue and depthless she felt as if she were falling.

The moment lengthened, tension gathering around them the way it had back in her office earlier. The gleam in his eyes intensified, became electric.

"Astrid…" His voice had become even deeper, liquid honey surrounding her.

She couldn't move. Couldn't look away from him.

He was very close, and he was so very tall, muscular, and powerful. And she didn't just want to lean into his strength; she wanted to inhale his scent, touch the fabric of his shirt, feel the hardness of the chest beneath it. Distract herself from the ache of guilt and grief in her heart, the feeling she'd let down the one person in the world she shouldn't have.

Just one touch. That would be enough, wouldn't it?

She lifted her hand and laid it on his chest.

He went very still, the electric gleam in his eyes flaring. And she thought he might pull her hand away or step back, but he didn't do either of those things. Instead, he lifted his own hand and laid it over hers, pressing her palm against him.

She could count the number of times she'd touched him, each moment glowing and warm, like pearls in a necklace of glass beads. Shaking his hand when he'd first introduced himself, and then again when he'd made her reciprocate up in the Moose yesterday. And then this morning, his fingers brushing her cheek as he'd pushed that curl back behind her ear…

And now this moment. His big hand enclosing hers, holding it against him, the scent of him around her, sandalwood and spice. His heat seeping through the fabric of his shirt and into her.

"Astrid." Her name again, his voice huskier now, deep and soft as velvet.

"What?"

"You should stop me."

"Stop you from what?" She couldn't look away from him. Couldn't tear her gaze from the astonishing blue of his eyes.

His other hand lifted, his fingers brushing along the line of her jaw, stroking her skin. Making her shiver. Threading into her hair, cradling the back of her head.

He was so gentle, handling her as if she was precious.

She trembled.

"Stop me from doing this."

Then he bent his head and his mouth covered hers, and Astrid was lost.

Chapter 9

DAMON HADN'T MEANT TO KISS HER. HE'D ONLY WANTED TO reassure her because he'd recognized the guilt in her eyes when he'd mentioned Connor, and seen the grief too. Knew the fear that had glittered in the misty depths of her gaze as she'd wondered if her son would talk to her. She was worried that she'd irreparably hurt him, and Damon got that. It was familiar. The questions he'd asked himself after Ella had gotten sick—Had he fed her the wrong thing? Let her come into contact with something she shouldn't? Not given her the vitamins she needed?—were the same things everyone asked themselves when they were responsible for someone else who ended up hurt or sick.

Most people wanted to do right by the people in their care and so did Astrid. It was written all over her face.

Connor hadn't said why he hadn't talked to his mom, but Damon could guess—mostly because he'd done the same thing with his own mother. He'd wanted to protect her, hadn't wanted to worry her.

But he hadn't thought Astrid would touch him, that her touch would make his breath catch and every part of him sit up and take notice.

He hadn't thought he wouldn't be able to stop himself from putting his hand over hers, from pressing her palm to his chest, the feel of it echoing through him, making him feel edgy and raw, the sensations sharp after years of blunted, muted feelings.

He hadn't thought he wouldn't be able to keep from reaching out to caress the soft skin of her jaw, watching as her eyes turned from misty gray into pure silver as the passion inside her came out to play. That tense, bristling energy turning into something much more fluid and supple, hot and needy.

She'd looked at him like she was desperate, and it had been a long time since someone had been desperate for him—since he'd *let* anyone be desperate—and no, he hadn't been able to stop himself.

Her mouth was soft opening beneath his, and she tasted as sweet and sugary as he'd imagined. And yes, there was a bite to her. But not like citrus. It was more a kick of something alcoholic, heady as summer wine and going straight to his head just as quickly.

He could also taste heat in her, the passion that he'd seen in her gaze. A secret she kept locked away, and yet now, as she pressed against him, a secret that was his too. He didn't think anyone knew about the fire that burned inside cool and capable Astrid James, and he liked that. Liked it far too much for his own good.

Her fingers spread out on his chest, and her mouth was hungry, as if she hadn't eaten for days and he was her first taste of food.

This was such a bad idea and he knew it. But the moment she'd set foot in the market, and everyone had looked at her, and she'd stood there looking back, her gaze finding his, her face lighting up.

He'd missed that. Missed having someone so pleased to see him that they glowed. The last person to do that had been his daughter, and since she had gone, there had been no one else.

Because you never let anyone get close enough.

And he shouldn't be letting this woman get close enough either, but he couldn't stop himself. She was too irresistible and he wanted her too much.

Her hands were both against his chest, pressed to his shirt, and she was kissing him back with a desperation that wound around his heart and pulled tight.

Backing her against the desk, he pushed his fingers deeper into her blond hair, the silky warmth of it flowing over the back of his hand as he eased her head back, allowing him greater access to the heat of her mouth. She moaned as he began to explore her, trying to stay gentle and in control because he always tried to whenever he was with a woman.

He'd never had to try so hard before, though.

She felt small and fragile against him, and yet there was nothing fragile about her kiss. There was a demand and a challenge in it that he found unbearably erotic.

"You should stop me," he repeated against her lips. "Because I don't think I can stop myself."

Her fingers spread out on his chest, caressing. "What if I don't want to stop you?"

"Astrid…" Her name came out low and rough. A warning.

She bit his lower lip, just a little nip, but it went through him like wildfire.

His hands clenched in her hair, and he kissed her again, harder, deeper, pressing her lightly against the desk, fitting those soft, slender curves tighter against him.

She sighed, her fingers winding into the material of his shirt as if she wanted him even closer. She smelled sweet and he wanted to bury his face in her neck, inhale her, fill himself up with that heady scent.

Hell, he'd never wanted to do that with a woman before. What was she doing to him? He really needed to stop. Because apart from anything else, she was still the mayor and Connor's mom, and completely out of bounds.

He lifted his head, holding on to her hair gently and stopping her as she tried to follow his mouth.

"No," he said, his voice rough. "Astrid, this is a bad idea."

Her face was flushed, her eyes glittering. The way she'd looked when she'd come out of her class this morning. He was right: kissing her made her look that way too.

"Why?" She didn't let him go, her fingers still twisted in the fabric of his shirt.

"Remember what I said this morning? About you being

Connor's mom? About you being mayor? Those things are still true."

"I know." The pulse at the base of her throat was frantic. He couldn't take his eyes off it. "I know they are. But...all I am here is the mayor, the librarian. All I am is Connor's mom. And don't get me wrong, I want to be those things. I'm proud to be those things. But it's been a long time since I've been anything else and I...want to be a woman for a change." Her gaze was open, letting him see the desire in it, burning hot. "Does that make sense?"

It did—more's the pity—and he wished it didn't. His body was already urging him to disregard his better self; he didn't need another reason to listen to it. Because it made him think of other things, such as exactly how long it had been for her since she felt that way, and why.

And why you.

Yes, that too.

His fingers tightened in her hair.

"How long?" He was unable to keep from asking. "How long has it been?"

She didn't look away. "Five years."

Everything in him stilled. "Five years?"

"Since I got to Deep River. At first I just didn't want to for... various reasons. And then... It's hard to find someone in a small town. And I haven't met anyone I've wanted to be with..." Her gaze was very direct. "Until you."

Something unexpected twisted in his chest.

"Don't go thinking I'm a good bet," he said roughly. "I'm not a saint, Astrid. And it hasn't been five years for me. It's been a couple of weeks, if that."

"I don't think that. And I don't care how long it's been for you. I don't want a saint. I don't want a relationship." The silver glitter of her eyes darkened. "I just want a moment. This moment. Right here, right now. I want you to make me feel like I'm something more than the things I am here. And it doesn't have to be anything but that."

He couldn't refuse her. How could he? She'd been through some kind of trauma, he could already tell, and even though he didn't know what trauma it was, he knew what trauma felt like. He'd been through his own special brand of hell, after all.

And sometimes a moment was exactly what you needed. A break from real life and its burdens. A moment to feel something good.

God, he really wanted to give her that. It might not have been a long time since he'd been with a woman, but it had been a long time since anyone had needed what he had to give. He could make her feel like she was something more. He could make her feel like a goddess.

"Not here. We should go to the Moose."

"No. People will see us and I don't want any gossip."

She wasn't wrong. Still, the library was a public place.

He released her, then moved around the desk, striding over to the door. Closing it, he flicked the lock so at least they wouldn't be disturbed, then he stalked back.

The desk was in the corner of the library, out of sight of the windows, and the big shelf that ran down the middle of the room would block them from view anyway. He didn't really care for himself, but he didn't want her to be uncomfortable.

Then again, given the way she looked at him now as he came toward the desk, she didn't appear uncomfortable in the slightest—only very hungry.

All of a sudden, he was harder than he'd ever been in his life.

She put her hands back on the desktop and pushed herself up so she was sitting on top of it. Her eyes had gone all silvery, her cheeks a deep pink, her mouth red from his kisses.

She wasn't just tempting. She was temptation incarnate. All that secret, hidden passion was flaming and he wanted it to flame higher, become a blaze.

Damon stepped forward, raised his hands and took her face between his palms.

Then he took her mouth.

The kiss was hot and unbearably sweet. It made him ache, like the echo of something profound that he'd lost and never thought to find again, only to discover it here, in this tiny town, contained in one cool, capable, sexy woman.

It was a deeper feeling than he was used to, but he couldn't pull away now. He wanted this to be good for her, to be special. Because if she was only allowing herself one moment, then he wanted to make sure it would be the best damn moment she'd ever had.

He explored her mouth gently, slowly, nipping and tasting, savoring her. She shuddered, her hands coming to his chest and pressing hard against it, kissing him back with a hunger that pulled at the leash that he had on his control.

But he was good. He kept the kiss a gentle tease that he only slowly began to deepen, turning it more intense, more consuming. Her hair against his fingers felt so good and the scent of her body was sweet and warm, wildflowers on a summer's day.

She gave a throaty moan, her hands sliding down over his chest and stomach, creeping beneath the fabric of his shirt, stroking his skin and leaving little trails of fire everywhere she touched. It made him breathless.

"No," he murmured against her mouth, releasing her hair and pushing her hands away. "No touching."

"But I want to—"

"No." He cupped her face between his palms, staring down into her glittering eyes. "Astrid, honey, if you touch me like that, it'll be over in minutes. And you deserve better than minutes." He stroked the soft skin over her cheekbones with his thumbs. "You want to just be a woman? Then let me make you feel like one."

She took a little breath, leaning into his hands, then sighed. "Okay."

He brushed a kiss over her mouth, then released her. "Lift your arms."

She obeyed without hesitation and he reached for the hem of her silky blue T-shirt, pulling it up and off her, leaving her sitting on the desktop in only a white lacy bra and jeans.

She shivered, an expression he couldn't quite read rippling over her lovely features.

Was that uncertainty? Discomfort? If so, he needed to know because he didn't want her feeling either of those things.

"You okay?" He put his hands on her hips, letting his touch ground her, his thumbs gently stroking the soft exposed skin just above the waistband of her jeans. "You need to tell me if anything's a problem."

"I will." She lifted her hands and put them on his chest again. "Nothing's a problem and I'm okay."

He studied her face, but there was only heat in her gaze now, whatever uncertainty there had been before dissipating. For the slightest of seconds he debated asking her about it, but he didn't want to ruin the moment, and besides, it was clear she was with him.

So he took an instant to look at her, because she was as beautiful as he'd thought she'd be, her skin pale as fresh cream, and then he smiled, letting her see how much he was enjoying the sight of her. "Beautiful," he murmured. "You're beautiful, Astrid."

She flushed and he couldn't resist another kiss. Her mouth opened beneath his like a flower to the sun, and again the taste of her filled him. God, delicious.

He stroked her, letting his hands trail up and down her sides, loving how she shivered in response. And then, when she was breathing faster, harder, he reached behind her, undoing the catch of her bra, pulling the material away from her.

She sighed and leaned against him, and he ran his hands up her back, tracing the curve of her spine, her body so warm and silky it made his already aching groin ache even more.

There was nothing hesitant in her now, and as he kissed his way down her jaw, she shivered, gasping a little as he found a sensitive vein at the side of her neck and followed it with his mouth, licking and nipping.

Her skin tasted delicious, as delicious as that kiss, and felt even better, and when he filled his hands with the soft weight of her breasts, she gasped again. Her nipples were hard and tight, pressing against his palms, and he circled them with his thumbs, making her groan.

She was so responsive, arching into his hands, her arms tight around his neck. Her golden lashes were half-lowered, her mouth red and swollen from his kisses. A beautiful sight. He caught it in his memory and held it fast. Because he wouldn't have it again, he knew that much.

This moment was for her, but he could take something for himself. He hadn't realized how good it felt to have someone need him the way she did.

He kissed her throat, tasting the pulse that beat wild and frantic under her skin, then he bent her back over one arm, trailing kisses over her chest, down to the curve of one breast, teasing her hard nipple with his tongue. She gasped his name, arching her back, and when he took that nipple into his mouth, sucking gently, she moaned.

Her fingers threaded into his hair, holding on tight, as if she didn't want to let him go, and he could feel his own heartbeat racing, his breath catching, the pull of desire inside him becoming more intense, more demanding.

He couldn't remember the last time he'd wanted a woman as intensely as he wanted her. She was like a flame in his hands, scorching him, filling him with wonder and awe.

Astrid James was a bonfire, and no one knew that but him.

He turned his attention to her other breast, covering the tip of it with his mouth and sucking, nipping gently as he slipped one hand down to the fastenings of her jeans and pulled the buttons open.

"Yes," she gasped, arching into his mouth. "Oh, Damon, please…"

He couldn't deny her. He eased his fingers beneath the waist-band of her panties, and down farther, between her thighs, finding her hot and slick. She groaned as he touched her, lifting his head so he could watch her flushed face.

He let her expression be his guide as he stroked her, teased her, listening to her catches in breath and her moans of delight, taking note of each little tremble and movement of her hips, watching ecstasy unfurl over her face.

She was so lovely. He wished he had her in a bedroom, entirely naked, and all the time in the world to explore and discover, see exactly which things made her pant and which things made her moan. But a bedroom and time wasn't what he had. All he had was her partially clothed, on a desk, in a library, and a moment. A moment to make her feel good, that's it.

It wasn't enough.

The thought streaked through his brain, bright as a falling star, then was gone. And he made sure it stayed gone. He couldn't start thinking like that. This was a moment, that's all, and once it was over, it was over.

So he ignored it, stroking and teasing, easing a finger into her slick heat, feeling her shudder and groan in response. Then he ran his hand down her spine as he gave her pleasure with his hand, inciting and soothing at the same time, until she tensed and turned her hot face into his neck.

And shattered in his arms.

―――――

Astrid leaned against Damon's broad chest, the aftereffects of the most intense orgasm she'd ever had rippling through her. It was bliss and all she wanted to do was float in that bliss for a while. She hadn't felt so relaxed or at peace for years, and it made her realize how tensely she'd been carrying herself. As if she'd been in pain for a long time and hadn't known it.

But there was no pain now—only Damon and the heat of his body. The hard strength of him beneath the warm, textured cotton of his shirt reassuring. He smelled good too, all musky and male, and she didn't want to move. She wanted to keep sitting here like this, relaxed and sated, feeling light, as if a burden had been taken from her shoulders. The warm skin of his throat was mere inches from her mouth and she knew all she'd have to do to taste him would be turn her head.

He'd told her she was beautiful and let her see the truth of it in his eyes. Then he'd touched her as if she were a precious work of art, carefully and with gentleness, like he didn't want to break her. And he'd paid attention to her, watching her carefully as he'd stroked and teased her, making it very obvious that her pleasure was important to him.

Aiden hadn't done any of that. He'd taken his pleasure self-ishly. After his initial seduction of her, he hadn't much cared about whether she enjoyed herself or not. And the only comments he'd made during the act had been critical ones, making her feel small and ugly and somehow as if she was doing everything wrong.

Warmth flowed through her entire body, and she turned her head, her mouth brushing the hot skin of Damon's throat, wanting to give back to him all the pleasure that he'd given to her. Because she'd never be like Aiden. He'd been all take and no give, but she wasn't.

Damon's fingers caught in her hair, tangling and holding her still. "Astrid," he said, his voice rough and soft as velvet. "Honey..."

"What?" She kissed him again, sliding her hands beneath the hem of his shirt to his flat stomach again, tracing hard muscle covered in smooth, velvety skin. "Isn't it your turn?"

His breath caught. Audibly. And it was intoxicating to know she had such an effect on a man, especially a man like him.

He's too good to be true. And you know what happens next...

A ghost of an instinctive fear whispered through her, but she ignored it. Nothing would happen next. This was only sex and he'd be going tomorrow, and this was the moment she'd allowed herself. Just the one. Where she didn't have to be the mayor or Connor's mom. Where she could be herself without fear.

And he'd given her that. It was glorious and so was he, and so she would take whatever she wanted for herself in this moment because this was all she'd have.

Will it be enough?

Of course it would. She'd gone five years without; she'd no doubt do it again.

"That was for you," he murmured. "And it's not about me."

"Why not?" She glanced up at him, letting her fingers trail down over the front of his jeans and the hard ridge behind them. "Seems to me you want something for you."

The handsome lines of his face were taut, his blue eyes gone electric. He looked like a man who'd gone without food too long and she was the feast set before him. "That wasn't the point."

"Well, now I'm making it the point." She grabbed the tab of his zipper. "I don't want to just take. I want to give too, so you can take what you need from me."

He stared at her for a long second, emotions she didn't understand rippling through his gaze. But the desire didn't leave. It burned hot and very, very strong.

Then all of a sudden he bent his head and his mouth was on hers in another of those astonishingly hot kisses, blanking her mind and stoking her desire. She'd thought she'd need more time to recover, but apparently not. Apparently she wanted him just as badly now as she had just before.

He tugged her to the edge of the desk, then pulled at her jeans, and she lifted herself so he could strip them down and off, taking her panties with them. His hands stroked her, building her pleasure, making her shake.

There was a brief, desperate moment where he paused to unzip himself and get out a condom, and she saw that his hands were shaking too. It thrilled her. And then she forgot about that as he gripped her hips, pulling her closer, so she was up against the hard, muscled heat of his body. That delicious scent of sandalwood and spice surrounded her, his hands firm; he was a man who knew what he wanted and how to get it and how to make it good for her. His certainty and confidence were unbelievably attractive.

He was a man she could count on. Who gave his word and kept it.

His hands were hot on her hips as he pulled her even closer, fitting her right up against him. The blue of his eyes had turned darker, like midnight, drawing her in; she couldn't look away.

He didn't wait, pushing inside her in one long, slow movement that tore a gasp of pleasure from her. He felt so good there, as if that's where he was supposed to be.

"Astrid." He said her name on a sigh, his voice impossibly deep, pausing as if he had to take a moment to get his breath back.

She knew the feeling. He felt insanely good.

Her arms tightened around his neck and she smiled. Heat flickered like a bonfire in his gaze, and he was looking at her with wonder and awe and a certain amount of amazement. It thrilled her. Had anyone *ever* looked at her that way?

His grip on her tightened, and he drew his hips back, sliding out of her before thrusting back in, a steady, driving movement. Pleasure broke through in a warm, golden wave and she gave a soft, gasping laugh at the sheer joy of it. "Wow. You're something else, Damon Fitzgerald."

His mouth curved in the most wholly beautiful smile she'd ever seen, but he didn't say anything. And he didn't kiss her either. He only looked down into her eyes, sharing the pleasure with her.

The world fell away; there was only him. Inside her, around her, everywhere. Only the pleasure that lifted her up and up, higher and higher with each thrust of his lean hips. Only the heat in his eyes that surrounded her, his astonishing smile that enveloped her.

This is special. This is something you want to have again.

But she dismissed the thought. Right now, the only thing that mattered was the pleasure that filled her, that she gave to him and he gave to her, an unbreakable current shared between them, getting more and more intense.

They didn't say anything. Nothing needed to be said. They understood each other completely.

Then he put one hand at the small of her back, steadying her as he thrust, deeper, harder, urging her closer as his other hand slipped between her thighs, stroking her.

The pleasure fractured in a wild rush, glittering golden shards scattering light everywhere inside her, making her gasp his name as she gave herself up to it, watching his face as it came for him too. Electricity flared in his eyes, his movements becoming wilder and out of sync. Then he stiffened and said her name hoarsely, ecstasy rippling over his beautiful face.

For a long moment afterward, neither of them moved. She found herself leaning against his hard body, her arms around his neck, her face pressed to the soft fabric of his T-shirt. Pleasure echoed through her and she wanted to enjoy it for as long as she could.

Because this moment was going to end and it would end soon.

Regret twisted inside her, bittersweet. But this was what she'd wanted and the only reason she could have it was because he was leaving. This pure, uncomplicated moment of pleasure was all she could allow herself, and now that she'd had it, she couldn't regret it.

His breathing was rough and ragged in her ear, his arms holding her steady. Then he lifted his head, and she knew from the expression on his face that the moment between them was ending. The regret tightened, but she ignored it.

Instead she smiled. "Thank you," she said, her voice husky.

He smiled back, warmer than the sunlight outside. "You're welcome." He brushed a ghost of a kiss over her mouth. "Now, let me make you presentable again."

He dressed her with care, and she let him because she liked him touching her. His hands were gentle as they eased her off the desk, helping her back into her panties and jeans and pulling them up. Then he handed her her bra and she put it on, letting him pull down her silky T-shirt over the top.

She smoothed her hair back behind her ears, while he got rid of the condom and put his own clothing back to rights.

Then there was nothing left to smooth, nothing left to adjust.

The moment was over.

She turned around, ignoring the pinching sensation behind her breastbone, concentrating on the next task at hand, which was Phil's books.

Damon said nothing.

She went over to the shelves, ignoring the deepening silence, pulling the books she needed off them before coming back to the desk. Then she issued them via the computer.

"There," she said, trying to ignore her heartbeat that was doing strange things inside her rib cage, speeding up and slowing down like a restless child who couldn't sit still. "Phil's books."

He'd put himself back together again, the only signs of the pleasure they'd shared the remains of a red stain on his high cheekbones and the crackle of electricity in his blue eyes. His hands were thrust into his pockets and his smile had faded. She couldn't tell what he was thinking. It was as if that instant of closeness had never happened.

Her heart twisted again, harder this time, and she turned away so he wouldn't see it. This was silly. Where was this feeling coming from? He wasn't her boyfriend and she wasn't in love with him. He was a handsome guy she'd known all of two days, whom she had amazing chemistry with. They'd had sex on the desk and it had been wonderful, and now it was over. The end.

She grabbed a pen and a sticky note, wrote down Phil's address, then stuck the note to the book on top of the pile. "That's Phil's address. It's half an hour's walk up the hill." She straightened, smoothed her hair again. "Well, I have some things to do so I better—"

His fingers caught her chin in a gentle but firm grip, turning her face toward him. "Astrid."

But she didn't want to know what he had to say. The ache in her chest was getting stronger and she had to get away from him, go and do something else, distract herself. Because the temptation to hold on to his shirt and beg him for more was rising and she couldn't stop it.

There are always consequences when you give in to what you want.

Oh yes, and didn't she know it? Her entire life was a monument to that little fact.

She pulled herself out of his grip, fighting to ignore the warmth left lingering on her skin from his fingertips. "Sorry," she said, though what she was apologizing for she had no idea. "I've got a busy day ahead of me. Better get on with it."

Her heart kicked in her chest as she turned toward the exit. But again, she ignored it.

He didn't speak again as she went to the door and unlocked it.

And when she walked out, he didn't stop her.

Chapter 10

DAMON SAT AT ONE OF THE TABLES IN THE MOOSE, A STACK OF papers in front of him, a cold beer beside him, and his concentration shot all to hell.

He was supposed to be working out which of the Deep River tourism proposals were the most financially sound, and yet all he could think about was Astrid.

Her in his arms, her cheeks flushed, her eyes gone brilliant. She'd smiled at him as he'd pushed inside her, delight written all over her lovely face. And amazement too, the same amazement he'd felt unfurl inside himself. At the feeling between them, the pleasure and the intense sense of connection.

There had been magic in the moment they'd shared and he could feel that magic still echoing through him. And it haunted him.

He wasn't sure why. Sex had always been easy come, easy go, and he'd been very deliberate about keeping it like that. Physical pleasure was the one intense feeling he allowed himself—as long as it didn't stray into the realm of emotional. So far, that hadn't been a problem. Then again, he'd always chosen partners who hadn't wanted anything from him but sex.

Astrid was different. Sure, she'd said she just wanted sex, but he'd seen the need in her eyes as he'd touched her. As he'd pushed inside her. Joy and wonder too. She'd looked at him as if she'd never seen anything like him in her entire life, and he'd felt himself respond.

He'd liked that. He'd liked that far too much.

You want it again.

The idea sat inside him and he let it for a second, examining it, because he tried to be honest with himself where he could. And he could admit that yes, he wanted it again. Wanted to touch her, hold her again. Be inside her again. Have that smile of hers again…

Damon grabbed the beer and took a sip, staring moodily at the wall next to him and the stuffed head of a brown bear that was stuck to it. The bear's glass eyes were deeply judgmental.

He glared at it.

No, he couldn't have any of those things again. That would be a mistake. Indulging himself in the first place had been a mistake. And perhaps she'd felt the same, because she'd walked out of the library very quickly afterward. He'd known something was wrong, but it was obvious she hadn't wanted to talk about it and so he'd let her go. No point in making the situation worse.

After she'd gone, he'd gathered up the books and taken them to Phil, the old guy who lived at the top of the hill behind the town. Phil had given him a look around his fledgling animal sanctuary and explained what he was trying to do. An interesting little operation, and given the quirk factor of Phil himself, it had definite tourist potential.

Of course, it would have been better if he'd paid attention to the old guy, but he hadn't. He couldn't. His head had been too full of Astrid.

The beer was cold on his tongue, the buzz of conversation in the bar around him loud. It was Saturday night and clearly the Moose was the place to be, packed as it was with town residents all talking and shouting and drinking.

Some idiot had put on *Sweet Home Alabama* on the jukebox for the third time that evening, the twangy sounds of the guitar competing with the *click* of pool balls and the sounds of loud laughter.

Damon found the noise irritating.

He'd been dead set on leaving tomorrow and he had no reason to change his mind, especially not after his mom's call earlier today. Two days and then he had to get back to her, that had been the plan. So why he should be feeling so unsettled and like he was making the wrong decision somehow, he had no idea.

Sex with a woman—even good sex—was not a reason to stay. He had to get back to LA. He couldn't keep relying on Rachel, especially not when his mother was uncomfortable with her being around; that wasn't fair.

What about your promise to Cal?

Well, what about it? He'd spoken to Connor, let the kid know he was around and available. Maybe he'd come and see him, maybe he wouldn't. Two days, that's what he'd told Connor. The kid knew where to find him if he wanted to talk.

And what about Astrid?

But his promise to Cal didn't include Astrid. And she was cool, capable, and strong. Yes, the sex had been fantastic, and perhaps if there hadn't been all those added complications he might have considered sticking around for a little more of it. But there were those complications and nothing had changed.

You're still thinking she's like all the rest and she isn't.

No, she wasn't. Five years since she'd been with someone, a long time for a woman as passionate as she was. Why was that? Was it fear of small-town gossip? Or had she just not met anyone she liked enough? And why the hell had she chosen him? Had he simply been convenient? Or was it something more?

Not that he wanted it to be anything more, definitely not.

"Hey," Silas said, interrupting Damon's whirling thoughts as he pulled out a chair opposite and sat down. "How's the financial stuff progressing?"

Damon gave him a long-suffering look. "Did I say you could sit there?"

"No." Silas put his elbows on the table and gave Damon a grin. "So? What's happening? Has Debbie gone into detail about Carl's beer coaster collection yet?"

Damon took another sip of his beer, not hurrying. "I'm going over options." Best to keep things noncommittal and not give away the fact that he'd been struggling to keep the Deep River tourism ideas at the forefront of his mind.

"Options," Silas echoed. "That's helpful. You want to talk about those options?"

"Not right now, no. Need some more time to think about it."

Silas's gaze narrowed. "Isn't time something you don't have?"

Well, this conversation could end up in some uncomfortable places if he wasn't careful.

Damon leaned back in his chair, hooking one elbow over the back of it and meeting his friend's gaze levelly. "I want to be sure that whatever advice I give is the right kind. I don't want any of these options to fail."

"Okay, then." Silas nodded his head in agreement. "But we need to make a decision about which ideas are viable and which aren't. People are getting antsy to get this sorted out so we need to do it soon."

That was all true.

He resisted the urge to rub a hand over his face. Hell, he really needed to get his head back in the game. He couldn't think about anything clearly when it was still full of Astrid.

"Yeah, I hear you," he said.

Silas was silent a moment, then asked, "You still planning on leaving?"

"Tomorrow, yes."

"Okay, well, I guess you'd better hurry up on it, then."

Irritated, Damon shot him an annoyed glance. "Thank you, I'm aware."

"The sooner we get this done, the better," Silas went on, apparently not picking up on the *please go away and leave me alone* vibes that Damon was projecting. "We need to get the ball rolling, keep everyone engaged and thinking about the future of the town and all the good things that will come to them, instead of thinking about the oil and what they could do with the money."

It was a fair enough concern. Phone calls from oil execs had been made to various townspeople, with money dangling from sticks like particularly juicy carrots. And he knew what people were like with money. It was a great motivator and not necessarily for the good, which was a concern.

He didn't like the idea of machinery everywhere, tearing up the landscape and ruining all that lovely scenery, destroying the peace and the magic of this place. Connor would be furious and upset, and that would in turn upset Astrid, and that would sure as hell bother Damon.

He wasn't sure when their feelings had started to be a concern for him. Their feelings in particular, as opposed to anyone else's...

"What does Astrid think?" Silas asked, apparently picking the thought right out of his head, the sneaky bastard.

"Still talking to her." Damon tried very hard not to let even the smallest part of that mind-blowing experience he'd had with her in the library this morning show.

"Okay, good. I'd like us to get a short list of viable projects together, organize a town meeting so everyone can get the info, then we put the issue to a town vote. People need to see something's happening."

"Fine, I can do that." And he'd pull his recalcitrant thoughts away from the beautiful mayor and back to the problem at hand while he was at it too. Then another thought hit him. "Hey, you hear anything from Zeke?"

Silas let out a breath. "Not a damn thing. None of my leads have gone anywhere either. It's like he's disappeared off the face of the earth."

"Great timing," Damon noted dryly.

"Tell me about it. I guess all we can do is carry on and hope that eventually he turns up."

"I guess so."

Silas gave him a meaningful look. "Which means you'd better

get moving on all those ideas and figuring out which ones are going to be the most likely to succeed."

Silas wasn't wrong. The sooner Damon dealt with this, the sooner he could get back to LA. Perhaps he needed to go for a walk, clear his head, then hopefully he'd be better able to concentrate on what he was actually supposed to be doing.

Damon swallowed his beer, collected his papers, stood up, and gave his friend a mock salute. "Roger that, chief."

After depositing the papers in his room, he came back down the stairs and stepped outside the Moose.

It was a particularly beautiful evening, the twilight getting longer in preparation for summer when it wouldn't get dark until almost ten at night. The light lay still and golden over the mountaintops, dancing off the rushing green water of the river. And once the heavy door to the Moose had shut behind him, silence fell. The kind of deep, heavy silence that only came with the wilderness and no cities around for hundreds of miles.

The kind of silence that sometimes made him very conscious of the silence within himself too. It could be oppressive, that silence. But it wasn't tonight, not with the warmth of Astrid's arms around him, the memory of that smile she'd given him as he'd pushed inside her. Looking at him as if he was something special. Magic…

Except he wasn't all that special, not these days. Maybe once he had been, to his daughter and to Rebecca, Ella's mom. But not to his own mother. He'd only ever been a burden to her, and he knew it.

Not that he wanted to be special to anyone, though. Being special demanded things emotionally from him, and he wasn't in any position to give those things to anyone. The surface life with no ties, nothing to pull him down under the water again, that's all he wanted. Nothing was going to change that. Nothing and no one.

Walking slowly from the boardwalk and onto the road that

ran behind the stores facing the river, he then came to a stop, distracted by the sounds of raised voices.

Glancing in the direction of the noise, he saw two figures standing on the sidewalk outside the back entrance to the mayor's office. One small, female, and blond. The other tall, gangly, and very teenage boy.

Astrid and Connor.

Astrid had her arms folded, a set look on her face, while Connor glared at her. Both of them were radiating the same sharp, prickly, angry energy.

"That's none of your business," Damon heard Astrid say, her voice very, very cool. "I'm an adult, Con, and it's got nothing to do with you."

"I'm just looking out for you, Mom," Connor said fiercely, waving a hand.

"I know, but you don't have to do that. I'm not your responsibility, and neither is the town."

"You're wrong. It *is* my responsibility. Who else is going to protect it? Those idiots?" He waved another hand in the general direction of the Moose. "They're strangers who don't care about this place like I do. And you've got no one to protect you except me, and I—"

"I don't need your protection, idiot boy," Astrid said furiously.

"Oh yeah?" Connor's voice vibrated with anger. "Do you really want another Aiden situation?"

Something like shock rippled over Astrid's face before giving way to fury.

A family argument, which wasn't his business. And it definitely wasn't his place to intervene. Yet Damon couldn't walk away. This was the type of fire that could spiral out of control if cold water wasn't poured on it, and the only person around here with that water was him.

"Hey, you two," he said calmly, strolling toward them. "Need help with anything?"

One pair of furious blue eyes and one pair of chilly gray turned in his direction.

"No, thank you." Astrid's voice was ice-cold, and she stared at him as if he were a complete stranger and not someone she'd shared mind-blowing sex with in the library that morning. "We're fine."

"No, we're not fine," Connor snapped at almost the same time, glancing at Damon, an expression on his face that Damon at first didn't recognize. And then he did.

The kid was looking at him as if he wanted Damon's help.

"Oh? What's the problem?" Damon came closer.

"It's nothing we can't handle," Astrid said in frigid tones. "I appreciate you want to help, Damon, but—"

"I want to stop school until this oil business is over," Connor interrupted, staring at Damon. "I don't want to be away for hours during the day when I'm needed here."

"Don't be ridiculous," Astrid said. "You can't just stop going to school completely. I won't have it."

"School's nearly over anyway, and who else is going to take care of this town?" Connor turned his furious gaze on his mother. "Who's going to make sure everything's—"

"Hey." Damon made sure his voice was calm but firm enough to get the kid's attention. "Need a chat, Connor?"

"No, he does not," Astrid said.

"Yes, I do," Connor said at exactly the same time.

Astrid glared at him. "I'm your mother. I'll make the decisions around here."

"Yeah, and you don't understand—"

"It's okay," Damon interrupted again, cutting across the kid's fury, meeting it with firmness and calm. "We can talk. Just give me five minutes with your mom here."

Connor gave Astrid one ferocious glance, then he nodded and stalked off to give them some privacy.

Astrid's face was white, her gray eyes gone dark in the evening light, not at all the lovely, flushed woman he'd held in his arms earlier that day. But the impact of her was still the same—a punch direct to his gut. She looked furious and beautiful and sexy, and he wanted to take her face between his hands and kiss her passionate mouth.

"You okay?" he asked instead. "What's going on?"

Her expression shuttered. "Connor has this ridiculous idea about giving up school while this oil business is going on."

Damon frowned. "Why?"

"Because you're leaving tomorrow, and he doesn't trust Silas or Zeke to do things right."

He muttered a curse under his breath. That hadn't been what he'd intended when he'd spoken to Connor earlier. Sure, get the kid to trust him, but also the others too.

"I don't know what you said to him before," Astrid continued, "but he seems to think you're on the level now and the other two are potential oilmen."

Damon sighed. "That's not what I had in mind, I have to say. Will you let me handle it?"

She gave him an unreadable look, then glanced away. She was angry and he could see why. But there was something more going on here, he was sure of it, and it wasn't only due to a stubborn teenager who wouldn't do what he was told. Maybe he needed to ask, because he couldn't help if he didn't know what was going on.

"Who's Aiden?" He kept the question very casual.

Silver glinted in her eyes, her whole body stiffening. Then just as quickly as the reaction had appeared, it vanished.

"Fine," she said flatly, completely ignoring the question. "You talk to him, then. See if you can make him see sense."

Without another word, she strode past him, heading in the direction of the road that led up the hill behind the town, her hair gleaming in the last rays of the sun.

Okay, so whoever this Aiden guy was, he was a subject she didn't want to talk about.

Damon didn't like that. He felt like he was flying in the dark with no autopilot and no navigation and heading straight into a cloud bank.

Looking around for Connor, he eventually spotted him standing just a little way down the street, his back to Damon, his attention determinedly forward. He looked big standing there, and broad. Not a kid. A man.

"So," Damon said as he came up behind him, "you want to tell me what's going on?"

Connor swung around. He looked furious. "You heard already. I want to quit school early. But Mom won't let me. She doesn't understand—"

He stopped short as Damon held up a quietening hand.

"I hear you," Damon said, wanting to prevent a deluge of irritation right here in the street. "Let's talk, but not here, okay?"

"But I—"

"You want people listening in on what you have to say? The whole town knowing your secret?"

Connor's chin jutted. "They can. Perhaps they'd take me seriously if they knew."

"They might," Damon allowed. "But what about your mom? That's going to affect her too, don't forget. Also, it's a hell of a way for your aunt to find out that her brother had a son she didn't know about."

Connor opened his mouth. Closed it. Then he looked away, thrusting his hands in his pockets. "Yeah, okay." He was still angry, that was clear, but there was a grudging admittance in his tone. "I hadn't thought of that."

Good kid. Unlike many teenagers, he wasn't just thinking of himself when it came down to it.

"Have you got somewhere we can chat without anyone listening in?" Damon asked. "Like, a hideout or something?"

"A hideout?" Connor's tone dripped with disdain. "I'm not ten."

Damon grinned. "No, but you're an angry teenage boy. You can't tell me you don't have a place to go brood on the injustices of life."

The kid rolled his eyes, but the tension around his mouth eased. "Maybe."

"Good." Already an idea about what he was going to do was revolving in Damon's brain. "Stay here a second. I'll be back."

Without another word, he turned around and made his way to the market. It was still open, so he went in, bought a couple of beers, then came out again.

Connor glanced then at the bottles in his hand. "Beer?"

"Serious conversation requires serious refreshment. My mom preferred whisky, but you're underage, so beer it is."

"You know beer has alcohol in it, right?"

Damon lifted a shoulder. "Hey, I'll drink both of them if you don't want—"

"Let's not be hasty," Connor interrupted quickly. "I didn't say that."

Damon laughed. "Didn't think you did. Come on, show me where this 'maybe' hideout of yours is."

Connor gave him a dark look, then turned and started heading down the street to the boardwalk, while Damon followed.

They stepped onto the boardwalk and walked down it, heading to the steps at the end that led to the path that ran along the bank beside the river.

The sun was going down, throwing out long streaks of gold and red and yellow light, bathing everything in a pretty twilight glow. It was starting to get cold, the unseasonable warmth of the spring day beginning to fade along with the light, making Damon draw his parka closer around him.

Stars started to glitter in the pale sky. When darkness fell, they'd be scattered across the night like jewels spilled from a treasure chest.

Connor continued on down the path and then abruptly veered off toward the river. Damon followed, curious.

The almost imperceptible trail led to a gravelly beach scattered with rocks. Connor scrambled over them like a mountain goat before disappearing around a particularly huge boulder.

Damon went after him, coming around the side of the boulder to find that the boy was gone. He had a moment of puzzlement and then he saw that the boulder had been hollowed out, the inside just big enough for a boy and maybe a companion.

Connor sat on the dry, sandy floor, pulling twigs from a stash tucked up at the back of the tiny cave and carefully piling them into a circle of fire-blackened rocks. A pile of dry driftwood sat next to the circle.

"This is something else." Damon looked around in approval as he sat down. "You've got a real man cave."

Connor reached into his pocket and pulled out a lighter, then hunched over the fire. "I found it a year or so ago. No one else knows about it."

Damon didn't say that probably lots of people knew about it; you didn't have something this cool within a couple of minutes of the town center and *not* have people know about it.

"I like it. It's the perfect hideout."

As Connor lit the fire, Damon took the tops off the beer bottles, then leaned over and put one in the sand beside Connor.

"Okay," he said comfortably. "Let's hear it. Why don't you trust Silas and Zeke to do what's right by the town?"

"Because Silas only came back a couple of weeks ago. I know he was born here, but he hasn't been around for years, so what would he know? And I don't know anything about Zeke." Connor's jaw was tight as he picked up more driftwood, slowly feeding it to the fire. "How am I supposed to trust either of them when I don't know them?"

Damon could see his point. As far as Connor was concerned,

Silas and Zeke were complete strangers who didn't live in the town and who didn't understand its ways. Hell, if he'd been Connor, maybe he wouldn't trust them either.

The difficulty was that Silas and Zeke were totally trustworthy men—he'd trusted them with his life and vice versa—and Connor didn't need to be worried. And the fact that he was was the issue.

What had happened in this boy's life that he'd somehow taken on the responsibility for the whole town? That he didn't trust two men who were totally trustworthy? Sure, Connor hadn't met Zeke, but surely Silas was okay?

"Do you need to know them?" Damon asked, keeping his voice neutral.

Connor reached for the beer, picked it up, and took a swallow. "Yeah, of course. You never know what some people are really like. And then when you find out, it's too late."

"Too late?"

Connor shook his head, looking at the fire, and didn't answer.

Damon remained silent, watching him.

This boy was afraid, Damon would have laid money on it. But where that fear came from, he didn't know. One thing he was sure of though was that he needed to find out. Because how could he help otherwise? How could he make good on his promise to Cal?

Is it just about the promise to Cal?

Well, of course it was. What else could it be? He cared about the kid but only as much as he'd care about anyone who was vulnerable and who needed his help. This wasn't personal. He couldn't afford for it to be personal for both his sake and the kid's.

"Connor," he said carefully, "I don't want to pry and I'm certainly not going to make you talk about things you don't want to, but...I have to ask: What happened to you and your mother before you got to Deep River?"

Connor looked away, an oddly devastated look flashing over his face.

A ripple of concern went through Damon. He'd suspected it was bad, and it looked like it was.

"I want to help you," he said quietly. "You and your mom have got some big stuff going on right now, and I get the feeling it's hard to talk to her. You don't want to worry her, right?"

Connor looked down at the fire and picked up some more wood, beginning to feed in some more twigs. "Yeah," he said slowly. "She shouldn't have to worry about me on top of everything else."

"I get it. So why don't you talk to me instead? I'm a neutral party and you don't need to worry about worrying me."

The kid picked up the beer again, swigging at it. "You should have brought the whisky."

Damon stayed quiet. He'd said what he needed to. Now it was up to Connor if he wanted to talk.

"We used to live with this guy called Aiden in Portland," Connor said finally, putting down the beer and picking up a stick, poking at the fire with it. "He was a good guy. I liked him. He was nice to me." The boy's jaw hardened. "He told me he'd always wanted a family and that me and Mom could be his family. I'd always wanted a dad and I thought he could be my dad." Connor jammed the stick into the flames. "He told me he wanted to adopt me and marry Mom so he'd be my dad for real, but Mom always said no and I didn't know why. Then he started…saying little things about Mom. Like how she didn't praise me enough or didn't allow me to have fun. How if she was really a good mother, she'd let me have more time on the computer or buy me toys or talk to me more. And that's when I started to realize that he…" Connor jammed the stick into the coals, sparks flying. "He wasn't a good guy after all. He was an asshole. And he hurt Mom."

Damon took a swig of his beer, hoping that the cool liquid would quench the slow-building fury that gathered hot and heavy in his gut. Righteous anger at an abusive guy was allowed, but this felt sharper somehow, deeper. This felt more personal than it had any right to be.

Some asshole had betrayed Connor and hurt Astrid, and now all he wanted was to go and find this bastard wherever he was and beat him to a pulp.

Except obviously that was going to help no one, so he got a grip.

"Did he hit her?" He kept the words stripped entirely of emotion, despite the anger that tangled and knotted inside him.

Connor, clearly oblivious to Damon's rage, shook his head. "No. I mean, I never saw him do it, and when I asked Mom, she told me he hadn't."

"Was she saying that to protect you, do you think?"

"I don't know." That devastated look flickered across his face again, and he turned away, his knuckles white on the stick. "I know she stayed with him because I liked him and she wanted me to have a dad." His voice broke like a boy's, squeaking a little. "If I hadn't—"

"No," Damon interrupted flatly, furious that Connor was blaming himself. "It's not your fault, you hear me?"

Connor went still, that strong jaw of his tightening.

"Connor," Damon said. "Look at me."

Slowly, the kid turned his head, his blue eyes full of fury and pain.

Damon held his gaze, because if there was one thing the boy needed to know, it was this. "It's *not* your fault. You know whose fault it is? It's his. It's Aiden's. Not yours, not your mom's. I've seen a lot of guys like him, think the world owes them a living. Think that people are their property. That they don't have to answer to anyone. But they're wrong. And they're assholes."

Connor bristled. "You don't understand. I *liked* him. He was a nice guy to me. If I'd—"

"Why are you trying to take the blame? When he was the one who broke your trust?"

The kid tore his gaze away, staring down at the fire again. Every line of him was tense and Damon felt that urge again to lay a hand on the boy's shoulder, tell him it was okay.

His fingers gripped the cool glass of his bottle instead, and he put every bit of certainty he could into his voice. "You're a good kid. And questioning yourself even a little bit makes you better than most. You're thinking of your mom and you want to do the right thing. You want to take responsibility. I admire that. I respect it. Some adults can't do that, let alone a fifteen-year-old."

Connor dug at the fire. He didn't look at Damon, but something in his posture eased. He was uncomfortable with the conversation, but also, it was clear, he needed to hear what Damon was trying to tell him.

When was the last time the boy had had some male praise? Just a guy telling him that he was doing a good job and that he'd earned some respect? It wasn't that praise from his mom wasn't important, but Connor was a boy, and he needed some male attention too.

Damon wasn't exactly the best man to get it from and he knew it, but he'd rather punch himself in the face than betray the trust of a child the way Aiden had. And he'd certainly never hurt a woman.

"But the fact is you *are* a fifteen-year-old. And back when this stuff was happening with Aiden, you were a little kid. You can't take responsibility for something that's not yours to take. Aiden was an adult. He should have known better. So I'm sorry you had to go through that, but there was nothing you could have done, understand?"

Connor stared moodily at the fire, sipping on the beer, but at last he nodded.

"Good. And as far as school's concerned, you need to listen to your mother. It doesn't matter that the year is nearly done. You still need to go."

"I knew you'd take her side." He sounded aggrieved.

"Yeah, well, sadly for you, I am also an adult and I know that staying in school is the best option for you long term. Can't protect a town without a decent education."

Connor scowled, clearly frustrated. "But I—"

"But I'll make you a deal," Damon interrupted, an idea forming in his head. "If you go to school, I'll keep you in the loop about the decisions and discussion we'll be having about the town. And if you have any suggestions, I'll bring them to the relevant people."

Connor's blue gaze narrowed, suspicious.

But Damon understood where he was coming from now and it made sense; the poor kid had trusted once and it had blown up in his face. How could he ever do so again?

The same will be true for Astrid...

The wary look in her eyes, the veneer of cool, the bristly energy that gripped her that she didn't do anything with, as if she was holding all her emotions inside...

Yes, it would be true for her too.

"You can trust me, Connor," Damon said with quiet authority. "I'm not Aiden. I won't betray your trust. When I say I'll do something, I'll do it."

Something flickered in the boy's eyes, that longing again. Connor wanted to trust him. He wanted to trust him desperately.

"I'll stay another couple of days," Damon went on, even though he knew he shouldn't. "I won't leave just yet. You can keep going to school, and I'll make sure Silas and Zeke do things right, tell you everything that goes on. And I'll take any concerns you have to them. I can't guarantee they'll do anything about them, but I'll make sure they listen. Okay?"

Connor stared at him, expressions rippling over his face, and Damon's chest tightened. He wanted Connor to trust him, he realized. Wanted it very much.

Careful...

Oh yeah, he knew. He couldn't let himself get involved. He

only had so much to give and no more. But surely this would be okay. Another couple of days to ease the kid's mind about all the oil stuff wasn't too much to ask. Rachel wouldn't mind keeping her eye on his mom just a little longer. And his mom would be okay with it, surely.

The silence sat there, deepening around them.

Then Connor said abruptly, "Okay. It's a deal."

And apparently it was as simple as that.

The tight thing in Damon's chest eased, a tension leaving him he hadn't realized was there. He didn't want to admit to being relieved, but he was.

Lifting his beer in Connor's direction, he waited for Connor to lift his and then they clinked bottles in acknowledgment.

"So," he said after they'd both had a swig to seal the deal, "do you want me to tell your mother the good news?"

Connor dug around in the fire again. "You can. She'll probably believe you more."

Damon was okay with that. Very okay with that.

"Good." He took another sip of his beer. "Right. Do you want me to tell you some stories about your dad?"

Connor's eyes lit up. "Yeah, I do."

Chapter 11

ASTRID WENT HOME AFTER DAMON HAD TAKEN CONNOR away for whatever man-to-man chat they were going to have, anger still fizzing inside her. That her anger wasn't wholly to do with Connor and his ridiculous insistence on skipping school didn't help.

She was aware enough to realize that a large part of it was due to spending the entire day trying not to think about Damon and what had happened in the library, and failing. Miserably.

She'd busied herself in her office, going over the ideas for tourist ventures that people had brought to her. She supposed she should be doing this with Damon, but there was no way in hell she was going to find him and talk to him now about it. Distance was better. She didn't want to think about those moments in the library when he had touched her, kissed her, been inside her...

Unfortunately, it had been next to impossible *not* to think about those moments. About him. About his smile and the light in his blue eyes when he'd looked at her. How he'd made her feel wanted and precious and cared for...

Astrid growled, mentally shoving away those memories as she flung open her front door. She'd had vague plans of a soak in the tub with a glass of wine, or watching a couple of DVDs she'd borrowed from the collection in the market—streaming was almost impossible without a decent internet connection—but she didn't feel like that now.

She ended up pacing around her living room, pausing every now and then to stare out the window at the little town below and the river rushing endlessly toward the ocean, trying to redirect her thoughts.

Connor coming to her and announcing his "decision" to skip

school for the rest of the year had really been the last straw. And it hadn't helped that he didn't want to talk about Cal or about why she hadn't told him that Cal was his father. He'd just insisted that the town was his responsibility and that he couldn't trust Silas and Zeke, especially since Damon was leaving.

It was clear that Connor now viewed Damon as someone less suspicious than the other two, and she didn't know how she felt about that. Damon wasn't staying and she didn't want Connor putting his trust in him or expectations on him for exactly that reason.

Her son's faith in men had already been broken by Aiden and she didn't think she could bear it if Damon broke it as well. She hadn't wanted him to take Connor away and talk to him, be nice to him, earn the boy's trust, only to have him go the next day. It just wouldn't be fair.

Eventually, sick of her own introspection, she went into the little kitchen she'd painted a clean, restful white and poured herself a glass of wine, got the tourism folder, and sat down at the battered wooden kitchen table, trying to redirect her attention to Gwen's eco-resort idea.

She was just finishing up her wine and running some numbers through her calculator when she heard the front door open then close, the sound of male voices echoing down the hallway. Her son's lighter tone and then a deeper, richer one.

Connor was home. And he'd brought Damon with him.

Astrid's heart gave a little kick in her chest, then started to beat faster, her body tightening in anticipation. Stupid. She wasn't going there again with Damon. That had been a one-off, so why she was feeling all dry-mouthed and excited she had no idea.

For a second she sat there, unable to decide whether to go and meet them or wait for them to come to her, her brain flailing around stupidly. Then, pulling herself together because she was thirty-two, not sixteen, she shoved her chair back, got up, and went down the hallway to meet them.

160   JACKIE ASHENDEN

They were standing just inside the front door, Connor making sweeping gestures toward various rooms, clearly giving Damon a tour of the house, while Damon stood next to him nodding.

The pair of them looked at her as she approached and almost instantly the same expression crossed their faces, the slightly guilty one all little boys get when they know they've done something wrong.

She might have laughed if her emotions hadn't been all over the place.

"Hey, Mom." Connor glanced at Damon meaningfully. "And that's my cue to leave."

Damon lifted both brows. "Sure you don't want to stay?"

"Uh, no." Connor grinned at him. "Thanks for the beer."

Astrid stiffened. "Beer? What beer?"

"Gee thanks, kid," Damon said.

"No problem." Connor, still grinning, sidled past her to his room and disappeared inside it, closing the door very firmly behind him.

Silence fell.

Immediately, her tiny hallway felt too narrow, its ceiling way too low. Damon was so tall, thoroughly invading her little space in a way that made her even more aware of him than she already was. And his scent wrapped around her, the warm spice she associated with him, making her feel hungry—and not for food.

He was still in that soft, black shirt and she knew what it felt like now. She knew what *he* felt like. His skin like velvet, the muscles beneath it steel. And all that male heat…

He was so sexy he ought to be illegal. What would he do if she pushed him against the wall and kissed his gorgeous mouth?

He would do nothing, because you're not going to do it.

No, she wouldn't. She'd had her moment, and there wouldn't be another one.

"You gave my son a beer?" She folded her arms, trying to stay cool.

Damon gave her that charming little-boy grin. "It was only one."

"He's underage."

"That's what he said."

"But did he drink it?"

"He's fifteen and a boy. What do you think?"

Astrid opened her mouth.

But Damon went on before she could speak, "I talked to him, Astrid, and we sorted some things out. The beer was just a way to ease the process." His smile became a little wicked. "It was either that or whisky, and I didn't think you'd approve of whisky."

Are you really going to stand here arguing about a beer?

That did seem pointless, especially considering there were greater problems to worry about.

"Okay," she said at last. "Fair enough. Come into the kitchen and we can discuss it."

She turned without waiting for him to reply, going back down the hallway.

"You've been doing some work, I see," Damon murmured as he came into the kitchen behind her, clearly noting the folder on the table.

"We need to make a decision about what ideas to take to the town, so yes, I have."

"Silas said the same thing to me earlier."

"Good to hear he's thinking the same." She indicated a seat. "Do you want some tea?"

"Sure. That would be great." Pulling out the chair, Damon sat down in a long, lazy sprawl.

She moved over to the stove where the kettle stood on the hob, picking it up and taking to the sink, filling it with water. Then she put the kettle back on the stovetop and turned it on.

Turning around, she leaned back against the counter next to the stove, braced herself mentally, then met Damon's mesmerizing blue gaze. "Okay, so tell me what's going on."

"Connor's very concerned about Zeke and Silas. He doesn't trust them and it's upsetting him."

"No kidding." She couldn't quite keep the bite out of her tone. "But he can't quit school."

"I know that and I agree. So I made a deal with him."

"What kind of deal?"

"If he keeps going to school, I'll stay on a couple of days more and keep an eye on the oil stuff, then report back to him about what's happening and take any concerns he has to Silas and Zeke."

Astrid blinked, a jolt of shock going through her.

Despite whatever responsibilities he had back in LA, Damon was going to stay for her son. And he wasn't going to tell him not to worry, that it wasn't his responsibility. No, he was going to include him in what was going on. He was taking Connor absolutely seriously.

That he would make the effort for her boy made her heart contract painfully, and she had to turn around again to check on the kettle, trying to hide her reaction. Tears pricked at her eyes, which was ludicrous. Why was she crying about a man being nice to her son? Didn't that mean she had to be more on her guard? Aiden had been nice to him too, and look what had happened there.

God help her, if Damon hurt Connor, there wouldn't be enough of him left to bury.

"I don't know how you managed to get him to agree." She fussed with the kettle, conscious of how thick her voice sounded. "He flat-out refused for me." And that hurt, she couldn't deny it. That her son would do for Damon what he wouldn't do for his own mother.

"Well," Damon said slowly, "he won't for you because he sees himself as needing to protect you. That's why he hasn't discussed things with you either. He doesn't want to worry you. He doesn't have to worry about me or care about my feelings, so he can tell me anything."

Okay, that made sense. She could understand that.

Letting out a breath and furiously blinking away her tears, she turned back to him.

He sat sprawled in the chair, long legs outstretched, watching her.

"So you said you'd stay." She folded her arms over her quickly beating heart. "Didn't you have responsibilities back in LA that couldn't wait?"

His eyes darkened. "Yeah, I do. But they can wait at least a couple more days."

Curiosity gripped her. He'd kissed her, held her in his arms, been inside her. But she didn't know a single thing about him except that his mother had been a single parent and had brought him up herself and that she apparently liked whisky.

"What do you need to get back to?" she asked, unable to resist the question.

Damon let out a breath. "My mom isn't well. I've got a house-keeper checking on her, but that's not ideal. I really need to be around for her."

Somehow, the answer didn't surprise her. She didn't know him, but she'd suspected that whatever was drawing him away from Deep River, it was something serious. Especially given how adamant he'd been about seeing Cal's last wishes carried out. He didn't strike her as a man who'd let something minor distract him from the things he considered important.

"I'm sorry to hear that," she said, and she meant it. "Should she be in the hospital?"

Damon hesitated. "She'll need a care facility at some point but not quite yet."

"That sounds difficult."

"Yeah, it's not great. Mom isn't the easiest person to deal with. She's very proud and doesn't like to admit that she's sick. The housekeeper can watch her for a little while, but she doesn't like having another person in her house."

"You don't have to stay here," she said, feeling bad for him. "Sounds like your mother needs you more than Connor does."

Damon shook his head. "Mom will be okay for another few days. And I made Connor a promise. I'm not going to leave before I fulfill that."

Her heart gave another painful contraction. He was a man who made promises and kept them. He'd kept Cal's and now he'd made another to her son, and she could see from the iron in his blue eyes he'd keep that one as well.

Dammit, why did he have to be such a good guy? Why couldn't he be awful? And for the love of all that was holy, why did she have to feel so incredibly attracted to him?

Too good to be true…

Oh, he was. Even now, even after she'd thought that particular curiosity would be satisfied, she couldn't take her eyes off the long, powerful stretch of his legs. Or the open neck of his shirt where his pulse beat. Or the sensual curve of his mouth.

He must have known the direction of her thoughts because suddenly his eyes glinted. "Kettle's boiling, Ms. Mayor."

Hell. So it was.

Astrid flushed and turned around, busying herself with making tea and trying to get a grip.

She fussed around, getting out the cups and dealing with the tea leaves—she preferred a teapot and leaves to teabags. Once she'd gotten it all together, she carried the teapot, milk, and sugar to the table, then came back for the cups. Or rather the mugs, since she preferred a bigger cup.

Damon watched silently as she carried everything to the table and put them down, sat, then poured out a couple of mugs. He nodded when she lifted the milk questioningly, before helping himself to some sugar. Apparently he liked his tea milky and sweet.

"So," he said as he stirred his tea, "Connor told me about Aiden."

Astrid went very still, her mug lifted halfway to her mouth. Her face had gone curiously blank. Slowly, she took a sip of her tea, then put the mug down on the table with some care.

"I don't know if that's something he should be telling people," she said, a chill in her tone.

She didn't want to talk about it, that was clear, and maybe he shouldn't push, given how painful it appeared to be for her. But he knew what it was like to have to bear painful things by yourself, how terribly lonely it could be, and how hard to get through it.

No one had been there for him when Ella had died. Rebecca had been too consumed with her own grief to take on his, and his mother, never good with the more difficult emotions, had simply refused to talk about it. He'd had to deal with his grief alone and it had been immeasurably hard. He didn't want that for Astrid.

Did she have anyone to talk to about it? Anyone at all? She'd been keeping Connor's secret a long time. No one knew here. So was this another secret? Another burden she had to carry?

"Well, he told me." Damon made sure his tone was matter-of-fact. "And you can tell me too, you know that, right?"

Her chin came up, her eyes flashing. "Why should I tell you? What right do you have to my secrets?"

She was guarded and he got it now. It made sense. That Aiden asshole had hurt her and hurt her badly. Connor had said that Aiden hadn't been physically abusive, but emotional abuse could be just as bad and she wouldn't trust easily, not after it had been broken like that.

And he wanted her to trust him. If he was going to help Connor, he needed to help Connor's lovely mother too.

It's not just about helping the kid, come on. You want to help her for yourself as well.

No, because this wasn't about him. This was about Astrid and

Connor and what they needed, not about what he needed. Not that he needed anything.

Whatever—if he wanted to gain Astrid's trust, it wasn't going to be as easy as sharing a beer. He was going to have to give her something else, something meaningful and precious. A secret of his own.

"I don't have a right," he said. "And you don't have to tell me anything. But secrets are hard to carry by yourself and I think you've been carrying Connor's for a long time."

She looked down at her mug, her hands placed on the scrubbed wooden tabletop on either side of it.

He didn't wait, though; he carried on because now he was committed. "I have a secret too that I don't tell anyone. Because it's hard to talk about." He could feel traces of a familiar tension gather inside him, pulling at his muscles. An old grief and the need to protect, even though the object of both that grief and that need was long gone: Ella, his daughter.

Astrid's head came up, her expression wary. "What secret?"

"I was like you a long time ago. I had a kid when I was only seventeen, a little girl."

Astrid's gray eyes went wide with surprise and not a little shock.

"She wasn't planned," Damon went on, the tension pulling tighter. "But she was very much wanted, and both Rebecca—that was her mom—and I did our best for her." The pain was still there despite the years, a deep, abiding ache that he carried close to his heart. And it felt wrong to tell Astrid about it, to put that pain on her, but he'd wanted her to have a secret of his, and his daughter was the secret that he held most precious.

"When she was two, she contracted one of those rare childhood cancers," he went on. "It was very aggressive and there was nothing the doctors could do. She died." There, he'd said it now. That was enough.

More shock flickered over Astrid's face, followed by a pain that was intimately familiar to him. The pain of a parent losing a child.

The grief had long since blunted so he didn't know why the sympathy in her eyes seemed to conjure it up again, and sharper than it had been in years.

He had to look away, his chest tight. This was crazy. Ella's death had been hard, but he'd gone through the darkness that had fallen around him after she'd died and come out the other side. So why should telling Astrid bring it all back? And why should he feel it so acutely?

A silence fell and he waited for her to tell him how sorry she was. Tell him she didn't know what to say. How she couldn't imagine how dreadful it was for him, all the trite bullshit that people trotted out when they were confronted by something they didn't want to face themselves. Before they changed the subject so they didn't have to talk about it.

But she didn't speak. Instead, she put out her hand and covered his where it rested on the table beside his mug. An instinctive, very human gesture of comfort. Her touch was warm, and there was a firm pressure to it, and he could feel the sensation of it flow up his arm and center itself in his chest.

No one had held him after Ella had died. No one had put their arms around him and given him a hug. No one had even touched him. And not one single solitary person had told him it would be okay.

So how strange that it should be a woman he'd known only a couple of days, with very real traumas of her own, who gave him the first significant, meaningful comfort he'd had in years. No platitudes. No trite phrases. Only a warm hand and a light pressure, an offer of strength, of wordless understanding.

When she spoke, it was soft and she didn't remove her hand. "Oh, Damon. I'm so sorry."

He looked at her at last. Her face was pale, but her gaze didn't waver. She wasn't afraid of his pain or his grief, that was clear, and was offering what she could: sympathy and comfort.

Deep inside him, so far down he was barely conscious of it, something jolted like he'd been given an electric shock.

"This isn't a quid pro quo," he said, ignoring the sensation. "I didn't tell you to force you into giving me something you don't want to give."

"Then why did you tell me?" The question was soft and genuine.

Damon met her misty-gray eyes. "Because Ella is my secret. And carrying her alone is hard."

Astrid's grip on his hand tightened and a small silence fell. Then she said, "I find it difficult to trust people. Especially men. And most especially men who seem to be too good to be true."

"Me?"

"Of course you."

Well, he wasn't totally evil, but he wasn't exactly a great bet either. "Is there alcohol in that tea? Or are you drunk on tannin?"

She smiled, her fingers warm against his. "Come on, surely you know how great you are? You're freakishly good-looking. You're very calm and very steady. You know how to tackle my son and you treat him with respect. You're ridiculously charming... Have I missed anything?"

"You missed that I'm excellent in bed," he added flippantly, because while he might be some of those things, that didn't make him a saint. And he had plenty of flaws.

"Oh, I hadn't forgotten." Silver glittered in her eyes.

Energy gathered in the space between them, every particle in the air charging with a hot, electric tension. The memory of their encounter in the library seemed to fill the room, making Damon's breath catch. His jeans were abruptly too tight, the blood in his veins pumping hard and strong.

Dammit, why had he mentioned sex? A stupid thing to do, especially when their chemistry was still tinder-dry and responding to any spark.

He turned his hand over beneath hers, giving her fingers a quick squeeze before withdrawing it. Probably best if they didn't touch for now.

She flushed and quickly grabbed her mug. "Anyway, where was I?"

"Me being too good to be true, I think."

Astrid leaned back in her chair, holding the mug. "Aiden was like that at first. He was a guy I met in Portland at a café where I was working. He was handsome. Friendly and charming. He was easy to talk to and he gave me lots of tips." She let out a breath, the expression on her face giving away how difficult the memory was for her. "Those were hard years. After I got pregnant with Connor, my parents kicked me out and I decided I couldn't stay in Ketchikan, so I went south. I ended up in Portland and had a neighbor look after Connor while I worked, but it was tough. The neighbor moved out, and I had to bring Connor into work with me at the café, which wasn't ideal. Aiden was so nice to him. One day he even helped me keep him entertained for a whole shift." She shook her head. "He seemed to be exactly what I needed. He was good with Connor, he was nice to me, and I was...lonely." Her gaze slid away. "It's hard being a single mom with no support."

"Yeah," he said quietly, because he was familiar with that. "My mom had it tough too."

Astrid took another sip of her tea. "Maybe if I'd had friends it might have been different, but I didn't. And Connor adored Aiden. He was five, looking for a father figure, and Aiden turned up and he was everything a little boy could want. Big and strong and a firefighter."

More things fell into place. Connor had told him that he'd liked Aiden and Damon had heard the guilt in his voice. But what little boy wouldn't look up to a man like that?

"But Aiden had a dark side," Astrid went on. "And only I saw it. About a year down the track, I started to be aware of how controlling he'd become. He didn't like me working too many shifts at the café, and he didn't like the few friends I'd made. He got very critical of me and the way I did things, especially with Connor. I dismissed it though, because he was supporting me financially and Connor really needed a father."

Pain ran through her voice along with an edge of guilt, though her expression was determinedly neutral.

"It was only when he started talking about adopting Connor that I started having thoughts about leaving. Because at the same time, he started being very critical of the way I was bringing Connor up, making me question myself. I started to think that maybe I wasn't a very good mother after all."

Anger coiled inside Damon, the same anger that he'd felt when Connor had talked about Aiden. Thick and hot and dark—sharp, so sharp. He hadn't felt anger this intense for years.

You haven't felt this intense for years, period.

Damon shoved the thought away.

"And then the criticisms started to get more personal," Astrid continued. "About me and my looks and…how we were together. It was very hard. I knew he was trying to undermine me, to make me dependent on him for everything, because that's what he wanted. A family who basically worshipped the ground he walked on." She sighed. "I put up with it for far too long, let him nearly cripple my confidence, but the last straw was hearing him tell Connor that he was better off without me." She stopped suddenly, her voice hoarse, and put her mug down, her knuckles white.

He wanted to touch her the way she'd touched him just before, offer her comfort and some reassurance. But touching was a bad idea, so all he said was, "That's a goddamn lie. Some kids are better off without their mothers, but not Connor."

Slowly, Astrid lifted her gaze. "I know. That's why I left. I just took him and drove away from Portland as fast as I could. I called Cal on the way, because I had no one else to turn to, and he told me to come to Deep River and he would give me a home here."

Her voice on the surface sounded firm, but he could hear the undercurrents of doubt; he could see the uncertainty in her eyes, and the guilt too.

"You did the right thing," Damon said, leaving no room for argument. "You saved your kid, Astrid. You protected him. It was absolutely the right thing to do."

"Was it?" Her silver eyes had gone dark. "Connor cried all the way to Deep River. He was heartbroken that I'd taken him away from Aiden. He'd wanted Aiden to be his father." She hesitated. "Sometimes I wonder if I should have stayed. Perhaps Aiden might have changed if I'd been a better partner, and at least then Connor would have had an actual father."

Chapter 12

ASTRID WISHED THE WORDS BACK AS SOON AS SHE'D SAID THEM. Those were her private doubts, her secret worries, the ones she barely admitted to herself let alone to another person. Let alone to *this* person.

She had to look away, unable to face him. Why on earth had she said that? It made her sound pathetic that she was making excuses for the way Aiden treated her, and she wasn't pathetic. She wasn't.

Damon was sitting back in his chair, his long, powerful body ostensibly relaxed, but she didn't need to face him to feel the anger radiating off him.

"Firstly," he said, his voice hard, "you didn't need to be a better partner. You're beautiful, caring, and loyal, while he's a total asshole. Secondly, if you'd stayed, what kind of man would Connor have grown up to be with a father like him?"

The guilt sat so heavily inside her, a boulder that she carried every day. And she hadn't realized just how heavily it sat until now. She'd told herself many times that leaving had been the only thing she could have done. So many times in fact that she'd mostly come to believe it.

But the doubt was always there, a doubt that Aiden had exploited, made deeper, wider. A doubt in herself that she'd had even growing up, that had been instilled by her reserved and distant parents, then exacerbated by Caleb's abrupt rejection.

Doubt in herself and her choices because it had been her choices that had led her to this moment. To Cal and his passion, a warmth that her teenage self had craved so badly. To a pregnancy that had blown her world apart. To Aiden who'd hurt her. To tearing her young son away from the only father figure he'd ever had.

Five years in Deep River had gone some way to restoring her faith in herself, but now, with the past flooding back, it felt like she was back to square one. Questioning herself as a partner and a mother. Questioning everything she'd ever done…

"You're right," she said huskily. "I know you're right. Leaving was the right thing to do, but…sometimes I can't stop wondering whether I made the right choice."

"You did." There was no equivocation in his voice. No hesitation. No doubt. And a fierce truth burned in his blue eyes. "You want to know the kind of man Aiden would have brought Connor up to be? A copy of himself. An entitled, selfish asshole who thinks people are his property and has no respect for anyone." Damon's chiseled jaw was hard. "And aside from anything else, if he'd had no qualms about hurting you, then eventually he would have hurt Connor too."

Astrid swallowed, her throat tight. "I know that. Intellectually. It's just that there are days when I don't feel it."

Damon didn't move, but the fierce light in his eyes held hers. "That's always the way. You can think one thing, but it always takes a while for the heart to catch up. Just know that you're a great mom, Astrid. You wanted to do the right thing by him and you did. He had a father figure for a time, but when that turned toxic, you ended it and brought him here. You protected him."

"But if I hadn't gotten together with Aiden—"

"You can't think like that. You were lonely and he was there. And you thought he was on the level. It's not your fault he turned out to be a manipulative bastard."

Isn't it, though? There's always something about you that people turn against…

As if he'd picked that thought right out of her head, Damon suddenly reached across the table and put his hands over hers where they gripped her mug. His gaze held hers, mesmerizing.

"It's *not* your fault, honey." There was so much conviction in his voice and a tenderness to the endearment that she wanted to reach for him and hold on tight. "There's nothing you should have done differently. Nothing you could have prevented. It's all on him, not you, understand?"

"My parents were distant," she said, her past spilling out of her whether she wanted it to or not. "They were older and I was unexpected. I think they had me more out of a sense of duty than anything else, but they weren't warm. And I wanted warmth. I used to wonder what I'd done wrong that they didn't like me, because it was clear they didn't. And then Cal came along and he was…like a fire. I couldn't resist him. Yet after I got pregnant, he didn't want anything to do with me, and then Aiden…" She was talking too much, but she couldn't seem to shut herself up. "I made so many stupid choices. Trusted the wrong people. Wanted the wrong things. And you know, sometimes I wonder if it's me. That there's something about me that turns people off."

Damon's thumbs stroked over her knuckles, and the warmth of his touch was like sunlight on her skin. "No. It's not you, understand?"

"How would you know? You've only just met me."

"True. But I've talked to people around this town and they all think you're the best mayor they've ever had. That you're tough and capable and fair and that you care about the town and the people in it. You're loyal and you care about your son so much. I can already see that."

Her heart swelled, pressing against her rib cage. She hadn't known the townspeople thought that about her. The inhabitants of Deep River weren't much given to praise. The only way you knew you were doing well was if no one complained.

Tears pricked in her eyes yet again, emotion making her throat tight. "I do care about him. But I should have told him about Cal. I should have let them meet. I was only afraid that Cal would let him down, and he'd already had his heart ripped out of his chest once by a man who didn't deserve him."

Damon's fingers gripped her tighter. "You were protecting him, that's only natural. You weren't to know Cal was going to get himself killed in a plane crash." The warmth in his fingers was in his voice too, and in the blue of his eyes.

He was such an understanding man. Too good to be true, she'd said, and he was. Of course, he'd clearly been uncomfortable with that, which had made her want to know why.

He'd had a daughter and lost her.

Her heart twisted painfully hard. He'd given her a piece of himself, a secret of his own and an agonizing one. And now he was giving her comfort and understanding, letting her talk selfishly about her own problems while he had his own very significant trauma to deal with.

"Damon," she said thickly, "I shouldn't be talking about this, not when you—"

"It's okay," he interrupted gently enough, and yet there was a thread of steel in his voice. "It happened a long time ago."

He knew that she meant his daughter clearly, and it was also clear that though it might have happened years ago, he didn't want to talk about it. Understandably.

She shouldn't push him, but he'd mentioned her name. Ella.

Her heart twisted again, like a towel being wrung out. No, not a good thing to ask him about. She was feeling emotional anyway, and hearing about his loss might be too much. It wasn't her grief to bear and he shouldn't have to bear hers.

So she gave a nod and his hands dropped away, leaving her skin feeling cold.

"More tea?" she asked, even though they'd both barely drunk from their own cups.

"No, I probably should be getting back to the Moose." His gaze lingered on her. "You okay?"

God, she liked the way he looked at her and that he'd asked. As if her well-being mattered to him.

He's not Aiden. And he never will be.

The knowledge settled down inside her, heavy and sure. A strange thing to be so certain of when she hadn't known him all that long. Nevertheless, she knew it like she knew her son.

He'd carried Cal's promise with him and he was here, making good on it. And it meant something to him. He'd put his mother's illness to one side for a time so he could help Connor, and here he was getting secrets out of her with honesty, a calm steadiness, and a reassurance she'd never experienced before.

It made longing uncurl inside her, a familiar kind of longing.

Cal had been a flash fire, burning hot and intense before flaming out, leaving her with nothing but dead embers and ashes.

But Damon was a home fire, burning strong and steady, providing comfort and safety, and then when the flames died down, those embers would continue to provide warmth and light. His was a fire that never went out, and she wanted to sit before it, hold her hands out to it, take that heat for herself.

Really? Again? When he's leaving soon?

But he wouldn't be leaving today, or tomorrow, if what he said was true. And the chemistry between them was still there and still strong; she'd felt it just moments before.

Yes, she'd told herself that morning had been a one-off, but why couldn't they have more?

She wanted that feeling again, the one she'd had in his arms in the library. Where she felt desired and precious and cared for. She wanted his fire to warm her up, chase away the cold that Aiden had left in her soul. And she wanted to give him something good in return for everything that he'd given her.

Because she had the sense that he too needed someone. He'd told her his secret, and even if he didn't want to talk about it now, he'd still told her. And that meant something. He wanted a connection as much as she did.

Neither of them were looking for an emotional one, but

perhaps a physical one could be just what they both needed. It was only sex. It didn't have to mean anything.

"Yes, I'm okay." She was conscious of how husky her voice had become. "You don't have to leave, you know. You could stay."

Heat flared in his eyes, then was gone. "If we're talking sex, I don't think it's a good idea."

"Why not?"

"Because this was a heavy conversation that I don't think either of us expected to have. And because you were very clear this morning that once was enough."

That was true, she had. She'd left the library as quickly as she could, too overwhelmed by what had happened to even want to think about it.

She flushed. "I know. I'm sorry. I didn't handle that very well. And I hadn't had sex for a long time. I'm out of practice…" She stopped, feeling she was digging the hole she'd fallen into deeper. "It doesn't have to mean anything. You're leaving soon anyway, so we can keep it casual and…" She swallowed, holding his gaze. "I think you need it as much as I do."

He didn't say anything for a long moment. His posture was casual, long legs outstretched, the light from the kitchen picking out the gold in the dark brown of his hair. A mountain lion sunning himself on a rock.

But blue fire flickered in his gaze.

"You said that sometimes you were a gentleman," she went on quietly. "And sometimes you weren't. I'd like to see you not being a gentleman for once."

He didn't move, but tension coiled around him suddenly. "What about Connor?"

"Connor's asleep. And he sleeps like the dead. Nothing wakes him up."

Electricity crackled around him and her heartbeat sped up.

"I'll have to be gone before he wakes up." Damon's voice had gotten rough around the edges, abrading her nerve endings in the most delicious way. "And before anyone else sees me sneaking out of your house."

That was definitely *not* a no.

"Okay." Her mouth had gone dry, excitement fluttering in the pit of her stomach.

"Are you sure, Astrid?"

She loved that he asked, but she didn't need him to.

"Yes." She met his gaze, held it. Let him see the heat in her eyes.

He was so still, and for a second it was like he'd turned to stone. Then in an explosive movement, he shoved the chair back, got to his feet, and came over to where she sat. Then he reached for her, pulling her straight up out of the chair and into his arms.

Astrid didn't hesitate or second-guess herself. She put her hands on his hard chest, lifted her chin, and let his mouth cover hers.

He tasted of hunger and the tea they'd been drinking, of heat and raw passion. She couldn't get enough. She let him in, let the heat deepen, the kiss intensifying. His fingers slid into her hair, closing into fists.

The gentle tug on her scalp went through her like lightning.

This wasn't gentlemanly. This wasn't gentlemanly at all.

She loved it.

She pressed both palms to his chest, feeling hard muscle beneath the warm cotton of his shirt, kissing him deeper, fitting herself closer against him. He was hot to the touch, his body lean and long and powerful; she wanted to strip his clothes from him, run her hands all over him. He was such a work of art, and she wanted to fully appreciate him in a way she hadn't down in the library.

Then she'd been greedy and desperate, wanting only to satisfy her hunger before putting it behind her. Now, she wanted more than that, wanted to take her time, learn him. See what gave him pleasure, what made him tick...

His fingers tightened in her hair as he lifted his mouth from hers and she made a soft protesting sound, not ready for the kiss to end. But he ignored it, holding her firmly. He wasn't smiling, the lines of his beautiful face taut with hunger, his eyes electric.

There was nothing easygoing or charming about him now. He looked unbearably intense, almost fierce. The way he had down in the library, when she'd pushed his control to the edge.

Was this the real man underneath all that easygoing charm? If so, he was thrilling. She loved his intensity, and she loved that she'd been the one to draw it out of him.

He said nothing, letting her go only to gather her into his arms as he stood up, looking down at her. "Where's your bedroom?"

"Down at the end of the hall." She relaxed against him. "I can walk, you know."

"I know."

But he didn't put her down, striding with purpose down the hallway to her little bedroom with its queen-size bed, the hand-made patchwork quilt she'd bought from Clare at the B&B, who did quilting as a hobby, thrown over the top. He kicked the door shut, then moved over to the bed, putting her down so she was sitting on the edge of the mattress.

Then he dropped to his knees in front of her.

Her pulse accelerated, her mouth going dry. They were at eye level like this, and the look in his eyes made her feel like she could hardly breathe, excitement crowding in her throat, her heartbeat loud in her head.

Damon didn't speak. He pulled her T-shirt up and over her head, then paused a moment, studying her. So she took a moment to study him too, the perfect planes and angles of his face, the sensual curve of his mouth, the darkness of his eyelashes shot with gold.

Beautiful man. Yet there was more to him than looks and charm as she'd already discovered. There was a deep well of caring inside him, and she had the sense that he was desperate to show it, to care for someone, though perhaps he didn't want to admit that to anyone. But she knew. She could see it in the way he'd involved himself with Connor. In the way he'd put his hands over hers in the kitchen.

In the way that he'd involved himself in the town, talking to people, helping out even though he had his own quite serious commitments back in LA.

Yes, he cared. He cared deeply.

She lifted a hand, touched the sharp, carved angle of one cheekbone. His skin was warm and smooth beneath her fingertips.

He stared at her from beneath those ridiculously long lashes, the burning intensity of his gaze taking her breath away.

She wasn't sure why she'd touched him or what she wanted to say—maybe that it was okay. That he could care for her son for as long as he was here. But perhaps that was too much, too soon, so she said nothing.

Then he leaned forward and kissed her, and every remaining thought she had vanished from her head.

His mouth was hot, the kiss demanding, and she gave back as good as she got. Letting him know that she was just as hungry for him as he was for her.

A sweet kiss, searing in its heat, making her open her mouth wider so he could kiss her deeper, harder. And he took complete advantage of the invitation, his tongue exploring her, tasting her, even as his hands fell to the buttons of her jeans and pulled them open.

Astrid took a breath, her hands on his shoulders before stealing around his neck, wanting to pull him closer. But he broke away all of a sudden, and before she had a chance to protest, he gripped the waistband of her jeans and pulled them down and off her, taking her panties with them. He undid her bra and pushed it off her shoulders, and when she was entirely naked, he pushed her back onto the bed.

Then he rose to his feet in a fluid, graceful movement and, keeping his attention entirely on her, began to take his own clothes off.

She made no move to cover herself, content to let him look at her. Because it was powerful to see the depth of his desire as he did so, as if he'd never seen anything more beautiful than she was in his entire life. And that made her feel beautiful too.

She rolled over onto her side, leaning on her elbow, head propped in her hand, watching him as he pulled his T-shirt off, revealing smooth, golden skin and, yes, the hard, carved muscle she'd felt beneath his shirt.

He was indeed the work of art she'd thought he was. He made her mouth go dry.

His hands dropped to the fastenings of his jeans, taking his time as he undid them, and she was fine with that, enjoying the slow reveal of sharply defined abs, narrow hips, and strong, muscled thighs. And his sex, long, thick, and hard.

Oh boy. He was something else.

A delicious tension coiled in the space between them, anticipation and the slow drawing out of that anticipation, making everything more erotic and more powerful.

Then he was naked and moving purposefully to the bed, getting onto it with her, his hands hot on her skin as he turned her onto her back before moving lower, pushing her thighs apart.

She shuddered as he settled himself between them and then leaned over her, his powerful body stretched over hers, his hands on the pillows on either side of her head. His heat surrounded her, his scent wrapping around her, the blue of his eyes her entire world.

"Damon," she whispered.

He bent, and his mouth covered hers and she was lost.

He kissed her hard, deep, but not for long enough, and she wanted to protest. But then his lips were trailing down over her jaw to her neck, pausing at the base of her throat, licking her skin, tasting where her pulse beat far too fast, before going lower.

Astrid's eyes closed slowly, a deep tremble shaking her, as his lips seared the tender skin of her chest, kisses like hot rain scattered over the swell of her breasts. He cupped one in his hand, making her shudder and her back arch as his thumb teased one hard, aching nipple. Then his tongue touched the other, licking gently before drawing it into the intense heat of his mouth.

She gasped, her hands on his shoulders, holding tightly onto him as pleasure raced along her nerve endings, bright and hot and wild. He sucked on her lightly, the pressure the most exquisite thing she'd ever felt, drawing tiny sounds of agonized pleasure from her.

Then he focused his attention on her other breast as his hands traced her sides and down over the curves of her hips, stroking her thighs.

His touch felt so good—so gentle, as if she were made of fine china and he had to be careful with her. It made her heart ache. Made her feel as if she was worth more than all the rejections she'd had and all the criticisms she'd received. Made her feel as if she wasn't the forgotten child, the rejected lover, or the abused victim.

It made her feel as if she was special.

Slowly, he drove her crazy and she was panting by the time he released her breast and moved lower, over the trembling plane of her stomach and down even farther.

Her breath caught as his hands settled on her thighs, pushing them apart even wider. And then he put his mouth between them, where she was hot and aching and needing him most.

She cried out as he began to explore her, again taking his time. Pausing to lick, to nip, to suck gently at her slick flesh, until she was panting and writhing beneath him, her nails digging into the heavy muscles of his shoulders.

There was nothing in the world but the pull of pleasure and the touch of his hands, the searing heat of his tongue and the warmth of his breath on her skin. She was desperate for him to end it, for the climax he held just out of her reach, and yet at the same time she didn't want it to end. She wanted the never-ending pleasure to keep going and to simply exist in it, to keep being the focus of his complete attention. To keep the feeling of being special and wanted and worshipped close to her heart for as long as she could.

No one had ever made her feel this way. Not one single person.

But of course it had to end. His hands settled on her hips, gripping her as he did something amazing with his tongue, and the world abruptly exploded into flame around her.

She cried out, her back arching, the orgasm taking her in firm hands and squeezing her, wringing every last gasp of pleasure from her. She was barely conscious of Damon shifting, moving from between her spread thighs. There came the soft rustle of clothing being moved and then the sound of foil ripping. Then he was back, the heat of his body covering her own, his hands stroking up and down her sides.

"Are you ready for me?" he whispered, and she could hear desperation for her in his voice. But his touch remained unhurried, waiting for her to give the okay. And she didn't hesitate.

"Yes," she gasped, even though she was still shaking from the effects of the last orgasm. And when he pushed inside her, she groaned again, arching up into him, trying to deepen the exquisite stretching sensation of him sliding into her. She wrapped her legs around his narrow hips, gliding her hands down his powerful back, glorying in the sheer sensual feel of his body on her, in her, surrounding her.

He felt so good. So incredibly good. He was a gift and she wanted to hold on to him for as long as possible.

His breath warmed her throat, and she hadn't realized she'd closed her eyes until he murmured, "Look at me."

And she did, opening her eyes to find him gazing down at her, the astonishing blue of his gaze colliding with hers. She'd thought it was the color of a winter sky, clear and light, but it wasn't. Around his pupil there was a darker midnight blue, drawing her, pulling at her, making it impossible for her to look away.

There were shadows in those eyes. Mysteries to uncover. Deep emotions that he hid and hid well. But she could see them. She could almost feel them herself.

She shifted her hands on his back, stroking him, loving the velvety feel of his skin beneath her palms and the weight of his body on hers, making her burn. Deepening that exquisite ache.

He didn't speak, only kept on staring at her as he began to move, a gentle, slow rhythm that had her trembling. Then he bent his head and brushed his mouth against hers, giving her soft butterfly kisses, little nips, sipping from her as the pleasure stretched out inside her, lazy and languorous.

She knew she shouldn't let all this get to her, that this was purely physical, but when his hands slid beneath her, gathering her even closer, it didn't feel purely physical. Held tight against him, close as a secret, it felt like more. And that should have made her want to put distance between them, made her want to pull away, but she was tired of distance. Tired of being guarded all the time. Tired of holding herself back, of being afraid to trust. Afraid of so many things.

But she wasn't afraid now. Here, in his arms, held tightly against his powerful body, she felt like she'd never be afraid again.

So she let herself go. Let the pleasure flow through her and the emotion too, let them turn her incandescent, burning bright like a torch. There was light in the darkness that had always felt like it was surrounding her; the darkness was now gone.

There was no darkness at all in his arms.

And when the pleasure exploded and lit up the night around her, there was only searing blue burning straight through her.

Leaving a mark forever on her heart.

Chapter 13

DAMON LEANED ON THE COUNTER IN THE LITTLE TOURIST information bureau, having a conversation with Sandy about cruise ships. The place was tiny, the walls covered with posters advertising Alaska fjord cruises, Alaska whale-watching expeditions, Alaska bird-watching trails, Alaska northern lights tours. Basically anything that it was possible to do in Alaska, Sandy had a poster for it. Including more of those mysterious "love in the middle of nowhere" posters that he'd seen in Astrid's office.

Talking about cruise ships wasn't a conversation he'd thought he'd ever have with anyone, but he was trying to whittle down the list of tourism ideas to a viable short list and Sandy was making sense.

She was an intense, sparky woman in her forties, with short black hair and dark eyes, and had approximately fifty million ideas about getting some tourism into Deep River. She'd once worked for the Alaska Tourism Board and still had contacts in the industry and had been busy regaling Damon with her plan to get Deep River on the list of cruise ship excursions.

It wasn't a stupid idea. Ketchikan and Juneau were already there, and sure, they were bigger and had more infrastructure, but why not Deep River? Maybe it could be a stop for people looking for places off the beaten track? Those who were wanting a taste of the "real wilderness." Sandy had further suggestions about playing up the town history and the fact that it was privately owned, not to mention suggestions for gold-rush-themed activities such as panning for gold.

All excellent stuff.

After he'd finished with Sandy, he checked his phone to see if he had any cell phone service and was pleased to find he had at least a couple of bars. So he called his mom to let her know he'd be leaving Deep River the next day. She sounded like her usual grumpy self, though toward the end of the call, she mentioned how she'd noticed a strange woman who kept coming in and cleaning up her kitchen.

Concern tightened inside him. It wasn't a strange woman, of course. It was Rachel, and he gently reminded his mother that she had a housekeeper, which then involved another repeat of the conversation he'd had with her earlier, about how it was for his peace of mind, not hers, and that of course she was fine.

She was not fine, that was clear. Which made his decision to leave the next day the right one.

Later, back in Hope and Silas's sunlit kitchen above the Moose, Damon sat at the plain wooden kitchen table, a coffee at his elbow, and laid out all the info Sandy had given him, along with the other ideas and information that he'd collected from various different people over the past few days.

Across the table from him were Silas and Astrid—they'd been going to meet in the mayor's office, but Gwen and several others had taken to hanging around outside the office entrance so they could impart "important" information about their pet projects—so to avoid them, Astrid had decided to meet at the Moose with Silas instead.

She looked particularly beautiful today. Her hair gleamed like spun gold in the early-afternoon sunlight coming through the kitchen windows, her gray eyes clear and cool. Except for the telltale silver glitter of passion that flickered every time she looked at him.

He'd left her early that morning, waking in the dark and leaving her sleeping as he went quietly out of the house. There hadn't been a sound from Connor's room and no one had been around outside either—it was Sunday, after all—so he'd managed to slip into the Moose without anyone seeing him.

If the moment in the library the day before had been magic, the entire night had been an enchantment. Even now he could feel the thrill of it winding through him and setting fire to him, tendrils of a spell designed for the most intense pleasure.

But not just physical pleasure.

No, it hadn't been. And that was the problem. He should have said goodbye to her and walked away, gone back to his bedroom in the Moose. Left her alone.

"I think you need it as much as I do," she'd said, and he knew she hadn't meant just sex, because if it had been, he'd have easily resisted. And he hadn't resisted.

It wasn't sex that he needed, but a connection, and a connection that went deeper than physical. That was about more than a joining of bodies. It was about the sympathy and understanding he'd seen in her silver eyes. Her lack of fear and the warmth in her hand as she'd laid it over his. The way she'd touched his face as he'd undressed her, something tender in her expression that he hadn't known he'd craved until he saw it.

He'd always been fine with his surface life, but something in him wanted more. At this moment, he felt the lack of deeper and more lasting. He was sick of drifting.

Yet deeper was something he couldn't have. After Ella had died and Rebecca had left him, his capacity for deeper had been burned right out of him. And if he'd felt small flashes of intense emotion in the past couple of days, he was pretty sure those were just the last electrical impulses of a dying brain.

His ability to care for anyone beyond the strictly impersonal was as dead and gone as his daughter.

Not that it mattered. He'd had a magical night with Astrid, where they'd both barely slept, and he'd remember it for a long time to come. But a night was all it could ever be. Tomorrow, he'd be going back to LA.

Silas cleared his throat ostentatiously. "You were saying?"

Damon, who hadn't in fact been saying anything, immediately glanced away from Astrid, who was blushing, and down at the table where all the papers were.

Right. Back on track.

"I've been talking to Sandy," Damon said, ignoring his pesky libido. "And she mentioned pushing to put Deep River in the cruise ship schedule. Juneau and Ketchikan already are, so there's no reason we can't be."

"'We'?" Silas raised a brow.

A flicker of irritation shot through him. Since when had he included himself as part of Deep River? He wasn't staying. There was no "we" about it.

He shrugged. "'We,' 'you,' it doesn't matter. The point is that getting this place on that schedule would be fantastic when it comes to getting tourists in the town."

"Sure," Silas said, "but how does she think that's going to happen? I'm not saying it isn't a good plan, but we're tiny and there's nothing here for tourists as it is."

"No, but isn't that the whole point of getting these tourism ventures together? To get them here?" He pushed a couple of the notes he'd made in Silas's direction. "Sandy's got some contacts from her old job with the Alaska tourism board, and she thinks she could reach out to some of the smaller cruise companies at least to make a case. Then we need to make sure we've got something to show them in terms of why they should make Deep River a stop. She thinks we could have something in place for the summer, even."

"I think that's a great plan." Astrid was smiling and it felt like the sun shining directly on him. "I've been talking to Gwen about the farmers' market thing she does in the community center and there's a few other people who wouldn't mind getting involved. Especially if there are tourist dollars on the table."

Silas looked skeptical. "Sure, but that's it? A farmers' market?

I wonder if we wouldn't be better placed to start with Kevin and Mike's fishing charters, since everything is in place for that already."

Damon sat back in his chair and eyed his friend. "Is there any reason we can't do all of it? Fishing charters wouldn't require much capital, since they already have the equipment. They'd only need a bit of promotion, and in conjunction with Wild Alaska running flights from Juneau to here, I don't see that it's a straight one or the other." He grinned, ideas beginning to form in his head. "I've got a few contacts in Juneau myself who could put out the word. We could do that, do a few interesting wilderness promotions—Sandy's got some great ideas for that too, by the way. She had this 'finding love in the middle of—'"

"'Nowhere' campaign, yeah," Silas interrupted. "I know. She ran it last year too. Didn't you have to get back to LA?"

"Yes, but email works," he said easily. "It's no drama."

Silas nodded. "Okay. And you're still wanting to sell your share of Wild Alaska?"

"Yeah," he said, because he had to. It was a significant amount of money tied up in a business he couldn't be part of. Money he'd need when his mom eventually had to go into assisted living. "I haven't got a lot of choice about it."

Silas was quiet a moment. "You ever thought about staying here?"

Damon frowned. "I can't, you know that. I have to be near my mom."

"You could bring her here. Or does she need hospital care?"

A nice thought, but impossible even if he'd wanted to live here. He liked Deep River and its people, it was true, and he was enjoying helping sort through tourism ideas. But he couldn't uproot his mother from everything that was familiar to her and bring her to live in the middle of nowhere. It wouldn't be fair to her.

It wasn't fair the way she basically abandoned you after Ella died.

The thought wound through him, poisonous and just flat-out

wrong. Sure, his mother hadn't been the most supportive, but she'd never been comfortable with strong emotion. She was very much a "suck it up and carry on" kind of person. Yes, it had felt like being abandoned at the time, but he'd put that behind him now.

Anyway, she'd sacrificed a lot to bring him up on her own. She'd taken care of him and now it was his turn to take care of her.

"No," he said carefully. "She doesn't need hospital care. But I can't just take her away from everything that's familiar to her."

Silas gave him a curiously direct look. But all he said was, "Okay. Fair enough."

His friend wanted him to stay, that much was obvious. Yet Silas wasn't going to make a big deal out of it, thank God.

Astrid fussed around with the open folder in front of her. "Perhaps we need to discuss a few of the less...conventional ideas?"

"Yes, let's discuss it," he said, ignoring the speculative gleam in Silas's gaze. "Debbie's very insistent about Carl's beer coaster collection."

Silas snorted and the conversation moved on.

The plan was to get a short list divided into long-term goals and then short-term plans the town could implement immediately without too much drama. Then there would be a town vote— apparently Mal put up a ballot box in the market and people came in with a ballot paper. It was all very twentieth-century.

Damon pointed out some of the financial issues with the ventures people had put forward, then outlined a few solutions. And after the bulk of the discussion had been had, he asked, "What will you do with people unhappy their idea wasn't chosen?"

Astrid was fiddling around with their provisional short list. "Oh, they'll have a vent and try to argue. But everyone abides by the vote."

"Apart from Mike," Silas added. "But his luxury motel idea could be a good one if it was done right."

"It could," Damon said, reflecting on it. "Could even tie in with Gwen's eco-lodge idea too."

They kicked around some more ideas after that and made some adjustments to the short list, then Hope came in with a couple of bags of treats from April's, along with some strong coffees. She had a couple of her own opinions about the shortlist and made sure they were noted.

Damon ended up in a good-natured argument with her which both of them enjoyed thoroughly, and that involved rejigging the short list yet again, much to Astrid's irritation. Then Hope mentioned that Clare at the B&B had had a call from some stranger interested in buying her out, which Clare had naturally refused. But it was a reminder of what they were trying to do and what they were up against.

"They're not going to stop, are they?" Astrid's expression was grim. "They're going to keep calling, keep bugging us until someone gives in."

Damon almost reached across the table to take her hand and hold it in his as a reassurance, because he didn't like the expression on her face. Her little safe haven for herself and her son was being threatened, so she was bound to find that worrying.

But he couldn't touch her without giving away their affair and he didn't want to start any gossip or make things difficult for her. So he kept his hands to himself.

Yet he was surprised at the anger burning inside him. On her behalf and Connor's and, surprisingly, for the inhabitants of Deep River too. Anger at the oil company and what they were doing and what they thought they could get away with.

More feelings he shouldn't be having. What the hell was wrong with him?

You should stay. Help them fight. Cal wanted you to look after Connor, after all.

No, he'd already made the decision that he couldn't. Besides,

Astrid and Connor weren't alone. They had Silas and Zeke and Mal and Hope. And everyone else in the town.

"Have we finished?" he asked, restless all of a sudden.

"Why?" Silas asked in surprise. "Somewhere you need to be?"

What could he say? That the thoughts in his head were driving him crazy and he needed to get out, get some air? Yeah, not so much.

"I have to get my stuff ready," he said shortly. "I'll be heading out tomorrow. Anyway, we have a short list now and Astrid will get a town meeting on the schedule. Is there anything else?"

"No, probably not." Silas glanced at Hope. "You want me to go talk to Clare? Get some idea about what they're offering her?"

"Yeah, sounds like a plan." She pushed herself away from the counter where she'd been standing. "I'll come with you."

After the two of them had gone, Astrid, who was still sitting at the table, raised a brow. "You think they did that on purpose?"

"What? Leave us alone together?" He grinned. "Possibly. Though Silas's already warned me off you."

"Really?" She didn't look pleased with the idea as she started to gather the papers back into her folder. "Why am I his business? It's got nothing to do with him."

"No, but it not being his business has never stopped Silas."

"True." Astrid rose, clutching her folder. She gave him a glance from beneath her golden lashes. "Since you're leaving tomorrow and your room's just up the stairs, I wondered if you wanted to… say goodbye properly."

The look she gave him would have set fire to a stone and he wouldn't have been a man if he hadn't gotten instantly hard.

There was no reason not to.

They hadn't had a chance to talk to each other since last night and he'd been assuming that, again, the night had been a one-off. Another of the those rare moments to hold on to, to take with him when he left, and he'd thought Astrid felt the same.

Except it was clear that she didn't.

"Are you sure that's a good idea?" He didn't know why he was asking her when he very much wanted to take her up on the offer. "It's broad daylight. People might notice us disappearing into my room together."

"No, they won't." Her mouth curved in a sensual, sweet smile. "There's no one else staying in the Moose, and no one's going to notice us leaving Hope and Silas's place."

He wanted to, and very badly. And he didn't understand where his reluctance was coming from…

No, he did know. Last night he'd held her in his arms and she'd looked at him with stars in her eyes, and those same stars were in her eyes now, bright and glittering.

She felt something for him.

It had happened so fast, him and the pretty mayor. Too fast. And now they'd gone beyond one pleasant moment, and 'pleasant' had become something more, something deeper.

It couldn't.

"Astrid," he said gently, "this is not—"

"I know what it's not. Look, if one night was enough for you, then I understand. I just thought…well…"

Of course she'd thought that. She had no reason not to, especially as he hadn't given her one. But…regret filled him.

He couldn't sleep with her again, even though she wanted it and so did he—quite desperately. Even though refusing her would hurt her. He wasn't going to mess around with her feelings just because his body wanted hers; that would make him no better than that asshole Aiden and he couldn't stand that.

"It's not that it was enough for me." He let her see what was in his eyes. "It wasn't. But last night…it was more than good, Astrid. It was special. And I don't think special is what either of us want."

Her mouth opened, then closed. Then she looked away. "No. I suppose not."

Disappointment laced her voice, and it caught at him in ways he wasn't expecting. He wasn't supposed to care about this. And yet he was, and it shouldn't be happening.

Living a surface life meant not caring too deeply, or at least not so deeply that it caused pain, yet he could feel her disappointment echoing in his own heart. Making him ache.

It was the phantom pain of an organ long dead, though. Her feelings might be engaged, but his weren't, and that was why he needed to end this and fast. Disappointment he could recover from, but anything else took far longer, and he didn't want to let it get to that stage.

"Don't make this into something it's not, Ms. Mayor," he said quietly.

Her jaw tightened. "I only asked if you wanted to go upstairs. How is that making it into something it isn't?"

"The look on your face when I said no."

"It was only a question." Her voice had cooled, the snow queen returning. "If you don't want to, you don't want to."

He shouldn't keep trying to explain himself, shouldn't turn this into a big deal. Yet he couldn't stop himself from wanting to ease it for her. Her history of men rejecting her had been an awful one, and he didn't want to be just another in a long line of assholes.

"I don't want to hurt you, Astrid. I just think this will be easier on both of us if we end it now."

Her beautiful gray eyes turned chilly. "You're assuming it's something and it isn't. It's just sex." The dismissal in her tone might have worked if she hadn't glanced away again, as if she couldn't meet his gaze. "Anyway, it's not like I don't have anything better to do."

"Astrid," he began.

"It's fine," she said before he could continue. "I'll see you around, Damon."

Then she turned and left him standing there.

Much later that afternoon, Astrid stood in the little Deep River library reshelving books when Connor came in. He was frowning, though not in an angry way, more as if he had a lot to think about.

She hadn't had a chance to talk to him today about how his conversation with Damon had gone or about school, since in typical teenage fashion he hadn't gotten out of bed until noon. By which time she'd been talking to Mal about some issues with the food co-op, and then she'd had that meeting with Silas and Damon.

Putting the armful of books she was carrying down on the library cart, she opened her mouth to speak, but he got in first.

"Mom," he said, still frowning, "I think I agree with Damon. I like the cruise ship option that Sandy was talking about with him. We should definitely be investigating that, and then we really need to be talking to Harry about—"

"Connor," Astrid interrupted, raising her hands in a stop motion. "Slow down. What's all this about?"

Connor came over to the library cart and poked at the books on it. "Damon came to see me and told me about the meeting you had with him and Silas." He glanced up at her. "He told you about our deal last night, right?"

Astrid's heart gave a small throb. Damon had been as good as his word. He'd included Connor in the plans for Deep River.

Did you doubt that he would?

Maybe. Just a little bit. But now the last shred of her doubt had gone.

"Oh," she said, trying to disguise the husk in her voice. "Yes, that's right. He did."

"So this deal." Connor idly kicked at one of the cart's big rubber wheels. "I'd go to school and he'd tell me what was going on with the oil stuff. And he'd tell Silas and whoever if I had any concerns."

This was important to Connor, she could see it in the earnest gleam in his blue eyes. It mattered that Damon had included him and that his opinions were being taken seriously. It was all about respect. And that was something that Aiden, for all that he'd been good to Connor, hadn't had.

Aiden wouldn't have respected Connor in this way, as an individual. No, as Damon had pointed out, Aiden would have viewed Connor as his property. And if he hadn't respected her—and he hadn't—then he certainly wouldn't have respected her son.

"You absolutely did the right thing…"

Damon had been so sure the night before; there had been no doubt in him, though a piece of her had still wondered. Yet it came to her, all of a sudden, that she didn't think that now. Looking at Connor, at his serious, earnest face, at the way he carried himself, not as if he were carrying the whole burden himself but as if he'd been given a part of it and that part was an honor…

Yes, she *had* done the right thing taking him away from Aiden and bringing him here to Deep River. To a place where he was safe and where he'd learned responsibility, to be part of a community, a help and a support to others.

One day, he'd make a great mayor.

"Mom?" Connor's frown deepened. "Are you okay?"

Astrid realized that her eyes were full of tears.

She blinked fiercely and smiled. "I'm fine. I'm just…so pleased you're going to keep going to school."

Connor inspected her. "You must be very pleased if you're crying about it."

"I'm sorry." The words burst out of her before she could stop them. "I'm so sorry I didn't tell you about your father. You were so upset when I took you away from Aiden and I was afraid to trust Caleb with you. I didn't want him to break your heart or let you down the way he did me. And I—"

"Mom," Connor interrupted gently. "It's fine." And then much to her shock, he stepped forward and wrapped his arms around her. He was big, her son, and getting broad, and though he could do with a shower, for a minute she closed her eyes and hugged him back, remembering the small, wriggly boy he'd once been. Who'd given her so much joy at a time when there wasn't much of it to be had.

He'd never let her down, this boy of hers. In a lifetime of people who had, he'd never done so.

"I'm sorry too," he said after a second, his voice muffled near the side of her ear. "I shouldn't have liked Aiden so much. I should have seen how horrible he was to you and I didn't."

"You don't need to apologize for that, Con. You were a kid and you wanted a dad." She squeezed him tight, then let him go and stood back. "Is that what all this protective stuff is about? About me and Aiden?"

He shrugged, stuck his hands in his pockets, and looked at the floor. For all that he could be uncannily perceptive about certain things, he was also still a teenage boy and uncomfortable about feelings.

"Yeah," he said slowly. "Damon said it wasn't my fault. That it was Aiden's."

A little rush of grief hit her. Of course. How could she not have seen that?

"Your fault for what?" she asked thickly.

"My fault for…liking him, I guess. For wanting to stay. I didn't know he hurt you till after."

She didn't want to cry yet again, so she looked at the floor too, emotion sitting like a stone in her chest. "I know you didn't. I didn't want you to know. But…" Blinking hard, she looked at him. "Damon's right. None of that was your fault. None of it. Understand?"

Her son's blue gaze met hers. Slowly, he nodded.

"It was Aiden's," she went on, the truth of it settling inside her as she spoke and it wasn't just intellectual this time. She felt it too, heavy and sure. "He didn't respect us. And he sure as hell didn't care about us. And getting you away from him was the best choice I ever made."

There was relief in Connor's expression and then he smiled. "You're fierce when you're angry, Mom."

The love she had for her son nearly strangled her, and she wanted to give him another big hug, squeeze him tight. But even one hug was rare for him and she didn't want to push it.

"Yes, and don't you forget it."

His gaze turned very direct all of a sudden. "Damon's a good guy. I like him."

The abrupt change of subject triggered a memory.

Damon, who'd stood there in Hope's sunny kitchen, tall and powerful, the gold strands in his dark hair gleaming, looking at her with hunger in his eyes at the same time he told her it wasn't a good idea. That she shouldn't make this something it wasn't.

She'd been hurt; she couldn't deny it. The rejection had made her feel like she had over the years with various different people in her life, asking for what she wanted only to be shot down. Only to be denied and refused or not to be listened to. And she'd done what she'd always done in those situations: she'd hidden her hurt, hadn't made it a big deal, turned and walked away.

And it wasn't a big deal, was it? It was only sex. And Damon was an amazing man, sure, but he would be leaving tomorrow. So maybe it was for the best that they left it at one night.

He'd been right, though: last night had been special.

"Yes, he is," Astrid said, turning away and direction her attention to the cart full of books. "But he'll be leaving tomorrow."

"I know. Actually…" Connor paused and took a breath. "I think he should stay."

Astrid looked up at him in surprise. "What?"

Connor's expression was as serious as she'd ever seen it. "He should stay."

"He can't, Con. His mother is sick and he needs to be with her."

"I know that. But…" Connor shifted on his feet. "I think he needs us."

For a second, Astrid could only stand there and stare at her son. "What makes you say that?"

He lifted a shoulder. "I dunno. He had a daughter who died, and when he told me, he had this look on his face…" Connor shook his head. "It was lonely. And he doesn't have a dad, he's only got his mom. Not that that's a bad thing, but…"

"A boy needs a man, right?"

Connor looked at her solemnly. "Yeah."

And a man needs a boy.

That might well have been true, but she remembered Damon's face this afternoon as Silas had suggested that he stay and that he bring his mother here too. His features had hardened and it had been clear he hadn't liked that idea one bit, which made Connor's observation wishful thinking at best.

That thought made her heart ache.

"He can't stay, Con." She didn't hide the regret in her voice, though it was only for her son's sake. Definitely not for her own. "There's better healthcare in LA than there is up here, and if she's sick, that's what she's going to need."

But there was a determined look on her son's face, the same kind of look he'd had when he'd told her that he was giving up school to keep an eye on the town. The same kind of look he always got when he had a plan about something.

"Connor," she said warningly.

"What?" His expression was the very essence of innocence. "You like him too, don't you?"

Heat rose suddenly in her cheeks and she gritted her teeth, trying to stop it through sheer force of will. "Oh? And what makes you say that?" She tried for cool.

"Your face when you opened the door after we came home."

Oh. Hell.

"He's a nice guy, like you said." She tried to sound exasperated and not as embarrassed as all get out. How annoying. The kid was fifteen. He shouldn't be the one making his parent uncomfortable, surely? "What are you implying?"

"Oh, nothing." Connor grinned suddenly and started to back away toward the exit. "Right. Gotta go see someone about…uh… something."

The door banged shut behind him.

What was he up to? Probably something that would end up backfiring.

She went after him, going to the door and pulling it open, but when she stepped out onto the library's porch, the road toward the town was empty. Connor had disappeared.

Astrid muttered a curse under her breath, turned, and went back inside. Whatever it was he was going to do, she'd no doubt find out eventually. And likely in the worst possible way, since that was how it went with kids.

Moving back over to the library cart, she picked up the stack of books and took them over to the shelves, slotting each book back in its place on the shelf as her thoughts turned to her son and that look he'd given her when he'd mentioned Damon.

You like him too.

And that was a problem. She did like him. She liked him a lot. Too much, probably. And Connor mentioning that he thought Damon needed them had only made things worse. Because now all she could think about was how he'd told her about his daughter and how he hadn't wanted to talk about it. And then this morning at Silas's, the way he'd looked at her…

She'd been hurt at his refusal, it was true, but it was also obvious that the problem wasn't that he didn't want her. It was…what? He'd made his refusal sound like he was protecting her, but was it really about her? Or was it more about himself? Did he not feel he could let himself have her? And if not, why? And why did Connor think that Damon needed them? Did he not have anyone?

Slowly, she put another book on the shelf, thinking, all the questions revolving in her head.

He had Silas and Zeke, and he'd had Cal. He had his mom in LA. But did he have anyone else? Perhaps he didn't. He'd mentioned that telling her about his daughter was a secret that he hadn't told anyone else. Why was that? Grief, yes, and pain, definitely. But not talking about her to anyone had to be such a terrible burden.

Yet...he'd told her, giving her a secret little piece of himself.

Emotion curled inside Astrid's chest, heavy and aching.

He was a caring, protective man, and she could sense that he had a lot to give and that he wanted to give it. Yet she got the feeling that he was holding himself back.

You can't keep giving without receiving.

It was true. Already he had given her a lot over the past few days, offering support and reassurance with her son, giving her passion and pleasure, rebuilding her confidence in herself as a woman. Yet she hadn't given him anything in return, and she didn't like that thought. Didn't like it at all. She wanted to help him the way he'd helped her. And it didn't have to be sex. It could just be the offer of a friendly ear and a shoulder to cry on. Reassurance that he wasn't alone. Because she got the feeling that maybe he was. That behind his direct blue gaze lay something lonely and hungry...

Determination settled inside her.

Yes, that's what she would do. She'd go to him tonight. He might not want to talk; he might only want sex and a night of distraction. Or he might just turn her away. But that didn't matter and she couldn't let her own issues get in the way. This was his last night here and this was her last opportunity, and she had to at least make the offer, let him know she was here if he wanted her to be.

It wasn't much. But it was all she had.

Chapter 14

DAMON SPENT THE REST OF THAT AFTERNOON TALKING TO Harry the survivalist in the man's sprawling log cabin in the bush. Harry had a quad bike that he used to get in and out of town, since his house was a few miles away—he and Gwen liked the isolation—and he offered to take Damon out to look at the place. Damon agreed because Harry's suggestions of wilderness survival skills was a good one and the guy wanted to give him a demonstration.

So he watched while Harry did various things like lighting a fire by striking sparks off his knife and onto a little pad of moss. Then building a shelter, before dragging Damon into the bush for a hunting demonstration. Afterward, since more rain had closed in, he and Harry sat on the porch while Gwen brought them herbal tea from herbs she'd dried herself.

He enjoyed himself far more than he'd expected to, mainly because it was an excellent distraction from thinking about Astrid.

Harry returned him to town much later, not to mention a bit the worse for wear after sharing with Damon some of his home-made whisky.

The Moose was full of people when he'd come into the bar, and he'd spoken to enough of the townspeople by now that they didn't give him the stranger stare. Instead, they called his name in greeting, several beckoning him over to join in conversations or waving beers at him in invitation to share. Hell, it was almost as if he was one of them.

Deciding that although more alcohol was definitely a bad idea, it was probably also a very good idea too, Damon went upstairs to change the clothes he'd got muddy hunting with Harry and to have a quick shower, planning to come back down to the bar. Because why not? It was his last night here after all, so he might as well make it a night to remember.

What about Astrid? And Connor?

He'd go see them tomorrow, say his goodbyes. Keep it friendly and light. They both deserved better than that, but friendly and light was all he had. Better they found that out now rather than later.

Regret cut at him, sharp-edged and painful, the way all his emotions seemed to be these days. But it wasn't anything to be concerned about. That phantom limb pain from his burned-out heart would go away soon enough. Once he left Deep River, probably. As if he needed another reason not to stay.

He stepped into the room, then stopped dead.

A slim, blond woman in a white T-shirt and jeans was sitting on his bed.

Astrid.

Her steady gray gaze met his and a rush of heat went through him, intense and unstoppable, making his heart race and his breath catch.

Goddammit. What the hell was she doing here?

Slowly, trying to get himself under control, he shut the door behind him.

"What's up?" The question came out a lot rougher and more demanding than he meant it to, but he didn't apologize. "You okay?"

"Not really." The setting sun shining through the windows lit in her hair, turning it into a blaze of gold. "I haven't been very good to you the past couple of days, have I?"

His heart was beating way too fast, and he had to thrust his hands in his pockets to stop them from reaching for her. Insanity. He'd made his decision not to touch her again and he wasn't going to change his mind.

"What makes you say that?"

"Because I've been quite selfish." Her hands rested on her thighs, her posture a little stiff. But her gaze was very steady. "Ever since you got here, you've put yourself out for me and Connor. You talked him through some crappy stuff, and then you did the same for me. You helped us. And I realize I haven't really given you anything back. So that's why I'm here. To give you whatever you need."

He smiled, conscious all of a sudden of how fake that smile was. Yet he couldn't control it; his mouth curled at the edges whether he wanted it to or not. "I told you last night. This isn't a quid pro quo. I mean, I appreciate the offer, but you don't have to give me anything."

"I know I don't. But I want to."

Inexplicable tension crawled through him, that goddamn smile starting to feel faker and faker. "I don't need it." He tried to keep his voice gentle. "Except maybe one of April's coffees."

Astrid didn't smile. Her gaze was very, very sharp. Like an X-ray, seeing through his skin and the fake smile that he plastered over everything, right down to the cracks in his bones.

"How sick is your mom, Damon?" she asked quietly.

He didn't know why he told her. Maybe it was because of Harry's whisky and he was just a little drunk. Or maybe he didn't want her looking at him like that, as if she could see the emptiness behind his smile.

"She has early onset dementia." He kept the words stripped of any emotion. "And last week she nearly burned her house down when she left a pot on the stove and forgot about it."

Deep sympathy glowed in her eyes. "Oh, Damon. I'm so sorry."

He wanted to turn away from her expression, but that would be to admit that her sympathy cut like a knife and he didn't want to admit that. He wasn't supposed to feel this pain anymore.

"It's fine," he said automatically. "It is what it is."

"But what does that mean for you?"

He made himself move, over to the nightstand near the bed, where the whisky bottle was. A glass sat beside it, so he poured himself a measure, because why not?

"It means that someone will have to live with her and make sure she's not going to accidentally kill herself. And since she doesn't have anyone else, that someone is me."

"So…you're leaving the life you have in Alaska to take care of her?"

"Yes." He lifted the glass and took a sip, the liquid burning down his throat. It probably wasn't a good idea to have more, but he didn't feel like behaving himself right now. "It's not a drama. Don't get me wrong. I like flying planes and working with the guys. But I'm not married to it. Mom sacrificed a lot for me, so it's the least I can do."

A crease appeared between Astrid's fair brows. "What about live-in care? Or assisted living?"

"She doesn't want that. She barely acknowledges the fact that she's sick as it is. And I don't want to force her. She's had a tough life and it seems wrong to stick her in a home like an afterthought." He swirled the whisky in the glass, looking down at it, since somehow that was easier than looking at Astrid. "I have some money set aside for private care when it happens, but I want to look after her as much as I can myself."

It was only fair.

Besides, it wasn't as if the life he had in Juneau was anything deep and meaningful. It was spent flying planes, having casual affairs, and drinking with the guys. There was nothing too intense, nothing too passionate. But that's what he wanted, a surface life, and he'd seen no reason to change his mind.

Not even for Astrid and Connor?

Why would they make a difference? When he'd only known them a handful of days? His promise had kept him here, nothing more. And if he'd had a few pangs from that long-dead heart of his, it was only phantom pain.

Hell, even if things had been different, he couldn't stay anyway. They needed more than what he could give them.

"I get that," Astrid said quietly. "That's tough."

A heavy silence fell, Astrid's fingers twisting together on her thighs.

"You don't have to stay, Astrid," Damon said and took another swallow of whisky. "Like I said, I appreciate the offer of help, but there's nothing you can do. It's my problem to deal with."

Yet she didn't move. "I know. But that doesn't mean I can't offer some support."

He was standing quite close to where she sat on the bed, the last rays of the sun falling over her and igniting in her hair. She didn't look so cool and capable now, the snow queen he'd first met only a few days ago. Now, her hair gleamed gold and there was warmth in her gray eyes. The snow queen melted, and for him...

He very much wanted to hold her. But it wasn't the right time for that kind of thing. He was drunk and his mood was off, and he'd be leaving the next day. Better to end it on the magic of the night before and not on him being drunk and tense and an ass.

Knocking back the rest of the whisky, he put the glass back on the nightstand and jerked his head toward the door. "It's best if you go, Ms. Mayor. I'm not in the mood for heart-to-heart chats."

Astrid merely gazed at him. The nervous tension that had been buzzing around her had vanished, and now an air of certainty and determination surrounded her. Which must be where her son got his from.

"Why did you tell me about your daughter, Damon?" she asked.

It was the very last question he'd expected, and it sent a jolt of shock through him. This time he couldn't stop himself from turning away and walking over to the windows.

"I told you why," he said, staring out at the river rushing by.

The rain had cleared earlier, leaving the evening newly washed and clean, the light glancing off the river and turning it a deep, endless green.

"You wanted to share it with me, and yet you didn't want to talk about it afterwards. So why tell me in the first place?"

"Hell if I know." He stared hard at the water. "Because it seemed like a good idea at the time?"

"You said that secrets were hard to carry all by yourself, so... it seems like you told me because that secret was getting heavy."

Why was he feeling so tense? Like he was inside enemy territory and looking around for the next attack? Ella had died years ago, and the sharp edges of that grief had dulled. It would always be with him, he knew that, but that's the way it should be. The extent of the pain measured the extent of the love, and feeling nothing at all would have meant that she was nothing at all. And Ella had never been nothing.

But he didn't want to talk about it. He didn't want to share her. After Rebecca had gone and the initial shattering pain of the grief had eased, he'd tried to talk about her to various people, his mother included. But no one had wanted to listen, and he'd hated that. He couldn't stand the thought of Ella's loss being dismissed because other people found it too hard, or didn't know what to say, or were too uncomfortable. Her memory was too precious for that. It was easier not to say anything at all in the end.

Caleb had been the only one who'd let Damon talk, the only one who'd listened. He'd understood because he'd been a father as well. Not even his mother had done that for him.

Astrid would listen.

His heart kicked hard inside his chest like a mule. Would she? He'd thought that of all the people in the world, the one person he could talk to would have been Rebecca, Ella's mother. But she hadn't even been able to face him. After Ella's funeral, she'd told him she was leaving, that being in LA was too hard. That bearing his grief as well as her own was too hard. She hadn't given him a chance to protest or even to comfort her; she'd simply delivered the news, then left.

He'd been angry with her for that. It was unfair of him, but he was. He'd been so full of memories of Ella, overflowing with the need to share them and share his grief, but there was no one around to listen.

The only other person he'd had to talk to had been his mother, and she'd told him in no uncertain terms that she didn't want to talk about it.

All those memories, all that pain he'd had to bottle up and keep to himself. Then it had ceased to become a necessity, but a choice. And he'd found it easier not to talk. Easier to keep it hidden because people's reactions were hard to deal with and he hadn't wanted to deal with them.

Easier to keep Ella as his own special secret, aching in his heart.

"You may not want to," Astrid continued in a calm, steady voice. "But if you want to talk about her now, you can talk to me. I'm here to listen. And I'd like to know."

There was a sunset outside, and it was beautiful.

He didn't move. He stared out the window at the river and the dusky purple of the mountains beyond, wrapped in the green of the bush and capped in snow. And he didn't mean to speak; somehow it just came out.

"I don't talk about her," he heard himself say. "Because no one ever wants to hear. It's too hard for some people to bear and it makes them uncomfortable. And Ella deserves more than that. I told Cal because he was a dad and he understood."

"Is that why he asked you to look after Connor?"

"Yeah, I think so."

Astrid was silent behind him, and she must have moved quietly because the next thing he knew, slim arms were winding around his waist, holding him tight, and there was warmth at his back. Warmth and the scent of wildflowers.

"Tell me about her," Astrid said softly. "You don't have to protect her from me."

His heart ached, a sweet and gentle grief these days. And he found he wanted to talk. He wanted someone to hear about his special girl, because she didn't deserve to be kept in the dark. She deserved to be talked about and remembered, and not with tension and anger but with love and happiness. Because that's what she'd given him.

And Astrid was right. He didn't have to protect Ella from her. She was a mother and she understood.

Damon closed his eyes. "She liked ice cream. And...she had this toy cat thing that I found in a thrift store for her because we had no money for brand-new toys. She really liked that cat. But she had a temper too. Hated it when I tried to dress her in clothes she didn't like." He could still picture her in his head, her blue gaze so like his own, and her dark brown hair. "She was so stubborn. When I told her no, she used to lie down on the floor and scream. An actual, literal tantrum. Couldn't take her anywhere when she was like that. I had to put her under my arm and carry her kicking and screaming."

"Hmmm, I wonder where she got that from?" Astrid's voice was full of warm amusement.

He was smiling, but he could feel moisture on his skin. It didn't matter. "Not me. That was all her mother."

"Sure, sure."

His hands were somehow out of his pockets now and he'd put them over Astrid's where they rested on his stomach. "She laughed a lot too, and she liked hugs. Liked being picked up and carried." Astrid's skin was warm against his palms. "She was very brave. She didn't like the doctors or the hospital but..." He stopped.

Astrid didn't prompt him, a calm, quiet presence at his back, giving him what he'd never had all those years ago. Comfort and strength. How strange that those arms around him, holding him tight, could be slender and yet so strong.

"There was nothing the doctors could do," he went on. "She slipped away without pain. I was with her at the end, and it was peaceful." His heart ached at the memory, but it was a welcome ache. A sign of Ella's presence in his life. "And it hurt," he said. "It…just fucking hurt."

Astrid said nothing. She kept on holding him, giving him the heat of her body and the warmth of her presence.

"The worst part"—he was unable to keep quiet now—"was not being able to talk about her to anyone. Rebecca, Ella's mom, couldn't bear being in LA. It was too hard and she couldn't stand my grief as well as her own. So she left and I never saw her again. Mom was… She came from a family that didn't talk about bad stuff and she couldn't talk about it with me. I tried to once, but she told me she didn't want to hear it. Life is hard, she used to tell me. Get used to it. Suck it up and carry on."

"Sometimes you can't suck it up and carry on." Astrid's voice was husky. "Sometimes you have to break a little before you can. And you can't do that alone."

Yet he had. He'd broken, and there had been no one to help him or give him comfort. But he'd gotten through it. And afterward, he'd pulled himself together and gone on.

"You can," he said. "It's just much harder."

"Yes, you can," she agreed. "But you shouldn't have had to is what I'm saying."

"Well, I didn't get a choice." He was aware of the bitter edge to his voice. Couldn't do a thing about it. "Anyway, you managed, didn't you?"

Astrid was quiet a moment. Then she said, "But I wasn't alone, Damon. I had Connor."

Of course she had.

He still had his eyes closed and he didn't want to open them. Didn't know what to say either. He could have told her that he was fine, that he hadn't needed anyone back then. That yes, it had been hard, but he'd sucked it up and carried on, just like his mother had told him to.

But the words sounded hollow in his head. As hollow as he was.

Because he wasn't fine and he knew it. His heart was a cold hearth full of dead embers and ashes, and there were no sparks left to coax it back into burning.

He'd never found it a problem—he'd never wanted to light it again. But…with Astrid's arms around him and her warmth soaking into him, there was a part of him that wished he could. That wished he could to set it alight for her.

And maybe she knew, because her arms tightened. "Whenever you want to talk about her, about grief or about how it hurts or about anything at all, you can talk to me, understand?" There was a ferocity in her voice that wrapped around him. "You don't have to suck it up and carry on with me. Everyone needs someone, Damon. And you have me. You will *always* have me."

———

Astrid felt Damon's big body go rigid, all his muscles tightening. Then he turned in her arms and she found herself looking up into his blue eyes.

She was trembling, and it wasn't with anguish or rage, but a powerful, fierce emotion she didn't have a name for. It was determination and protectiveness and an urge to give comfort all in one, and it was concentrated on him.

She hated how he hadn't had anyone, because she knew what it was like to feel alone. To have nothing and no one to turn to. That was what her entire pregnancy and early motherhood had been like.

Sure, she'd had Connor in the end, but initially she'd been alone, with a baby and no support. And everything she'd done, she'd done on her own. She'd had no one to talk to and no one to care, and she knew how lonely that could be.

It broke her heart that the same thing could happen to such a caring, protective man as him, and she didn't want to ask herself why that hurt so much; it just did.

He shouldn't have had to be alone. He should have had someone.

And now he did.

He didn't look away, his gaze burning with a fire that found an echo in the powerful intensity currently flooding through her. And it wasn't only desire she saw there, but something that went deeper. A longing and a hunger, as if she was the treasure he'd been searching his whole life for.

"Why?" His voice was stripped right back to bare rock and gravel. "You barely know me, Astrid. Why should it matter to you so much that I have someone to talk to?"

"Because I've been there, Damon. Yes, I did have Connor, but not at the beginning. When he was first born, it was just me in a crappy apartment that I shared with four other people because I couldn't afford to have my own place. Everyone would complain when Connor cried, so I had to make sure he didn't. No one wanted to hear me talk about him, and they certainly didn't want to hear me talk about how lonely I was, or how frightened."

His gaze was shadowed, his hands coming up all of a sudden and cupping her face between them. "Oh, honey…"

But this wasn't about her. This was about him.

"Like you, I got through it. I survived." She wrapped her fingers around his strong wrists. "But I don't ever want to go through anything like that alone again, and neither should you. And it matters to me because you matter to me."

She hadn't realized it until the moment he'd walked into the room. Hadn't fully understood her own feelings, though after the night before, maybe she should have.

He'd seen her sitting there and heat had flared in his eyes. Then he'd shut it down, tension in every line of him.

He seemed to be a man at war with himself, a man in pain even though he possibly didn't realize it himself. And she wanted to help him so badly. Put her hands on him and make it better, because under those easy smiles and charm burned something intense and fierce. He felt things so deeply, and he should have had someone to hold him, ease his grief and his pain. Someone to listen to him talk about his daughter.

He should have had someone to love him when he'd needed it and it was clear he had needed it.

But there had been no one, not even his mother, and that was so unfair.

He'd had his trust broken as badly as she had. The people who should have helped him had abandoned him, leaving him to deal with his grief alone.

"Astrid." His voice was still gravelly and raw. "You shouldn't let me matter. I'm not staying. I can't."

Too late, too late...

Oh, she knew that. She was fully aware.

"I know that." Her voice was as raw as his. "But you gave me a moment, so now I'm giving you one. You can let yourself matter to me, Damon. Right now, here in this room, you can let yourself be important to me."

He'll be important to you long after this moment.

Yes, she knew that too. But if a moment, a night, was all he'd let himself have, then that's what she'd give. He'd done it for her, after all.

Damon stared at her but didn't speak, and she wondered if he'd do it. If he'd really allow himself to have it. She wanted him to so much, because he deserved it. But it all came down to trust, didn't it? He had to trust her that she meant what she said.

She held his gaze, let him see the truth in her eyes.

He slid one hand to her nape and then up to the back of her head, his fingers curling in her hair, drawing her head back.

Then his mouth was on hers.

The kiss was fierce and raw, hungry and hot. And it went on and on for endless minutes of heat and fire. Until he let go of her hair, his arms coming around her, strong as iron bands, pulling her up against him.

She didn't fight, didn't resist. She could feel the need in him, that longing for a connection and so she gave it to him. He'd given her what she needed the night before and so she'd hold nothing back from him now.

And she deliberately didn't think about the small voice in her head that kept nagging at her, that kept reminding her about how important he'd become to her when this was only supposed to be about sex. When he'd be leaving anyway.

She didn't listen to it. And when he picked her up and carried her to bed, putting her down, then stripping their clothes away before dealing with protection, she ceased to hear it at all.

She wanted to touch him, to run her hands all over him, but this wasn't for her—not now. This was for him. So all she did when he came down onto the mattress with her, pushing her onto her back and spreading her thighs, was slide her arms around his neck and hold him.

He didn't wait, pushing inside her hard and deep without any preliminaries. She wrapped herself around him, pulling him close, and when he leaned down to kiss her, hungrily, desperately, she held him tight, her legs wrapped around his waist, her arms wrapped around his neck.

It was more than a meeting of bodies and more than simply a pursuit of pleasure. He needed contact, a connection, and so she gave it to him without restraint or reservation, wrapping not just her body around him but her heart as well. Because he was as vulnerable as she was, and he deserved to be kept safe. He deserved to know that he wasn't alone.

She wouldn't have cared if he'd taken his pleasure without

thinking about hers. It wasn't about keeping score. It was about him taking and her wanting to give, and an orgasm didn't matter, not in the greater scheme of things.

But Damon had never been selfish in bed and he wasn't now. He moved faster, harder, pushing deeper, his mouth ravaging hers. Then he slid his hand down between her thighs, stroking her until she could feel the orgasm beginning to splinter around her.

She sobbed as the pleasure pulled unbearably tight and then let go, making her shudder and twist and gasp beneath him. And then it was his turn, his rhythm fast and getting faster, before he groaned her name, his big, rangy body shuddering as the climax came for him too. But her grip on him was strong, and it was she who held him tight as he fell apart in her arms.

Chapter 15

DAMON LEANED AGAINST THE WALL OF THE COMMUNITY center and watched as the entire population of Deep River trooped in and sat themselves down on the long wooden benches that had been set out, all of them talking loudly and interestedly about the meeting that was about to take place.

Connor had come to stand beside him in companionable silence as the buzz of conversation rose and fell around them.

The short list for tourist plans had gone out the day before, the announcement for a town meeting going up at Mal's that afternoon, and while there had been some grumblings about the short list, word was that most people were keeping an open mind. This was going to be important for the town—historic even—and while everyone was united on keeping out big oil, Deep River was in need of direction. *Tourism* couldn't be a dirty word any longer, not when the future of the town itself was at stake.

A sense of purpose, a sense of community, that's what the people of Deep River had always been best at, and that's what would save them now.

Or at least that's the speech Silas had given him just a few hours earlier. It had been pretty inspiring.

Damon shifted his attention from the chattering townspeople to the woman who stood silently at the front of the hall. Her arms were crossed, and she had that no-nonsense mayoral look on her lovely face.

His heart tightened behind his ribs, no matter that it shouldn't have.

Last night, she'd held him in her arms, keeping him together as he'd talked about his daughter. Giving him the gift of her presence, letting his little girl live again as he'd shared his memories of her.

"You can let yourself matter to me, Damon," Astrid had told him. *"Right now, here in this room, you can let yourself be important."*

He wasn't sure why those words hit him as hard as they had. Or why he'd gone against his better judgment and given in to the need inside himself. The longing for something deeper, the need for a connection to someone that went beyond physical.

He shouldn't have. He'd told himself he wouldn't. Yet she'd offered him that moment and he'd taken it with both hands.

Perhaps it was because it was for a limited time and they both knew it. Or perhaps it was because he just wanted her and hadn't been able to hold out any longer.

Selfish of him to put his own needs first, but she'd wanted him to and it had made her happy. And afterward, they'd lain in each other's arms, and more stories came flooding out. They'd shared the hardships of being a teenage parent and yet the wonder of having a child, and then had spoken about their own parents.

She'd told him about her father, how cold he'd been and how her mother had simply followed his example, while he'd talked about his own mother and the difficulties of being the child of a proud single parent who worked every waking hour to make ends meet and who didn't take handouts.

It had felt good to talk, to hold her, to know that she was listening and that it mattered to her. That he mattered to her.

She was special, was Astrid James.

You could stay here. With her. And with Connor.

No, he couldn't. All of that changed nothing. If anything, it only clarified things for him even more. Astrid and Connor needed and deserved someone who could give them everything. And he'd given his everything already.

He had nothing left to give.

"So," Connor said from beside him. "Um, I know you might get mad about this, but...I kind of called your mom."

Damon went very still, shock echoing through him, the hum of conversation in the hall fading into the background. Slowly, he turned to face the teenager standing next to him.

Connor's expression was determined, though he'd gone a little pale, as if he knew he'd probably stepped over the line.

Which he had. Significantly.

"Say that again," Damon said.

"I called your mom." Connor's jaw had a pugnacious slant to it. "I know I probably shouldn't have—"

"Probably shouldn't have?" There was too much anger in his voice, but he couldn't stop it. "Probably?"

Connor had gone even paler, but the determination in his gaze did not lessen one iota. The kid wasn't backing down.

The anger inside him gathered into a tight, hard knot. He really needed to put a lid on it, because it wasn't a good idea to start chewing the kid out for invading his privacy and contacting his sick mother in a room full of people.

But he had to know just what the hell Connor had been thinking.

"Outside," he ordered curtly, jerking his head toward the doors.

There were people still coming in and the meeting was about to start. But he wanted answers and he wanted them now.

Connor turned without a word and headed toward the exit, Damon following. He passed Morgan West coming in, whom he'd met at Cal's funeral, and she gave him a smile, but the look on his face must have given her pause because she didn't say anything, letting him move past her without a word.

Outside, late afternoon was starting to set in, the sun on its way down. The late spring air had a hint of chill to it, the last gasps of winter coming down off the mountains.

Connor walked out into the gravel parking area. The line of

people going in had lessened, the hum of conversation drifting out from the open doors ensuring people probably wouldn't hear them.

The kid came to a stop, then turned around, facing him and the community center, the stubborn look on his face pure mule.

Damon stopped too, fighting to get a handle on the anger pooling in his gut. "Okay, so you get that calling my mother without telling me is a huge breach of her privacy, right?"

Connor said nothing, a muscle in his jaw leaping.

"How did you even get her details, anyway?"

"Silas. He had next-of-kin details for you."

Okay, so that was good. At least the kid was giving him the truth and wasn't hiding it. But still...

"So, what? You just asked him and he gave you that information without consulting me?"

"Yeah, he did." Connor's blue eyes glinted with challenge. "He agreed with me."

Right, so now he was going to have to kill Silas. And then maybe stick his head over the bar in the Moose.

"Agreed about what?" Damon snapped, the iron of the officer he'd once been in his voice. "Tell me, Connor, and it had better be good."

Connor didn't flinch. He stood there the way he'd stood near the Nowhere pole when Damon had stumbled out of bed that first morning. All confrontation, challenge, and stubborn determination.

"We want you to stay," Connor said flatly. "Me and Silas. We want you to stay in Deep River. And I know your mom is sick. Silas told me that you don't want to take her away from her home, so I thought I'd call her and tell her what a great place Deep River is. How she'd be really happy here because there's a porch to sit on and mountains to look at. And I'd visit her. She wouldn't be lonely. Everyone here would visit her."

The dead hearth of Damon's heart felt sore, a longing rolling over him so strong he could hardly breathe. Because he could see his mother sitting on that porch, could see Connor coming to visit her, the pair of them sitting and chatting. His mother was a social person, she liked talking to people and particularly young people. They made her feel young too, she'd once told him...

No, it was impossible. Familiarity was important and there would be nothing familiar to her about Deep River. The confusion was already starting and it was only going to get worse, plus there were implications about being so far away from health services. The whole idea was ridiculous.

"So you call my sick mother, whom you don't know and who doesn't know you, without my knowledge, to sing the praises of some tin-pot little town in the middle of goddamn nowhere." His voice was rising now, his anger getting hotter. "Tell me, Connor. If I'd done that to your very sick mom, how would you feel?"

Connor's face had paled. "She didn't sound sick. She said she liked the idea of it."

"She's got early onset dementia," Damon said harshly. "She probably thought you were me."

"No, she didn't. I told her my name and where I was from and how I knew you. And I told her that I wanted you to stay here, with us. With me and Mom."

Damon's anger stretched out, dark as a shadow inside him, but he didn't move.

Why are you so angry? When you weren't supposed to care?

He ignored the thought. He didn't want to frighten the kid, but Connor had to know that he'd overstepped. That he was messing with things that didn't concern him and when those things concerned Damon's mother, then he needed a reality check. A hard one.

"You had no right to do that," Damon said coldly. "You had no right to invade her privacy and mine. You should have talked to me first."

"Sure, I could have talked to you. And you would have said no."

"You're damn right I would have said no." Tension crawled through him, every muscle in his body tightening. "This is none of your concern, Connor."

"Bullshit. It is my concern." Connor moved suddenly, taking a few steps forward, coming closer, his blue eyes full of a fury that matched the fury inside Damon. "My father chose you, Damon. He chose you to come and look out for me, but now you're leaving. You stayed four measly days and now you're going home. How is that looking out for me?"

The anger in his gut seemed disproportionate, but he couldn't seem to shove it away. It ate at him, burned him. Felt like someone had lit a fire under him and was holding his skin to the coals.

"What do you want from me?" he demanded roughly. "You're a great kid, you've got lots of confidence and common sense most of the time. You've got your mom and the town looking out for you. You don't need me."

"What do I want?" Connor shifted on his feet, crunching gravel under his sneakers. "I want a guy I can just...talk to about stuff. You know, things I can't talk to Mom about. I know you're not my dad and I'm not looking for one. But a friend would be good."

Damon's heart twisted, his anger turning inward on himself. A friend, that's all the kid wanted. That's all. How could he deny him that?

"I can give you my number. We can email or I can call—"

"Email?" Connor's voice was sharp with disappointment and anger. "That's seriously all you got? Going to be really effective out here where there's no service."

Shit.

You goddamn coward.

Damon gritted his teeth, set his jaw. No, screw that; he wasn't a coward. And Connor was right; email or phone calls were half measures, and the boy deserved more than that from him. A hell of a lot more.

But he didn't have it to give. All he could give him was the truth.

"I'm sorry, Con." He held the boy's gaze. "I can't stay. I know it sucks, but I have to think of my mom. She's got no one else to take care of her and she needs to stay in LA, where the hospitals are."

Something seemed to go out of the kid then, the light of determination in his eyes dying. He looked away, his shoulders hunching. "Yeah, I get it."

The hopeless note in Connor's voice made Damon feel as if someone had punched him in the stomach.

"Connor," he began.

But the teenager only shook his head and walked past Damon wordlessly, stiff and furious as he strode back to the community center and up the stairs, disappearing inside.

Good going, asshole.

Damon cursed under his breath and strode forward a couple of steps, taking a couple of deep breaths, trying to corral his fury and frustration.

The early evening air was cool and fresh in his lungs, carrying with it the scent of the river and the faint spice of cedar and spruce from the forest.

His temper eased a little.

Why did he feel Connor's disappointment so acutely? The boy wasn't his son. He'd known him less than a week, so the sharpness of the feeling didn't make any sense.

Perhaps it was because he knew what it was like to be lonely. To need someone to talk to. His mom had worked two jobs to make ends meet, leaving him on his own a lot. Which he hadn't complained about, especially considering she was working hard to keep him fed.

So yes, it had been lonely. But he'd sucked it up and gone on because he'd had to. Because he'd had no one else.

Because life was hard and some things you had to do by yourself.

He'd managed it; Connor would have to do the same.

"Damon?" The voice behind him was soft and feminine.

Astrid.

He turned sharply. She came down the steps from the center's porch and onto the gravel, her footsteps crunching. Her hair gleamed, a soft golden halo. She wore worn jeans and a deep-blue long-sleeved button-down shirt with a parka thrown over the top, the color tingeing the gray of her eyes, making them look like thunderclouds.

She was so beautiful. But it wasn't her beauty that made his heart catch inside him. It was the look on her face, full of concern.

Everyone needs someone, Damon. And you have me. You will always have me.

The memory of what she'd said to him the night before drifted through his head like a song he couldn't remember the words to, the tune haunting him.

He ignored it.

"Yes?" He tried to sound neutral but couldn't hide the rasp of emotion that lingered in his voice. "Is the meeting starting?"

"I'm going to give it a few more minutes." She took another couple of steps, then stopped, her gaze roving over him. "Are you okay? I saw Connor come in looking upset. Did he do something he shouldn't?"

It took conscious effort to relax his tight muscles. "He just told me that he called my mother. He got her details from Silas and called her to tell her how great Deep River was and that she needed to move there with me."

Shock rippled over Astrid's fine, precise features. "Oh, for the love of... That kid... I'll kill him."

"It's not his fault." Damon's hands ached where they were clenched in fists, so he thrust them in his pockets. "It's Silas I'm planning to kill. He had no right to give Connor Mom's number."

"No, he didn't." Astrid folded her arms. "But I think Silas wants you to stay."

"Yeah, I know he does."

"And so does Connor."

"I can't, Astrid. You know I can't."

"No," she said quietly. "I know."

The acceptance in her tone caught at his anger somehow, inflaming it though he couldn't think why. Because he didn't want her insisting that he stay, right? He didn't need another voice to add to the chorus.

"That doesn't sound convincing," he said before he could stop himself.

She frowned. "What do you want me to say, then? You have your mother to care for. I understand that."

"Do you?" He didn't know why he was asking her. He didn't know what he wanted her to say.

"Of course. What does it matter what I think, anyway?" Her gaze was cool, the mayor in charge. But he could hear a note of challenge in the words, as if she wanted him to dispute it.

Which he would. He wasn't going to let her opinion change his mind, but that didn't mean she wasn't important or that she didn't matter. And he wanted to hear what she had to say.

"It matters," he said. "Tell me."

She stared at him, expressions he didn't understand flickering across her face. Her eyes had darkened almost into the deep blue of her shirt. "No," she said at last. "I don't think you should stay."

His gut lurched, though again he wasn't sure why. Because wasn't that a good thing? It was better for her if she didn't want him to stay.

"Why not?" The question was out before he could stop himself.

"Because you don't want to."

"What makes you say that?"

She held his gaze, unflinching. "I can see it in your eyes, Damon. I think if you'd wanted to stay, you'd move heaven and earth to make it happen."

There was no accusation in her tone, but it was so determinedly neutral it needled him. "There's no way I can—"

"Please," she interrupted, and this time he heard a small tremor in her voice. "Don't use your mother as an excuse."

Shock moved through him, lightning rooting him to the spot.

"I'm not," he said hoarsely. "You think I should leave her alone? Let her burn her house down? Wander onto the road and get hit by a car? Or just forget to eat? You think I should do that instead?"

She shook her head. "No, of course not. But you could bring her here if you wanted to."

"I can't just uproot her from her life and her familiar—"

Astrid took a step up to him and raised her hand, her fingers touching his face, making the words die unsaid. Her touch was very soft, very warm. "You love her very much and I understand. She's sick, and she needs care. But what are you trying to prove to her, Damon?"

It was too much, the touch of her hand and the look in her eyes. It was that sharp look from last night, seeing into his soul. Seeing the lonely little boy who'd watched his mother run herself ragged to keep him fed, selfishly wanting more from her, some crumb of affection or praise. Seeing the angry young man, furious at his mother for walking away from him right when he'd needed her most.

He turned from Astrid in a jerky movement, taking a few steps toward the trees. His heart was beating far too fast and he felt like he couldn't breathe.

"She never needed me," he said, even though he hadn't meant to. "And she never let me need her either. But she does now, and I won't do what she did to me. I won't walk away."

"You could bring her here."

"No." He stared up at the sky and the long spears of light cast by the fading sun. "I can't, Astrid."

Behind him there was silence, but she would ask him. Astrid had never flinched away from the truth.

"Why not?" Her voice was quiet.

He didn't want to see her face, not with what he had to tell her, because it would hurt her. But she was right. His mother was an excuse. The only thing he had left to give her was the truth, and he wasn't going to give her that with his back turned.

Slowly, he spun around, facing her.

The light fell full on her lovely face, and those stars were in her eyes again.

He so badly didn't want to cause her pain, but he had no choice.

"Because of you, Astrid," he said.

―――――――――――

Damon's beautiful face was set in hard, harsh lines and his blue eyes glittered, his whole posture radiating tension.

Her heart beat fast. Nothing he said was making any sense.

She shouldn't have come out here, not with the meeting nearly ready to start, but she'd seen him and Connor leave and then not too long afterward, Connor had come back inside, his face white.

Worried, she'd wanted to go straight to him and ask him what was wrong, but he'd positioned himself on the other side of the hall, next to a friend, and she didn't want to have a discussion like that in the middle of a town meeting.

So she'd gone outside in search of Damon instead.

She shouldn't have pushed him about why he was leaving, but Connor had obviously been upset and he at least deserved the truth. And maybe she did too.

Except now all she could do was stare at him in shock.

"Me?" she asked blankly. "What do you mean because of me?"

Damon's gaze speared her right through. "You know why."

"No, I don't. Perhaps you'd better spell it out for me."

He didn't move, as if he were turned to stone. "I can't stay because I can't give you what you want, Astrid."

She blinked, not understanding. "I don't... What do you mean you can't give me what I want? I don't want anything."

"Yes, you do. It's written all over your face. I see it every time you look at me."

He's right. You're in love with him.

There was no instinctive denial at the thought, no protest. Just acceptance. Because yes, she was in love with him and had been since the night he'd made love to her in her bedroom. Crazy considering she hadn't known him all that long, but that didn't make it any less true.

A deep, calm feeling swept through her, a strength she hadn't known she had.

Folding her arms, she held his gaze steadily. "And how is that a problem?"

Fire flickered in his eyes. "How do you think? What would happen if I stayed? Would our affair go on? And would it be secret? And if it wasn't secret, what would you want? Us living together? Or staying apart and seeing each other casually? And if that, then what would the town think? Could you deal with gossip?" The questions were like a rain of sharp stones. "And if not, if we ended it, would you be fine seeing me every day? Talking to me every day? It's hard to stay distant in a small town."

She didn't flinch. "Again, how is that a problem?"

"Seriously?" A muscle flicked in the side of his strong jaw. "You can't see the issue?"

"Those aren't issues, Damon. Those are all excuses. Not that they're relevant anyway, because you're not staying."

His eyes went dark. "And if I did?"

The calm surrounding her faltered, a fist squeezing her heart as she imagined what it would be like to have him here every day. Waking in the morning with him beside her, working during the day and meeting up for coffee at April's. Then going home to find him and Connor sitting in the kitchen while he helped the kid with his homework.

Him teasing her as she made dinner. Her kissing him to shut him up.

Oh, it would be so good to have him here. It would be heaven. But it would also be a lie. Because for that to happen, he'd have to want to stay. And he didn't.

"But you won't," she said quietly. "And I don't want you to anyway."

He stood so very still, like he'd been carved from rock. A statue left alone in a place no one ever visited. "Why not?"

"Because if you did, it wouldn't be because you wanted to. You'd stay for the promise you made to Cal. And for the sake of me and Connor." She took a small breath. "It wouldn't be for yourself."

His expression twisted and he looked away, but not before she caught the pain glittering in his eyes. "You can't know how much I wish things were different." His deep voice sounded scraped raw. "How much I wish I could give you and Connor what you both need and what you both deserve. But…I can't. I've got nothing left, Astrid. Nothing at all." He glanced at her then, and the look in his eyes made her throat close. "If I can give you nothing else, just know that I would have loved you if I'd been able. But love isn't something I can do anymore. I'm sorry."

It hurt, she couldn't deny that. It felt like he'd picked up a sword and run her through with it.

But what could she say? She understood what he'd gone through and the cost it had exacted. And it made sense that he didn't want to allow himself to feel for anyone else. Because it wasn't that he couldn't; it was that he wouldn't.

He'd been betrayed too badly and been hurt irreparably, and she couldn't fix that.

All she could do was let him go.

Slowly she walked across the gravel until she was right in front of him, then she tipped her head back and looked up into his sky-blue eyes.

"It's okay," she said quietly. "I'll just have to love you twice as much."

Something shifted in his eyes, flaring bright, an intense, deep longing. He wanted what she had to offer, wanted it badly—she could see the need inside him. But she also knew he wasn't going to let himself have it for whatever reason.

"No," he said. "Don't."

"I told you last night it was too late." Her voice was surprisingly calm given how much her heart ached. "And I'm not going to ask anything of you. If you have to go, you have to go. I won't stop you or demand that you stay. But know this." She held his gaze. "If you ever need anyone, Damon Fitzgerald, you have me. And you have Connor too. We care about you. We're here for you. And we're not going anywhere."

Emotion rippled over his face, but she couldn't tell what it was. And then suddenly it was too hard to stand there, too hard to face him. Too hard not to reach for him and pull him to her.

"I think the meeting's about to start," she said, then turned around and headed back to the community center.

He didn't call her name, and she didn't stop.

She went in and closed the door behind her.

Chapter 16

DAMON FOLLOWED ASTRID IN—HE HAD NO OTHER OPTION. The meeting was important and especially so since he was there to add his thoughts on the financial implications.

Connor was on the far side of the hall and he didn't look in Damon's direction, not once.

Astrid called the meeting to order, her face betraying nothing of what had happened between them outside in the parking area. Or at least nothing anyone else could see. But he noticed the pale cast to her skin and the tightness around her mouth, her eyes gone dark, the sharp glitter dulled. And that tension was back, bristling and edgy.

I'll have to love you twice as much.

His chest squeezed, like someone had closed their fingers around his heart, and it made anger churn in the pit of his stomach.

Why did she love him? He hadn't asked for it, hadn't wanted it. She said she wouldn't ask anything of him, but he could feel her love pulling on him all the same, demanding things from him. Things he couldn't give.

It's not her you're angry with.

He leaned his back against the wall, the tightness in his chest unrelenting.

No, of course it wasn't her. He had enough insight to know that. It was himself he was angry with. Because he'd told her the truth. If he still had the ability to love, he would have loved her. He would have stayed with her. Would have brought his mother to live here in Deep River with them. Would have created a family with her and Connor, a life that wasn't just lived on the surface. That was about something more, a tree with roots that went deep, not a leaf drifting in the current of a river.

But it would never happen. Love wasn't something he could feel anymore.

"Okay, everyone settle down," Astrid said, raising her voice enough to cut through the chatter and then waiting until it was mostly silent. "So, tonight we're going to hear from those who've put forward some ideas on how to get some tourism dollars into Deep River. I've sat down with Damon over there, who you all know by now and who's one of the new owners—"

"Hey, you can't be an owner if you don't live here," someone piped up from the back. "Them's the rules."

Astrid glanced at Damon, raising one pale eyebrow, inviting him to speak. She seemed so together, but he could see how soft her mouth was, the vulnerability she hid from everyone. Yet even now, after he'd refused her, she was doing her job, carrying on.

She was so strong.

"I know the rules," Damon said, his voice gravelly as the entire hall turned to look at him. "I'll be passing my share on to Silas."

A murmur ran through the crowd, several people turning to look at each other and whispering. April frowned in disapproval, while Harry shook his head.

"Well," Mike Flint, the local grump and skeptic, said, "I don't think that gives you the right to choose which ideas get to be voted on."

"I didn't, Mike," Damon said. "Astrid and Silas were the main drivers. I gave them some financial pointers. As I told you when we had this conversation a couple of days ago."

"You leave him alone, Mike Flint." April turned around to give Mike a glare from her place in the front row. "And don't take it out on him just because no one liked your motel idea."

"Actually, his motel idea was a good one." Damon nodded at Mike. "I've got it down on the long-term project list. As Mike already knows."

Mike snorted and folded his arms, remaining silent.

"What about Morgan?" someone else called out, and there were a few murmurs of agreement that whispered around the hall.

Morgan, sitting next to Hope, pulled a face, then stood up, her strawberry-blond hair glowing in the light. "I'm not an owner, as you guys already know." She gazed around at the gathered townspeople. "And my brother didn't leave Deep River to me because I didn't want it."

A shocked silence fell.

Yet Morgan didn't look apologetic in the least. "I have a vote, just like the rest of you do, but no more than that. And I'm fine with it. For what it's worth, though, I trust Silas and his friends, and Caleb wouldn't have left the town to them if he hadn't trusted them as well."

Without another word, Morgan gave a nod, then sat down.

That Cal hadn't left Deep River to Morgan had puzzled them all back in the shocked days after Cal had been killed. But they'd all agreed that he probably had a reason for not doing so, and it would have been a good one. Cal never left anything to chance.

Only his son and the woman he abandoned.

Damon's gaze was drawn helplessly back to Astrid, standing at the head of the hall, unmoving and indomitable. She'd seemed fragile to him when he'd first met her, but not now. That strength was there inside her, an iron will like his own. The same kind of will that had made her go on after she'd been left with nothing and no one, with a tiny baby to look after. That had driven her to escape an abusive relationship, to swallow her pride and contact the man who'd rejected her for help, and all to find safety for her son.

She was a woman worth any price.

A woman worth loving.

Yes, and that too. But another man would have to love her. It wouldn't be him.

People were starting to chatter again, the buzz of conversation rising, and Astrid called people to order and the meeting went on.

It went well.

Kevin Anderson turned out to be a surprisingly good speaker, talking eloquently about the fishing charter business he and a few of the other fishermen were planning. Gwen waxed lyrical about expanding the farmers' market she'd started in the community center and how she'd roped in Clare from the B&B with her quilting, Filthy Phil with some carving, and Lloyd, the old trapper, with some of his homemade lemonade which he made in addition to his moonshine. And then Phil, who'd made the trip into town specially since he didn't often come down from his little house on the hill, made a rambling presentation about the wildlife sanctuary that he'd begun building on his property. There was a bit of friction with Mike, who'd gotten up to speak about the luxury motel can of worms, that he'd once put to a town meeting a few years ago and that everyone gave the big thumbs-down to, but then Mike seemed to generate friction purely by existing. Sandy was a welcome breath of fresh air as she stood up to present her ideas for tourism promotion, including making Deep River a stop for cruise ships and other campaigns, appealing to people in big cities who might want a taste of the wild outdoors.

There were mutterings about tourists and crowds and not wanting things to change, but people generally accepted that if Deep River wanted to survive as a town, they were going to have to pull together on some things. And there was something positive about taking charge of their destiny themselves and not leaving it in the hands of the big-city suits.

They were a bunch of good people. Quirky and a bit different, but they all had good hearts—even Mike Flint. And they all wanted this to work for their town's sake.

After the meeting had ended, Damon slipped out of the hall. He'd been planning to get the plane back to Juneau by the time night fell so he could leave for LA the next day, and he still had to get his stuff together back at the Moose. He'd do a round of good-byes once he'd packed. No doubt everyone would be in the bar by that stage anyway, which would make things easier.

Twilight had settled over the town as he made his way back to the Moose, bathing everything in a golden glow. The river looked deeper and greener, the bush on the mountains lush and dense. Even the cluster of buildings at the water's edge looked less ramshackle and more quirky and whimsical. Pretty, even. A place where people could take some time out from big city life. Where they could sit on the boardwalk with a beer and take in the silence and grandeur of mountains around them, let the peace of the wilderness settle inside them.

Yeah, this place would be okay. And Astrid would be too, and so would Connor. Perhaps he'd helped them, perhaps he hadn't, but one thing was for sure: they'd go on without him just fine.

The thought should have encouraged him, but instead it felt bleak. A bleakness that had always been with him, that he hadn't ever really shaken after Ella had died.

He needed to get back to LA; that was the answer for it. Submerge himself in caring for his mother. Watching out for other people was always preferable to thinking about himself and his goddamn issues, that was for sure.

He went down to the boardwalk and into the bar, climbing up the stairs.

It didn't take long to pack his bag. He hadn't brought much to start with, but by the time he came back downstairs again, the Moose was heaving with seemingly the entire town.

There were stares as he strode up to the bar, but he ignored them. Hope was standing behind it, regarding him with a steady, dark gaze. "You leaving then, pretty?"

He smiled, very conscious of how empty it felt. The way it had the night before, as if he were pasting it on like plaster over drywall covering up the cracks. "Yeah, gotta get back to Juneau."

"Sure," Hope said, clearly skeptical. "Will we be seeing you back here, then?"

No. I'm never coming back.

"Maybe." He kept that stupid smile on his face as he felt the cracks inside himself widen, deepen.

Someone came up beside him and leaned on the bar.

"So I presume I get a goodbye?" Silas asked.

"Yeah, well, that's why I'm standing here." He glanced at his friend. "You shouldn't have given Connor my mom's number."

Silas's expression was unrepentant. "Let's go into the office and have a conversation."

He didn't want to. He wanted to head out and not talk to anyone. Get in his plane and fly away. Then maybe get himself a pretty woman and a drink, work on finding his way back to the surface of life, because he had a horrible feeling that he'd sunk beneath it somehow and his air was running out.

But hell, he wouldn't mind giving Silas a piece of his mind before he left.

Silas turned and led the way into the back office, and Damon followed without a word, shutting the door after him.

His friend had gone to sit in the chair near the desk, his arms folded, and was now gazing at him dispassionately. "You want to know why I told Connor?"

Damon gripped the strap of the bag he'd slung over his shoulder. "I think you owe me, considering that was private information and you had no right to give it to a teenage boy."

"I didn't give it to him," Silas said. "I dialed the number and handed him the phone so he could talk, and I stayed here and made sure he didn't say anything stupid."

"That's not the point."

"I know that's not the point." Silas's green gaze was very level. "Connor and I at least wanted to know if all that bullshit you were talking about your mother was true."

Anger coiled inside him.

"It's not bullshit," he said flatly. "And why the hell would you think I'd lie about that?"

"I don't know. You tell me."

"Why should I? I don't have to explain myself to you, Silas."

A heavy silence fell.

His friend looked at him, then let out a breath. "Look, I'm not trying to be a dick. And I'm sorry. Letting Connor call your mom probably wasn't the right way to go about it. But I want you to stay, Damon."

"Why? What does it matter to you what I do?"

"Because I'm your friend, asshole. And I think you have a lot to offer that this place could use. People like you, which is unusual here, believe me. Usually it takes years for them to take to a stranger. You managed it in four days."

The heavy feeling that had been sitting in Damon's chest shifted and the anger inside him shifted with it. His friend had his back, that was for sure, but then that was Silas. He was always wanting to help people, do the right thing by them.

"Okay, well, I appreciate it. But you know I can't."

Silas said nothing for a long moment, then he asked, "So what's the deal with you and Astrid?"

Yeah, he wasn't having that discussion.

"There's no deal," he said curtly. "You got anything else to say? Because I need to get out to—"

"You think I didn't pick up on the tension between you two up in the kitchen yesterday?" Silas gave him a sharp look. "It was so thick I could have cut it with a knife and spread it on my toast for breakfast."

"It's none of your business," Damon snapped.

"I know it isn't. But I like Astrid and I don't want to see her get hurt."

What could he say to that? And he knew the expression on Silas's face. The guy wasn't going to leave this alone.

He let out a breath and scrubbed a hand across his face.

This was all getting too complicated. Because if he went into talking about Astrid, he'd have to talk about Connor. About Cal. And from there, he'd have to tell his friend about Ella...

So?

Something shifted inside him yet again, a certain knowledge. About secrets and the burden of them and how it felt to share them. To know that you weren't alone.

Astrid had done that for him. She'd been the catalyst and then, when he'd told her about Ella and she'd told him about Aiden, they'd been there for each other. And though it had been painful, it had also been good. It had made him feel strong in a way he hadn't felt for a long time.

Damon took a breath and looked at his friend. Silas was a good guy, one of the best, and they'd all had each other's backs in the army.

Why wouldn't he have your back now?

Good goddamn point.

"The deal with Astrid is that you know what's been going on," he said before he could think better of it.

"Ah." Silas let out a breath. "So you've been sleeping with her."

Sleeping with her... It sounded so...casual. A cheapening of what was actually between them. But what else had it been? It was nothing at all now.

"We had an affair, yes. But we both knew it was temporary, and we agreed it wasn't going to be serious."

"Didn't look not serious yesterday."

Damon glanced away, pain settling in his chest. Astrid's steady gray gaze, telling him that she would always be there for him...

"I have to leave," he said. "I can't give her what she wants."

"Uh-huh. And what's that?"

Damon opened his mouth. Then shut it. If he was going to tell Silas about him and Astrid, then he had to start from the beginning. He couldn't tell his friend about his promise to Cal, not yet, because it involved Connor and he wasn't going to give away the kid's secrets without asking him first. But he could tell him about Ella at least.

"It's complicated," he said at last.

Silas nodded as if that was something he already knew. "Hey, I'm not going anywhere."

"Okay then." Damon dropped his bag on the floor, leaned back against the door, and began at the beginning. With his mother and Rebecca and Ella.

"Shit," Silas said in the silence that fell afterward. "That's…" He trailed off, his green eyes full of sympathy.

Damon waited for the awkward change of subject or for Silas to simply turn around and leave, because after all, who wanted to talk about the death of a child?

But Silas went to the desk, pulled open the bottom drawer, and took out the bottle of Harry's whisky that was in it. Then he grabbed a couple of glasses that were also in the drawer, poured them both a dram, and held out the glass. "Here. I think you could do with this."

A tension that Damon didn't even realize was gripping him eased. He should have told Silas before, he really should have. It was about trust in the end and he did trust his friend, he really did.

Damon took it and lifted the glass, ready to drink.

Then Silas raised his own glass and looked his friend in the eye. He didn't say a word, but then Silas was a man who didn't waste them. And there were too few words that would encompass what Damon had just told him, and none of them were right.

"To absent friends," Damon said, because it wasn't only Ella who was gone, but Cal too.

Silas nodded and they both drank. Then Silas said, "Anytime you want to talk, you can."

Okay, so he'd been an idiot not to tell Silas, not to trust him either, and he'd been a dick about it, no question. All of this would have been simpler if he'd just been straight from the beginning, but old patterns of behavior were tough to overcome.

"I appreciate that," Damon said gruffly. "But as you can imagine, all of this has made it complicated when it comes to Astrid."

"Yeah, okay," Silas allowed, putting his glass down on the desk. "But how?"

"Because I'm not up for the kind of relationship she needs. Or any kind of relationship, in fact. Which means sticking around here will only make it difficult for her."

Silas nodded slowly. "I get it. You're trying to protect her."

"Yes." He stared back at his friend. "I don't want to hurt her."

"Well, sure," Silas agreed. "But you know, sometimes when we think we're protecting people, it turns out that the only ones we're protecting are ourselves."

Damon stiffened. "It's not like that."

He's right.

No, that was bullshit. Silas was wrong. And Damon wasn't protecting himself; he was protecting Astrid and Connor from hurt and disappointment, because they'd both been hurt and disappointed too many times already.

He couldn't love them. He couldn't love anyone. And it was better that he stayed away so they could both find someone who would.

Liar. She loves you and you're dismissing it like it means nothing.

He shoved the thought away, bending to grab the strap of his duffel and hauling it up and over his shoulder.

"You have to think of her," Silas said quietly. "Hurting her because you're too scared to man up is never a good look."

Okay, that was enough. He was done.

He straightened. "It's not about fear. It's about knowing you can't give someone what they need and that they deserve better than that."

Silas's gaze turned assessing. "You're in love with her, aren't you?"

Icy shock slid through him, like he'd plunged headfirst into a pool of glacier meltwater, though he had no idea why. How could he be in love with her? It simply wasn't possible for him.

"No." He met Silas's green gaze without flinching, because the guy was just flat-out wrong. "I'm not. I can't. And that's the reason I'm leaving."

Silas only stared at him for a long moment, then he nodded. "Okay, have it your way. I take it you'll drop the plane at the hangar in Juneau?"

"Yes. And I'll call you when I get back to LA. We'll sort out the ownership stuff then."

Silas just nodded, and that was that. There wasn't any more to be said.

Damon turned and went out, entering back into the crowded Moose, nodding at Hope as he passed by the bar and then flashing a smile at the various people who greeted him and waved. He didn't stop, even though politeness dictated that he should. He just didn't have the energy.

Outside, the twilight was starting to deepen into night, and despite the cool night air, there were a few people standing in groups on the boardwalk. He glanced around, trying to spot Astrid because he wanted to say goodbye properly to her and Connor at least.

A flash of movement by the Nowhere pole caught his eye, and he could see Connor leaning against it. The kid was staring fixedly at him, the expression on his face utterly cold, just like his mother's.

Damon took a step in his direction, but Connor turned his back very deliberately and walked away.

The pain felt like claws. Damon had let him down, and he knew that. But it was for the best. Better a short, swift lesson now and then the kid could put it behind him. He needed a much better father figure than Damon would ever be.

Turning back to the groups of people, he took another scan around, but Astrid definitely wasn't there.

Dammit, he didn't want to leave without saying goodbye.

Cursing, he hauled his duffel higher and made a circuit of the town, trying to find her. He didn't want to go up to her house, because he didn't want to impinge on their space, especially given Connor's level of pissed-offness.

Then he spotted her just on the point of going into her office.

"Hey," he said quietly, moving toward her, then stopping.

She glanced at him and a ripple of some bright, painful emotion moved over her face. "Coming to say goodbye, then?"

"Yes. I have to go to Juneau tonight, drop the plane off."

"Okay." Her gaze roamed over his face, as if she was memorizing him. "I suppose you won't be back."

It wasn't a question, and he saw no reason to answer. It was the truth after all.

"I'm sorry," he said, knowing it was pointless. Knowing it didn't mean anything but saying it anyway. "It's better this way."

Her gaze was very steady in the fading light. "I'm sorry too."

He wished he could say something that would make her feel better, but he couldn't think of anything that would help. "If things were different…"

"But they're not different," she finished. "It's okay." She turned away to the door of her office, and then stopped. Then she turned her head to look at him, and for a second her eyes glittered. "No, actually, it's not okay. I know we haven't known each other very long and you've had a really hard time. But I think you were wrong when you said love wasn't something you could do anymore."

His heartbeat thumped in his head. "What?"

"You said you would have loved me if you'd been able to, but love wasn't something you could do. I think you're wrong, Damon.

You've done nothing but care since you got here. Caring about Cal and what he asked you to do. Caring about Connor. Caring about this town. Caring about me." She gazed at him as if she was seeing things in him that even he didn't know about. "You have so much love inside you, Damon Fitzgerald. I can see it every time I look at you."

He stiffened in instinctive denial. "No. Whatever you think you're seeing…it's not that."

"It is. But I get why you think it isn't." She gave him the saddest smile he'd ever seen, and it almost broke his heart. "Just remember that love isn't finite and you don't ever lose the ability. It's always there, always part of you. It's just that sometimes fear gets in the way."

"I'm not afraid," he said through gritted teeth, as if he said it enough times it would be true.

Astrid let out a breath. "Don't worry. I'll let you go now." She turned away, pulling open the door. "Goodbye, Damon," she said and disappeared inside.

He stared at the closed door, pain tearing at his chest. He'd let her down and he knew it. But there wasn't another way.

She was wrong about all of it.

Damon turned on his heel and walked back to the boardwalk, heading for the docks.

Kevin Anderson only nodded as Damon approached to ask for a trip over the river. It seemed to take too long and yet no time at all, and then he was moving in the growing dark to the hangar, where the Cessna sat waiting.

He began the usual preflight checks and then stopped. He hurt. Everywhere. And there was no good reason for it. No reason at all.

Astrid was wrong. There was no love left inside him, no spark in that dead hearth. It was all gone, sucked out of him by the endless demands of Ella's illness and then her death, by the grief that had swamped him and by the lack of support that he'd had afterward. There was nothing left but meaningless smiles and empty charm.

His phone beeped in his pocket. He took it out, glancing down at the screen to find that he had service. And then prompted by an urge that came from God only knew where, he found himself pressing his mother's number.

She answered almost straightaway.

"Hey, Mom," he said.

"Damon? Is that you?" Her voice was so familiar, that Texas drawl she'd never left behind.

"Of course it's me," he said. "Who else calls you 'Mom'?"

"Huh, well, you never know."

"Look, I'm heading to Juneau now, which means I'll be back in LA pretty soon."

"Good," she said. "I need to talk to you about the strangest phone call I got yesterday."

Oh hell.

Damon closed his eyes briefly. "What phone call?"

"From a child. At least, I think it was a child. He was telling me about some town in Alaska called Deep River and how wonderful it was, and that you were there and you liked it."

His mother knew where he was, but sometimes she forgot.

"Yeah, I'm there right now. But I'm leaving to come home."

"He said I would like it. That there was a house with a porch and a chair on it. And there were mountains I could look at. And he would come visit every day." She sounded curious. "I don't know why he would, but I do like talking to young people."

"He shouldn't have called you," Damon said through gritted teeth.

"Why did he? I wasn't sure what he wanted."

Damon sat down on the concrete of the hangar floor and leaned against the little plane's front wheel. The pain refused to leave him, sitting heavily in his chest like the mountains surrounding the town, and he knew he shouldn't have this conversation. His mother had never been able to deal with her own emotions very well, let alone his, and it was unfair of him to unload his issues on her. But he was tired of holding it all inside. So goddamn tired.

"He wants me to stay in Deep River," Damon said. "And I told him I couldn't because of you."

That's not really why.

He ignored the thought.

"Huh." She sounded unfazed by this. "Why because of me?"

"Because you're sick, Mom. And you need someone to take care of you."

She gave a snort, as if that was the most preposterous thing she'd ever heard. "Where's his father?"

Of course she didn't want to talk about her illness. She never did.

"His father died," Damon said flatly.

"What about his mother?"

The pressure in his chest became wrenching. "He lives with her. She's a single mom, brought him up on her own. Very strong. Very capable."

"She sounds decent," his mother pronounced. "Why does he want you?"

Anger suddenly coiled inside him, hot and raw, and he didn't have the energy to keep it down, not right now. "I don't know, Mom. Why would he want me? There's no reason, is there? I'm no use to him. No use to Rebecca. No use to Ella. And I certainly was no use at all to you."

There was a long and terrible silence.

He'd never shown his temper to her. He'd shown her nothing but patience and calm. Sucking it up and carrying on the way she'd always taught him.

But he didn't want to suck it up and carry on anymore. He was tired of pretending. Tired of forcing down what he felt and locking it away. Because that's what he'd been doing the past few days, wasn't it?

Only the past few days? Try the past few years.

His breath caught and he stared out over the river, unseeing, his thoughts whirling.

Years? Had he really being doing that for years? Forcing everything down? Locking everything away?

You know it's true. Sucking up and carrying on is what you've been doing ever since Ella died.

It felt as if the very ground he was sitting on had shifted beneath him, rearranging itself into a landscape he didn't recognize. A place where his emotions hadn't been burned out, where his heart hadn't died. Where the feelings he had weren't the last electrical impulses from a dying limb or the last sparks in a dead hearth full of ashes. Where those feelings had always been there. Forced down and locked away—because that's what he'd been taught to do—but still there. Always still there.

His heart felt painful, his chest full of glass, and this time he didn't ignore the agony or tell himself he didn't feel it. He sat there with it, examining it.

He knew where it was from. He knew why it was there.

You're angry and you're in pain, and you can't stop thinking about her, can't stop wanting her. Because you're in love with her.

Love isn't finite and you never lose the ability, that's what she'd told him. It was only that fear gets in the way.

Was she right? Was this pain all because he loved her and was too afraid to admit it?

"Of course you were of some use," his mother said at last, oblivious. "You couldn't help Ella, and it wasn't your fault that woman left. She should have stuck by you. I certainly never approved of her leaving." She made a chiding noise. "Anyway, what's got your goat?"

Damon took a slow, silent breath, pain seeping into every part of him. But it was different this time. It wasn't the last gasp of his dying heart. It was more like the pain that came from sensation returning to limbs that had been frozen for a very long time.

"My goat," he echoed, a strange amusement filling him. "You really want to know what's got my goat?"

"I wouldn't have asked you otherwise."

"Fine. Why did you always say 'suck it up and carry on'?"

There was another long silence.

"Because life is hard. I told you that." She paused a moment, then went on, "And you were such a caring little boy. You felt everything so deeply and I hated to see you get hurt. My daddy always told me that carrying on was the best way when life got tough, that you had to develop calluses, otherwise you'd just fall down dead where you stand. And he was right."

He'd heard that same story for years. About how tough life was and how you had to be hard to survive it. And he'd internalized all those lessons.

But now that story felt different, because he was seeing it differently. His mother hadn't been cutting him off or abandoning him. She'd been trying to protect him the only way she knew how. Teaching him things that had worked for her because of her life and her choices.

You don't have to do that, though. Your life is different and so are the choices you make.

The earth slowed and came to a dead stop. A moment hanging in time, endless, depthless.

Yes, he *was* different. And he could make different choices.

For years, he'd chosen the surface life. Choosing to drift with the currents and never go deeper. Giving only so much and no more. Never committing, never giving his all, because he was afraid of returning to that black place after Ella had died, where he was alone with his feelings and there was no one to help him through it.

But had he really come through it? Sure, he wasn't in the darkness, but he wasn't exactly in the light either. He was in a kind of half world, in limbo, where everything was muted and gray. Where there was no pain, but no joy. No sadness, yet no happiness. Nothing to regret, and nothing to look forward to.

He was a kite with no string, and it was freeing being that kite. But sooner or later, the wind was going to shred you or you'd crash into a mountain or the rain would make you come apart.

You needed a tether. You needed something to ground you. To hold you when the wind got too strong. To shield you from the rain. To watch for mountains in your path.

You needed joy and happiness and a future, even if it meant pain and sadness and anger. Because otherwise, what was life? What was the point?

You might as well fall down dead where you stand.

The truth dawned on him, slow and clear, like the first streaks of dawn after a cold and lonely night.

It wasn't sucking it up and carrying on that protected you.

It was love.

And he could choose that if he wanted. If he stopped being afraid. If he opened himself up and didn't hold back. He could put down roots and tether himself. Feel all the pain that love brought, but all the joy too, because he'd forgotten that there was joy.

Ella's arms around his neck, her smile lighting up his world. His mother making him hot chocolate on a Sunday night as they watched TV together. Connor clinking bottles with him. Astrid holding him. Astrid smiling at him. Astrid's gray eyes full of stars as they looked at him.

Astrid...

She was a woman who'd been dealt one of life's shitty hands, but she hadn't run away or given up. She kept going, but it wasn't because she sucked it up and carried on. It was because she loved her son. Love had kept her going, through her own personal darkness and into the light. And she hadn't just found that light; she'd created something beautiful with it.

She'd become part of a community who supported each other, who had each other's back. A family—together.

He wanted that. He wanted the light, the community, and a family. He wanted her with every single part of his soul. And not because of a promise he'd made to a dead friend or because he wanted to save her, protect her.

It was because he loved her.

"Damon?" his mother asked. "Are you still there?"

"Yeah, Mom." His voice was gravelly as a dry riverbed. "I'm still here."

A silence. A long one.

"You like this boy?"

"Yeah, I do." He looked out over the river, to the hill behind the town and the scattering of lights on it, trying to find one specific light. "And I'm in love with his mother."

"Oh." His mom sighed, and he didn't know whether it was shock or disappointment or something else. "Does she feel the same?"

"Yes, she does."

"Oh," his mother murmured again, and this time he heard a note in it that he was sure was relief. "Oh…I'm so pleased. You've been so unhappy. And don't think I haven't noticed. You try to hide it, but I can see. You haven't been quite right since Ella died."

Damon closed his eyes again. Of course his mother cared; she always had. He'd just been too blind to see it.

"I just want you to be happy, Son," she went on. "That's all I've ever wanted for you."

Damon took a breath and opened his eyes. "Then will you come here, Mom? Will you come and live in Deep River with me? Meet Astrid and Connor? Let me take care of you?"

"Yes," she said without hesitation, and he could hear the smile in her voice. "I believe I will. Like I said, I always wanted to see the mountains."

———————

Five minutes later, Damon ran down the gravel path to the dock. He didn't know what he'd do if Kevin's boat wasn't there, but for some reason, it was still bobbing gently at the end of the dock.

Kevin was coiling ropes on the deck and he looked up as Damon approached. "Back again, are you?"

Damon stepped onto the ferry. "You were waiting, weren't you?"

"It was an even bet." Kevin shrugged. "Some folk can't bring themselves to leave, and some you never see again. I figured you might be one who stayed."

Damon smiled, and this time it felt genuine. It felt real. His heart was full of light and the heaviness had gone. "You're right. I am."

"Damn straight," Kevin replied and went into the wheelhouse.

Fifteen minutes and they were on the other side. Damon sprang out of the boat, climbed up the stairs from the dock, then ran hell-for-leather all the way up the hill to Astrid's.

He charged up the steps and hammered on the red front door.

It opened and Connor stood in the hallway. Shock rippled over his face as he took in Damon before it changed into sheer, blue-eyed fury. He opened his mouth.

"I changed my mind," Damon said before he could speak. "I want to stay here with you and your mother. And I'd very much like to be your friend. If you still want that."

Connor shut his mouth. Fury cycled through to shock, then something else more intense. "I don't know. It depends."

"On what?"

"On whether you're going to leave again."

"I'm not," Damon said fiercely. "I made a mistake. I thought leaving was the best thing for both of you, but I was wrong. I want to stay, Connor. And it's not for some promise I made to your dad. I want to stay because I need someone at my back to look out for me. Someone I can trust. And I'd really like you to be that someone."

Connor stared at him and slowly all the fury dissipated, replaced with a dawning hope. "Seriously? You really want that?"

"Yes," he said. "I've never been more serious about anything in all my goddamn life."

Joy broke over the kid's face, and Damon had the impression that Connor kind of wanted to hug him but was holding back, too uncertain.

But Damon wasn't uncertain.

He stepped over the threshold, pulled the boy into a brief, hard hug, then let him go.

"Friends?"

Connor grinned. Hugely. "Friends."

"Oh," Damon added. "One more thing. I'm going to marry your mother."

Chapter 17

ASTRID WAS SITTING IN THE KITCHEN, STARING INTO THE glass of wine she hadn't touched, trying to tell herself that she was okay. That yes, she'd had her heart broken, but she'd been okay before and she'd be okay again. She'd go on; she always did.

She'd known that the last meeting she'd had with Damon hadn't made any difference to him, and sure enough, it hadn't. Not that she'd expected it to. He'd made his decision, and if there was one thing she knew about Damon Fitzgerald, it was that once he'd made his mind up, he didn't change it.

He would be at his plane now, ready to take off into the sky. Flying away from Deep River.

Flying away from her.

She'd never particularly been one to indulge in tears, but she couldn't stop one as it escaped and rolled down her cheek.

No, it would be fine. Some sadness now, and then she'd be better. She'd recover and get over him. She had so much to do: the food co-op and nutrition classes, the oil stuff...

No, you won't. You won't ever get over him.

Someone hammered on her front door.

She ignored it, picking up her wine and taking a sip.

Connor must have answered, because she could hear voices drifting down the hall. Her son's and a man's deep tones. Rich and so achingly familiar.

Astrid went very, very still as a sudden and very real fury went rushing through her.

It was Damon, wasn't it? He hadn't left. He was here, at her house, talking to her son.

The fury climbed higher. Why the hell was he back? After

making such a big deal about leaving? God help him, if he broke Connor's heart again, she would skin him alive, stuff him, and stand him beside the door of the Moose as a warning.

Shoving back her chair, she stormed out of the kitchen and down the hall to find Connor standing in the entrance, grinning like a lunatic, and Damon Goddamn Fitzgerald standing beside him, also grinning like a lunatic.

Both of them turned as she approached.

The bright expression on her son's face would have broken her heart if it hadn't been broken already, while Damon's eyes flared a brilliant electric blue, a familiar determination settling over his handsome features.

"I...uh...gotta go," Connor said, still grinning. "Go easy on him, Mom." Then before she could say another word, he took off out the front door and ran down the steps.

Damon closed the door very deliberately, not taking his eyes off her.

Her broken heart seized in her chest, making the flood of fury climb even higher, bursting out of her before she could stop it.

"What the hell are you doing here?" she demanded, her voice shaking. "You said that you were leaving, that you were very sorry but you couldn't—" She broke off abruptly as he stalked slowly toward her.

"What are you doing?" Her heart began to race.

"What do you think I'm doing?" He didn't stop.

"Damon..." She was breathing very fast, and the look in his eyes was very intent, very sure. "Damon."

But he didn't stop. He came even closer, and she knew she should back away and run, protect herself somehow, because she'd said goodbye to him and she was barely holding it together as it was. She didn't need him coming back for whatever reason.

She opened her mouth to tell him to get out of her house and never come back, because seeing him again hurt; it just hurt so much. But before she could get the words out, he dropped to his knees on the floor in front of her.

Astrid stared at him in shock.

"I know you're angry," Damon said, his gaze holding hers. "And you have every right to be. You gave me your heart and I threw it away. And I'm sorry, Astrid. I'm so goddamn sorry that I hurt you, and Connor too." His expression was intense. "You were right. You were right about everything. I was scared. I didn't want to go back to the place where I was after Ella died. I didn't want to feel anything so deeply again because it nearly killed me the first time, so I told myself the ability to feel was gone. And that a life with no ties or connections would suit me just fine." Blue fire flamed in his eyes. "But then I met you and I started to feel again, and it scared the shit out of me. I told myself a lot of lies about what I was feeling. I did what my mom taught me to do: I ignored it and tried to carry on. But I was wrong, honey. I was so wrong."

Astrid's throat had gone tight, her vision blurring. All she could do was stand there, staring at him as he knelt at her feet. Her beautiful man...

"And you were right." His voice had gotten thicker, rougher. "You were right about me. Love isn't finite and I never lost the ability to feel. It's still there. I was just afraid of it. And I'm tired of telling myself the same old lies. Tired of sucking it up and carrying on. Tired of pretending I don't feel anything. Tired of having nothing in my life. I want something different. I want something meaningful. I want you." He stared at her as if she were the center of the universe. "I want to stay here with you and Connor. I want to bring my mom here too. I want a life full of ties and connections and community and friends. And not because of Cal or any other kind of promise. I want it because I love you and my life is nothing without you in it."

The tear that had rolled down her cheek before was joined by another, and then another. Which was just silly, because she hated crying. And here she was, standing in her hallway, with the most beautiful man in the world kneeling at her feet, and she was crying because she was happy. How stupid was that?

"Damon," she said in a thick voice, blinking furiously. "Why are you kneeling?"

The smile he gave her was so full of warmth and tenderness she couldn't breathe. "I'm trying to be a gentleman. And gentlemen always kneel when they ask for a woman's hand in marriage."

A hiccup of laughter escaped her. "You can't be serious."

"I'm not getting up until I get an answer."

It didn't matter, the tears. Nothing mattered. Nothing but this man in front of her, who wasn't leaving after all. Who was here and not for some promise or because he wanted to protect her or look out for her. He was here because he loved her.

Damon Fitzgerald *loved* her.

Astrid wiped her face. "You hurt me."

"Yes," he said quietly.

"You broke my heart."

His blue gaze searched her face, full of tenderness and regret. "I know. I'm sorry."

"Well, someone's going to have to stay and help me repair it." That heart of hers was beating very fast and she knew that taking another step toward him would change things irrevocably. But things had already changed. She was in love with him, and nothing would alter that. And she was okay with it. She was more than okay with it.

Astrid took a step and then another, until she was right up close to him. There was love in that blue gaze of his. Love and joy and hope. All the things she'd had small tastes of but never been able to hold on to.

But she could now, couldn't she? She could have them.

They both could.

"Yes," she said quietly, looking into his eyes. "I'll marry you, Damon."

For a second, he stared at her, as if he wanted to memorize this moment. Then he surged to his feet and reached for her, pulling her into his arms. "Oh, honey," he murmured, his breath warm against her ear. "I'm never leaving you. I'm never leaving you ever again."

Astrid put her arms around his neck and turned her face into the warmth of his T-shirt, inhaling the familiar, delicious scent of him. "And I love you," she whispered. "I love you so much."

Then his fingers were in her hair, and he was pulling her head back, and he was kissing her, hot and desperate, the salt of her tears mingling with the rich, heady taste of him. And she wanted it to go on forever.

But all too soon he was lifting his head, his eyes blazing blue. "One last thing before I take you into your bedroom and lock the door for the rest of the night. Would you mind if I brought my mother to Deep River?"

Astrid leaned into his heat, loving the hard strength of him. "Oh God, of course not. Connor talked to her, didn't he?"

"Yes." Damon's smile lit up the entire world. "I called her just before I was going to get into my plane and we had an honest chat." His fingers wound tighter in her hair. "I think I've been angry with her ever since Ella died, for leaving me without support. She thought she was protecting me. That carrying on would help."

"And you told her it didn't?"

"I think she knew that anyway." He leaned down and brushed her mouth with his. "I told her that I was in love with you and that I wanted to stay here. And she said that all she wanted was for me to be happy."

Astrid's heart squeezed tight. She knew what that meant to him. "Oh, Damon, did she?"

"Yes." His eyes were so very blue. "She wants to come here and see the mountains."

Astrid smiled, her throat tight with emotion. "Then we'll show her."

"We will." Damon's arms tightened around her. "But not yet. First, I need to show you something."

"Show me what?"

"Show you that I'm really not much of a gentleman."

She laughed as he picked her up in his arms. "Just as well. I don't much care for gentlemen."

━━━━━━━━━━

A month later...

Connor leapt excitedly up the wooden stairs to the porch of Laura Fitzgerald's new house, Laura herself trailing along behind him.

She moved more slowly than she once had, Damon noted, and with more hesitation, but she still walked tall, her chin lifted. She still was a proud woman.

It had taken them a month to move her from LA to Deep River, and it had been a bit of a mission.

A few days after he'd made his decision to stay, he and Astrid had thrown an engagement party at the Moose that the whole town had attended. It had been raucous and fun, and Silas had been totally disgusted that Damon had beat him to it with an engagement.

Damon didn't care. He had his mother to move, which had involved a trip to LA to help her pack up her apartment. He tried to go alone, but Astrid and Connor had insisted on coming with him, the three of them helping Laura with her packing.

His mother had been a little cool with Astrid and Connor initially, but it hadn't taken either of them long to endear themselves, Astrid with her practicality and Connor with his sheer exuberance.

Damon had determined that Laura living with him and Astrid and Connor wasn't an option because not only would she not want to, but the house was too small anyway. However there was a small house next door to Astrid's that was empty, and it had the same amazing view of the mountains that hers did. It was also very close, so Damon could keep an eye on Laura easily enough.

Now Connor stood at the top of the porch stairs, turning to offer Laura his hand. She waved it away irritatedly. "I can manage on my own quite well enough, thank you very much."

Connor only grinned, not at all fazed by her temper—he himself was fairly irrepressible, as it turned out—moving over to where he'd placed the chair for Laura's use and rearranging the pillows on it for the umpteenth time.

He'd been very particular about what kind of pillows were needed and what kind of chair, since he'd been the one to promise her those things. A nice wooden rocking chair, with red pillows since red was her favorite color—or so Damon had told him.

"Here you are, Mrs. Fitzgerald," Connor said, patting the pillows. "I hope it's comfortable for you."

Laura sat down carefully in the chair. "Very nice," she murmured. Then she turned a bright-blue gaze, almost the same color as Connor's, on him. "You're a good boy."

Connor grinned, taking that as his due, and stepped back as she settled herself.

Damon came up the stairs, then stopped, Astrid beside him. "You don't want to look around inside first, Mom?"

"No. Why would I want to look around inside?" She nodded at the view. "When I have this to look at?"

And what a view it was. The surrounding mountains, still capped with snow even though it was mid-summer, cradling the town and the river, the dark green of the forest a perfect contrast. And Deep River itself, the ramshackle collection of buildings that made up the town clustered at the river's edge.

"Can't argue with that," Astrid said, amused. "Come on. Let's get her bags inside."

"Thank you, dear." Laura sighed. "Bring out some whisky, would you, Damon?"

He smiled, small threads of tension that he hadn't realized were there unwinding inside him. When his mother wanted a whisky, it meant she was home.

So he and Astrid went inside and put the bags down. Then Damon got the whisky while Astrid got some glasses, and they went outside again to where his mother sat on the porch, talking with Connor.

It was the perfect time for porch sitting, with the long summer twilight lying over the town and the air mild—or at least as mild as it would ever get in Alaska.

Astrid put the glasses on top of the wide wooden railing for Damon to pour them each a measure.

"One for the boy too," Laura said, frowning.

"No," Astrid and Damon both said at the same time.

Connor scowled.

Laura reached for her glass, then handed it Connor. "Just a sip, mind."

Oh, his mother—she was going to be a problem.

But Damon didn't care. How could he? When he had the three most important people in the world in his life?

Laura leaned back in the chair, and for a second nobody moved or spoke as she stared out over the river and the mountains beyond.

"You were right," she said at last, glancing at Connor and then over to her son. "It sure is pretty here."

And the last shred of tightness in Damon's heart disappeared.

He gathered the woman he loved tight against him and stood with the boy he regarded as a son and the mother he adored, a family with roots that would soon grow deep, nurtured by love and compassion, joy and understanding. A tree that would grow tall and strong for years to come.

And together they watched the sun go down over Deep River.

Epilogue

MORGAN WEST CYCLED HOME FROM DEEP RIVER TOWNSHIP, the early-summer-evening sun shining on her back and making her feel warm under her uniform.

It had been a long day, but an excellent one and Morgan was full of a sense of well-being.

Sandy had just reported at a town meeting that one of the smaller cruise ship companies had agreed to add Deep River as a day stop on their way to Juneau, much to everyone's delight.

Well, perhaps not quite everyone. There were still a few worries about tourists and strangers being around, but most people agreed that the Deep River tourism ventures were off to a great start.

It made Morgan happy. Being home made her happy.

That first day after she'd gotten back here—after the time she'd spent first on bereavement leave, and then on a police course for some distraction—and she'd put on her uniform…well, she'd felt like herself again. As if the normality that had been suspended after Cal's death had reasserted itself.

And that was good. That was what she wanted: to be home in the place she loved, doing the job she also loved, protecting the people she cared about, and hopefully with no more drama in her life.

Morgan hummed to herself as she turned her bike into the driveway of the West house and coasted down the hill, letting the slight breeze generated by her speed cool her face.

But it wasn't until she'd pulled up in front of the wide wrap-around porch that she noticed the man standing right beside her front door.

The *extremely* tall man. And broad, like he routinely wrestled lions in his spare time. He had dark hair, dark eyes, and enough stubble to outline his very strong, hard jaw.

Handsome too, in a kind of wild, uncivilized way.

He had his hands in the pockets of a pair of very worn jeans and the expression on his face was that of a man who was set on getting his own way no matter what.

She recognized him. She'd met him at Cal's funeral, and Damon and Silas had spent the last couple of weeks looking for him without much luck.

What was *he* doing here? Standing outside her front door?

Morgan got off her bike, leaned it up against the side of the house, then folded her arms across her chest and gave him a very stern look. "Where on earth have you been, Zeke Montgomery? Don't you know everyone's been looking for you?"

Keep reading for a sneak peek at the next book in
Jackie Ashenden's Alaska Homecoming series

SUNSET ON
Deep River

Chapter 1

ZEKE MONTGOMERY KNEW MORGAN WEST WAS GOING TO BE trouble the minute he laid eyes on her.

She stood at the foot of the steps to her own front door—the front door he'd been waiting outside of for the past couple of hours, not that he'd been counting or anything—with her arms folded, looking sternly at him like he was a little kid who'd just drawn on her walls with a crayon.

She was very small and wore a not particularly flattering uniform of dark brown pants and khaki shirt, with a dark brown parka that nearly swallowed her thrown over the top. And her strawberry-blond hair, the color of which reminded him of apricots, was in a very severe ponytail down her back.

She wore no makeup, her face freckled and wholesome, with those bright blue eyes, the ones he remembered from Cal's funeral that had been red from weeping then but were much brighter now. They were also very, very direct.

And she was still the prettiest thing he'd seen for months, if not years.

All of which spelled trouble with a capital *T*.

She said crossly, "Where on earth have you been, Zeke Montgomery? Don't you know everyone's been looking for you?"

He had to admit, he was surprised. He didn't think she'd remembered him from Cal's funeral, but she obviously had. Which was good.

It was going to make this whole situation a hell of a lot easier.

"I could ask you the same thing," he said, choosing to ignore the question for the moment. He'd tell her why he was here eventually, but in his own time. He didn't like to rush important things.

Anyway, he hadn't minded the two hours he'd spent sitting on her front porch waiting for her to come home. He could have gone searching for her, but he hadn't wanted anyone else to know he was here—at least not yet.

He was a man used to waiting, though, and he'd liked the peaceful quiet as the afternoon had lengthened into a long summer twilight. The house was surrounded by spruce and a few firs, and he'd spent a good bit of time observing a couple of squirrels arguing in the branches, their loud complaining broken only by the rush of the river nearby.

Still, he'd hoped she'd have come back earlier from wherever it was she'd been because he had a feeling she wasn't going to like what he was here to say and generally people handled unpleasant things better in the middle of the day rather than at the tail end of it.

Couldn't be helped, though, and he wasn't going to go away and come back later to have this discussion.

Already he'd waited too long.

Morgan frowned, apparently unbothered by the unexpected appearance of a man she'd only met once and in very trying circumstances.

"What do you mean you could ask me the same thing?" she said. "I've been at work. What do you think I've been doing?"

Not a woman who was easily ruffled, obviously.

But then Cal had mentioned to him on more than one occasion that she was competent, professional, and tough. Not to mention that she was also a Village Safety Protection Officer, the rural equivalent of an Alaskan State Trooper, so she wasn't likely to be a pushover.

All of which could prove problematic considering the reason he was here.

Zeke eyed her. "You remembered my name," he said.

"Kind of hard to forget when some big, bearded mountain man approaches you out of the blue at your brother's funeral and tells you to call him if you need anything." Morgan's bright blue gaze did not even so much as flicker. "And then forgets to leave you his number."

She'd leaned the bike she'd ridden down the driveway against the porch, and the late-afternoon sunlight crept across the green lawn that surrounded the Wests' sturdy, two-story house. It was mostly in good repair, but he hadn't only been watching squirrels. He'd also used part of the waiting time to have a look around the place, and there were a number of things that needed doing.

Take care of Morgan, the letter he'd received after the reading of Cal's will had said. *Once I'm gone, she'll have no one.*

It wasn't exactly what Zeke had wanted to hear, but since he felt partly responsible for Cal's death, he owed the guy big-time.

Stupid of him to forget giving her his number at the funeral, but he hadn't been thinking straight. He wasn't the best at dealing with people on a good day, let alone a bad one.

"So I did," he said. "Well, you don't need it now. I'm right here."

"Uh-huh." Morgan's stare narrowed. "So, are you going to tell me why you're on my front porch? When your two friends, who've been looking for you for weeks, are back in the Happy Moose?"

Zeke had arrived in Deep River, the tiny, quirky, little Alaskan town he and his two best friends had inherited after Caleb's death, a couple of nights earlier. He'd made a camp for himself in a clearing in the bush just out of town—he'd preferred a bedroll to staying in a hotel since he always slept better on the ground. And yeah, he should have announced himself to Silas and Damon, the ex-army buddies that Morgan was talking about, but he wasn't a man who charged into a situation without doing a bit of reconnaissance first.

Which was what he'd been doing. Reconnaissance. Of Deep River itself. Again, he was a man who took his time and didn't like to rush into things. Especially given that oil reserves had been discovered underneath the town and he knew for a fact that those oil reserves were of interest to...certain people.

People connected with him.

Luckily, though, he'd handled that issue, so now the only things he had left to do were finish up his mission for Cal and then go see his friends.

He'd figured that finishing up his mission for Cal and taking care of Cal's little sister was more pressing than seeing his friends, so here he was.

Zeke dismissed the question of said friends for the moment. "I'll see them later. In the meantime, I'm here to make sure you're looked after."

Surprise rippled over Morgan's pretty face. "Make sure I'm looked after?" she echoed. "Why would I need looking after?"

He shrugged. "Your brother asked me to."

Morgan's arms dropped. "Oh. How wonderful." She didn't sound as if she thought it was wonderful. She sounded extremely irritated.

"I appreciate it," Morgan was saying, "but as you can see, I'm pretty good right now and I've been pretty good for a number of years, both with and without Caleb."

Her response did not surprise Zeke. Cal had mentioned in his letter that his relationship with Morgan was a fraught one and that she wouldn't appreciate someone muscling in on her territory, especially if she knew that Cal had ordered Zeke to.

Of course, Zeke could have just not told her that part of it, but

SUNSET ON DEEP RIVER

he wasn't a liar and he didn't play games. He was straight up, and that's the way he preferred everyone else to be too.

He eyed her. She did look pretty good, he had to admit, and in more ways than one. And it was also clear that she was annoyed about her brother. Then again, it had been his experience that people said one thing while meaning something else, so he could never take anything at face value.

"You are, huh?" he said.

"Yes." She eyed him right back. "So you can consider your job done."

At Cal's funeral and afterward, at the crappy bar they'd gone to, she hadn't seemed that great. She'd seemed small and vulnerable and folded in on herself with grief, which was why he'd offered to help her out.

To be fair, though, that had been a couple of months ago. Now it seemed as if the worst of that grief was over, and he couldn't imagine a woman more competent and able to handle herself.

She was a West, like Cal, and the Wests had owned Deep River for over a century, so no wonder she didn't need him. This was her town through and through.

Then again, the Wests didn't own Deep River now, and Cal's letter had been clear. And even though he was a man who preferred being alone in the great outdoors to being around people in cities, when the proverbial shit hit the fan, he'd be there.

Cal had been a good friend, and since Zeke could count the number of good friends he had on one hand, he wasn't going to let him down.

"Place looks like it could use some work," he said, ignoring her assurance. "Roof needs some shingles. Got a few cracks in the boards here." He nodded his head toward the wall of the house. "Some of the trees need a prune too. I'll start with those."

"That's very kind of you, but—"

"I've got a camp nearby. I won't need to stay here. Though if you feel safer if I do, I'm happy to." He'd seen signs of bears around the Wests' property, which he was sure Morgan probably knew about, but still. They weren't grizzlies, but black bears could be dangerous if you weren't careful.

You always had to be on your guard in the bush. Complacency led to an early death if you underestimated Mother Nature.

Zeke hadn't been a Boy Scout for a very long time, but if there was one thing he was, it was prepared. Always.

Turning, he scanned the trees that clustered around the house and then the bush beyond. "Should have brought my rifle. You never know what could be hanging around."

Morgan muttered something under her breath and came abruptly up the stairs, planting herself in front of him and tipping her head back to look up at him.

Damn, she really *was* a pretty little thing. Wholesome as a pint of milk. Clear, pink skin, freckles, a soft rosebud of a mouth, and a button nose. Not a cop's hard-bitten face. A long strand of that apricot-colored hair had come loose from her ponytail and now draped itself over her shoulder. It almost glowed.

Not that he should be noticing her skin, or her hair, or her prettiness right now. She was Cal's little sister for Christ's sake. And a cop.

"Zeke," she said very firmly. "As much as I appreciate the thought of you helping out, I'm quite happy with the state of my house, no matter what Cal told you." She crossed her arms over the curve of her—rather lovely now that he looked—breasts, giving a very good impression of a woman who would not be moved come hell or high water. "Have you let Si and Damon know you're here? They've been worried about you."

He hadn't told anyone that he was here, mainly because he'd wanted to scout out the lay of the land, so to speak, before he got into any difficult conversations with his friends. But Damon and Si knew that about him. They also knew he preferred the wilderness and often took off for weeks at a time on various expeditions, so would they really be worried about him?

Perhaps they were. He found it difficult reading emotions in people and sometimes he got it wrong—at least, he had in the past. He thought he was better at it these days, but maybe not. Then again, he was getting Morgan West's irritation loud and clear.

"I'll let 'em know," he said, hoping that could close the subject. "Roof's going to be a problem come winter, though."

More irritation flickered across Morgan's pretty face like the wind ruffling the surface of a milky pond. "Did you somehow miss the fact that I said you're not doing anything to my house?"

She was right in front of him, making it very difficult to move past her without pushing her out of the way, and he didn't want to do that since he was not a man who felt the need to prove himself physically.

He looked down at her. There were little sparks, like fireflies, in her blue eyes.

His sister, Izzy, had once said, crossly, he could out-stubborn a mule and that was no joke. He'd once insisted on sleeping in a tent instead of his bedroom for entire month back when he'd been a kid, which had annoyed the crap out of his mother.

But that was one of the beauties of living in the bush; he never had to concern himself with other people's feelings.

"Why not?" he asked bluntly. "If it needs fixing?"

She frowned. "Well, for a start I don't know you from Adam."

"I'm not Adam. I'm Zeke. And besides, you already met me at the funeral."

"Sure, but that wasn't exactly the perfect moment for chatting."

"You don't need to know me in order for me to fix your house."

Her pretty eyes widened a little. "Seriously?"

Zeke didn't like having to explain himself constantly since it was a pain in the ass. He preferred his actions to speak for themselves. Then again, perhaps he was going to have to actually do some explanation here. Cal's letter had been very clear after all: *Be a brother to her now I'm gone.*

He hadn't been a great brother to the one sibling he did have, so he wasn't sure why Cal had chosen him for the task. Still, he seemed to recall that being a brother involved a lot of pissing siblings off, in which case he was obviously doing something right.

"I know it's your house," he said. "But I'm only going to fix it, not knock it down."

Morgan looked him up and down, unimpressed. "I still don't know you. What if you're a serial killer?"

Seemed an odd question to him. Wasn't it obvious he wasn't a serial killer? "I'm not."

"Of course since you've said you're not one, you're definitely not one." A crease appeared between her red-gold brows. "Though, if you are, you'll be kicking yourself because I can arrest you, you know. I am the law in Deep River."

Tough little thing, wasn't she?

Zeke looked down at her. "You might be the law, but there's only one of you and sorry, but you're not very big."

He'd only stated the truth, but she still looked affronted. "I've done a lot of physical training, and I can and have put cuffs on people bigger than you. And if the worst comes to the worst, I have backup from the detachment in Ketchikan." She gave him a very stern stare. "So don't cross me."

Okay, so he was blunt, but it seemed as if Morgan was one of those people who didn't appreciate his bluntness. Which wasn't good since if he was going to do what Cal had asked of him and take care of her, he needed her to not view him as a serial killer at the very least.

Still, he was glad she'd let him know where her line was, because he hated game players. He also rather liked her tartness, like an almost-ripe peach.

He stuck his hands in the pockets of his jeans. "People bigger than me, huh? What did you do? Bite them on the ankles?" He wasn't sure what else she could do.

She didn't appear charmed by this response. "You're assuming I'm not carrying a weapon."

"I'm not assuming you're not carrying one. I'm assuming that you don't use it on people who aren't actually threatening you."

Her cheeks went pink and for some reason she looked very cross. "As it happens your very presence threatens me. Which means you have two choices. You can leave now and I won't arrest you for trespassing. Or you can stay and I'll shoot you with my Taser." Her little chin came up, confrontational as hell. "Well? What's it to be?"

―――――――――――――――

Zeke Montgomery was turning out to be the most stubborn-ass man Morgan had ever met, and as she lived in Deep River, a town noted for being full of stubborn-ass men, that was saying something.

He towered over her, solid and immovable as a rock wall, all black hair, unshaven black stubble, and the fathomless black eyes that she remembered from the bar back in Juneau, the night of Cal's funeral.

He had his hands in his pockets and he looked just as wild and uncivilized as he had a couple of months back. Perhaps even more so. He wore a worn-looking, long-sleeved black Henley, a pair of dark jeans with holes in the knees, a battered parka, and hiking boots, and he had the unkempt, rumpled air of a man who'd spent considerable time camping out in the bush.

She had no idea what he was doing on her porch, and to be honest, his appearance was a bit of a shock. But given how her brother's pal Silas had arrived in Deep River, and then his other pal Damon a couple of weeks after that, it had only been a matter of time before Zeke turned up.

Since he'd basically told her that night he'd failed to give her his number in the bar that anything she needed she only had to call, it made a weird kind of sense that when he had turned up, it was to stand on her porch like a large, rumpled black bear.

Her reaction to him, though, did not make sense.

The night in Juneau, when she'd first met him, she'd only been aware of a vague kind of…unsteadiness in his presence. But that she'd put down to grief.

Yet even though grief had lost its sharp edge now, she still felt unsteady and had no idea what to make that—or of how she'd blushed under his steady, dark stare.

She never blushed. She was a village public safety officer (VPSO), and she was the law in Deep River, and not only that, she was a West—the family that had once literally owned the town— and no one tended to tangle with her.

Which was just the way she liked it.

Men, though. They were far too much trouble.

Exhibit A standing on her porch, for example. Who'd inexplicably made her blush like a teenage girl and who also wasn't taking no for an answer. He also didn't appear to be leaving.

What had her stupid big brother been thinking? Why had Cal thought she needed "looking after"?

Ridiculous, not to mention ironic coming from the man who'd ceased being her protective big brother the moment he'd left Deep River for Juneau. Certainly, him getting all worried about her from beyond the grave was a little late in the piece.

Especially when she was a grown woman of twenty-six, who'd been taking care of herself for years already, not the thirteen-year-old girl she'd been when he'd taken off.

Zeke still hadn't said anything, midnight eyes giving her a thousand-yard stare. Another woman might have been intimidated by his massive height and his heavily muscled torso, not to mention the whole beard thing he had going on, but Morgan had never been that woman.

Plus, although Cal had left Deep River years ago, he'd kept in intermittent contact and had told her a little about his friends. Zeke, he'd said, was very stubborn, a man of few words, and didn't much like people. However, he was also protective, generous, and very honest. A good guy to have in a tight spot.

All well and good if you were in a tight spot, but she wasn't. She was home and what she wanted was to go inside, make herself some dinner and relax after a busy day, not make a tour of all the things wrong with the house purely to entertain Cal's annoying, taciturn, and erstwhile missing friend.

The missing friend who didn't seem to be all that bothered that his other friends, Silas Quinn and Damon Fitzgerald, had been getting worried about him, though they tried to pretend they weren't.

Morgan let out a silent breath while Zeke simply stood there. Silently. Like a granite statue of a man. Making curiosity tug lightly inside her about why he'd decided to turn up now, at least a couple of months after Cal's death, and what he'd been doing in the interim since Cal had left Deep River to him, Silas, and Damon.

The other two now lived here, Silas with his fiancée, Hope, who owned the Happy Moose bar, and Damon with his soon-to-be wife, Astrid, Deep River's mayor.

Morgan had been going to ask them if they wanted her to open a missing person's investigation, but it hadn't quite gotten to that point.

No need now, since he'd arrived here all by himself. A camp, he'd mentioned, which indicated he'd been living in the bush for...how long? And why? Why hadn't he let them know he was here? And why hadn't he gotten in contact with her earlier if Cal had supposedly told him to "look after her"?

Zeke's eyes glittered in the late-afternoon light and she thought he might say something about her threatening to shoot him with her Taser, at least.

But he didn't. He simply turned around without a word and

walked down the porch, disappearing around the corner of the house.

For a second, Morgan could only gape after him.

Perhaps it was a dream he'd been there. Perhaps the single beer she'd had at the Moose just before she'd headed home had been one too many. Then again, could you really say one beer was one too many? And more importantly, what in God's name was he doing?

The porch wrapped around the house and she went after him, peering around the corner. This side faced the river, and on summer days, if you sat on the chairs outside the living room windows, you could see the green water rushing by, glinting off rocks and sparkling in the sun. Her favorite view in the whole wide world.

It was that time of year now, the Deep River filling the afternoon with a liquid sound, the same soundtrack that had punctuated all the important moments in her life.

Along with the noise of the river came the spicy scent of the bush that surrounded the house, mixed with warm, dry earth and the green dampness of the river itself. The scent of home. It was a familiarity she never got tired of and never would.

Zeke had gone down the steps and out onto the lawn that lay between the house and the river and was now looking back up at the house. The sunlight threw his shadow against the stand of spruce and fir at his back, making him seem almost as tall as they were, a giant...

No, not a giant. A bear. A big black bear wandering into her home and sniffing around like he wanted to make it his den.

Pesky things, bears. There'd been a one hanging around the house lately, but her approach to the plentiful wildlife in Deep River was that if you left it alone, it would leave you alone.

Sadly, she didn't think that applied to stubborn-ass men.

She walked along the porch, then went down the stairs that led onto the lawn and came up beside him.

"What part of 'I'm going to arrest you for trespassing' or 'shoot you with my Taser' didn't you understand?" she said.

Zeke ignored her. "See there?" He pointed to the roof. "Definitely going to need some new shingles. Guttering, too, needs work." His pointing finger lowered. "And the second-story windows. Some of the frames are going to give you trouble come winter." Then he pointed at the pipes that ran down the side of the house. "And I'm thinking that the downpipes over there might need replacing too."

Morgan glared at him, annoyed at his continuing inability to listen. "You want me to get the zip ties?"

"You can try." Zeke didn't look at her. "Cal asked me to take care of you. And that means fixing up the house."

Ah. That explained things.

"Well, why didn't you just say?" she muttered, her irritation lessening somewhat, since she was very familiar with the male tendency to want to fix things to show they cared. That had been Cal's default too. Still, she didn't want this particular male hammering at her guttering right now.

"It's fine, Zeke," she said. "You don't have to—"

"I should take a look under the house, make sure the plumbing is okay. How's your wood supply?"

Morgan frowned. Persistent, wasn't he? "Are you listening to me?"

"About as much as you're listening to me."

She gritted her teeth. He still wasn't looking at her, his dark eyes narrowed as he kept on scanning the house like an engineer looking for structural faults.

Really, she wasn't sure why him offering to fix her house bugged her so. Because all the things he'd mentioned were things that she'd been going to fix herself, but hadn't gotten around to it due to the fallout from Cal's death.

Oil reserves had been discovered lying beneath the town, oil that now belonged not only to Cal's three friends who'd inherited the town from him, but to all the people who leased land in Deep River—a.k.a. the entire town. The leases were bought and sold for nominal amounts of money, since when Jacob West had founded the town over a century earlier, during the gold rush years, he'd intended Deep River to be a haven for those who weren't comfortable anywhere else.

A refuge and a sanctuary for those who needed it, even those who had no money.

Morgan believed very strongly in her ancestor's vision and so had Cal, and the oil discovery had been a shock. Especially since Cal had kept it a secret from her.

She wasn't sure why he hadn't told her, but whatever, the town deciding to take up Silas's suggestion of kickstarting tourism to replace oil dollars and getting some projects started had eaten up her time.

That and the usual duties of a VPSO—fire safety, search and rescue, first responder duties, plus all the paperwork—didn't allow for much rest and relaxation. She also involved herself in the day-to-day running of Deep River, so yeah, busy.

But still, she could be handy with a hammer. She was an independent person who much preferred taking care of others to being taken care of herself, especially by persistent men with painted-on ears.

"Zeke," she said, striving to keep a grip on her patience. "If I need help with the place, I'll be sure to let you know. But right now—"

Zeke walked off abruptly yet again, going back to the porch and climbing the stairs.

What. The. Hell?

"Hey," she called, going after him and hurrying up the steps and onto the porch. "Where are you going?"

He vanished around the corner again and so she followed, catching up as he strode to her front door.

"Hey!" she repeated. "Zeke, you can't just—"

Zeke pulled open the front door and stepped inside as if he owned the place.

The bear is in your house now, Goldilocks.

Ignoring that aggravating thought and trying to hold on to her thinning patience, Morgan went after him.

He stood in the entranceway, giving everything another of those slow, careful scans. The space was high ceilinged, with big wooden beams crisscrossing overhead, and it had always felt echoing to Morgan, especially when she'd been a kid. Like a church, her mother, who'd never liked the house, used to mutter darkly. But with Zeke's massive form standing there filling the space, it felt... small almost.

He glanced up at the big chandelier a West ancestor had made out of deer antlers that her mother had always wanted to get rid of but her father had insisted needed to stay.

"Light fitting could use replacing." His voice was very deep and rumbling, a bit like the river when it flooded. Or an avalanche. "I bet the electrical work in this place could do with a look over."

Morgan put her cop face on. "Zeke Montgomery."

"What?" He didn't even spare her a glance. "If you're gonna arrest me, then get on with it."

But she'd gone off that idea. It wasn't worth the aggravation.

"I'm not sure I can be bothered." She eyed up his tall form. "Are you always this annoying?"

He frowned at something he'd obviously spotted on the ceiling. "Yes." Then he turned and walked calmly through the doorway to the left that led into the big living room.

Lord, give her strength. What was with this guy?

Morgan found herself following him yet again, this time into the living room. "You know that walking away from people without a word is rude, don't you?"

Zeke had gone down to where the fireplace was, looking at it and frowning yet again. "I didn't walk away without a word. I said yes." Crouching down in a surprisingly fluid movement for a man so large, he then leaned forward into the hearth to peer up the chimney.

There had been no sarcasm in his voice, or at least none that she could detect, so maybe he genuinely thought that his curt "yes" wasn't rude. Maybe he genuinely thought that turning and walking away before a conversation had ended was fine too.

Taciturn and stubborn, Cal had told her about Zeke. A man of few words.

She gave him a more appraising look, the tug of curiosity deepening.

The way he'd twisted himself revealed that it wasn't only his jeans that had holes in them. The faded black Henley he wore underneath his parka also had some holes, through which she could see bare, bronzed skin.

For some reason, the sight made heat rise in her cheeks.

She shoved it away, concentrating instead on the holes and not on the skin beneath it. Huh. Looked like he'd been living rough for quite some time, at least if the state of his clothes was anything to go by. Where had he been? And why?

Perhaps that was why he was also being such a stubborn, persistent ass. Perhaps he hadn't been around people in a while. Sometimes that happened to hunters and trappers who'd been in the bush too long. They simply forgot how to interact.

Morgan's annoyance, though intense while it lasted, never lingered, and it quickly faded now.

Out of the three of Cal's friends he'd owned the supply and transport service Wild Alaska Aviation with, she knew Silas the best since Silas had grown up here. Damon was a transplant from LA, whom she'd only gotten to know once he'd moved to Deep River weeks earlier, but Zeke had remained an enigma, no matter what Cal had told her about him.

She wasn't really a fan of enigmas, not when oil had been

discovered in her town and she had people to protect. The towns-folk had taken the oil news pretty well and had successfully managed to resist the lure of the oil company flashing money about in return for their leases and drilling rights, but it still paid to be vigilant.

Her family might not own the town anymore, yet she still had a duty to it.

Morgan chewed on her lip, examining Zeke's muscular form.

One of Cal's friends wasn't going to be a threat to the town. And hey, if he wanted to do a few odd jobs around the house, why not take advantage of the free labor? Especially when he seemed hellbent on doing them.

But he could give her a little something in return too. Information about himself for example.

Zeke shoved himself back from the fireplace and rose to his full height, dusting his hands off on his jeans. "Chimney's good."

"Well, thank God for that," Morgan said. "I might have a giant stranger with painted-on ears in my house, but at least the chimney's good."

He studied her from beneath ridiculously long, thick black lashes and didn't smile. "Yes, that's what I said."

Right, so in addition to being rude, he didn't have a sense of humor as well. Had he somehow lost it out in the bush? Or had he never had one at all?

The curiosity inside her deepened further, along with a weird echo of the unsteadiness she'd felt out on the porch. A small flutter, like a firefly flying around in a jar.

Strange. She had no idea where that had come from.

"Where have you been, Zeke?" she asked. "And why are you here now?"

He hooked his thumbs into the pockets of his jeans, a classic dude pose. "I told you. I'm here because Caleb asked me."

Morgan gave him her cop stare. "I'm afraid I'm going to need more than that."

Chapter 2

MORGAN HAD HER ARMS FOLDED AGAIN AND WAS GIVING HIM that very stern, no-nonsense glare. Which would have been effective if she hadn't looked as cute as an extremely irritated china shepherdess.

Not that she didn't have reason to be irritated. Walking away from her without a word was rude. Then again, he wasn't sure what he was supposed to say. *Goodbye* wasn't appropriate since he wasn't actually leaving and telling her to follow him seemed redundant. Anyway, he'd thought he'd answered her questions.

Still, getting her riled wasn't a great idea. He didn't want to cause an issue. But he didn't want her to stop him doing what he'd been asked to do either, which was to look out for her.

You might have to make more of an effort with her.

Zeke didn't like that thought. People could take him as he came or not at all, an attitude that had worked out pretty well for him so far. He had a great job that he loved, that consisted of guiding hunters and hikers in the wilderness, a bit of search and rescue, climbing expeditions, as well as flying planes. Of course, he'd found himself dealing with more people than he would have liked, but since those people didn't care that he didn't talk much, didn't seem to need him to be polite, and certainly didn't give a shit about what he wore, it wasn't a problem.

Morgan, though, wasn't one of those people. And he didn't think she'd appreciate conversations about how to start a fire when the weather was wet, which type of mushrooms could be eaten safely, or what were the best types of bivouac construction.

He was going to have to think of some other things to say that wouldn't actively piss her off. Unfortunately, right now, he couldn't think of any.

"I don't know what you're talking about," he said at last. "I told you why I was here."

Her eyes really were the brightest blue, a noonday sky in the middle of summer. And they were full of summer lightning too, electricity snapping and crackling.

"Because Cal asked you to, right?" One delicately arched apricot brow arched even higher. "And do you always do what Cal asks you to?"

"No." He pleased himself mainly. "But you're his little sister and you were important to him."

Her mouth opened, then shut. An unreadable emotion flickered over her face and unexpectedly, she looked away.

A heavy feeling turned over in his gut. Okay, maybe he shouldn't have said that. Perhaps she hadn't liked him mentioning Cal. Still, they'd mentioned him before and she hadn't seemed bothered. And surely she couldn't be that surprised that she was important to Cal. Maybe she was still grieving...

Of course she's still grieving, asshole. He was her brother and it's only been a couple of months.

Zeke's gut clenched tight. He didn't want to hurt anyone, especially not someone he was supposed to protect, like Morgan.

"It was a last request," he said, hoping that more explanation might help. "In the form of a letter sent to me after the reading of Cal's will. And since I'm basically the reason he's dead, I couldn't ignore it."

She glanced back at him, her expression unreadable. "What do you mean you're the reason he's dead?"

"I was supposed to do the supply run that day, not him."

"Oh, right. Yes, Si told me about that at the funeral." Her brow creased. "But...you know that's not your fault, don't you?"

Zeke shrugged, not sure what to say to that. Intellectually, yes. It was the feelings that were the issue. It was *always* the feelings that were the issue.

"Anyway, that's all very well for him, but what about me?" she went on. "Cal didn't ask me if I wanted to be looked after, because if he had, I would have said no. I can look after myself."

Again, Zeke wasn't sure what to say. His instinct was to walk away the way he had done before, take himself out of the situation before he made it worse. But that wouldn't help Morgan.

"That's between you and him," he said at last. "I just know I got a letter from him wanting me to be a brother to you now he's gone."

"A brother," Morgan repeated blankly.

"That's right." Zeke frowned. Was that shock on her face? And if so, why? He and Cal hadn't had any heart-to-heart chats that weren't about planes, the bush, or Zeke's guiding schedule, so he wasn't sure what kind of relationship Cal had had with his sister. Perhaps it had been a fraught one?

Not that he could do anything about it, since relationships fraught or otherwise were hardly his specialty. Especially family relationships, not when his own had been so difficult.

His mother had required him to be pleasant and biddable and friendly, so she could show him off to her country club friends, while his father had wanted a businessman, who could charm and manipulate like he did.

Zeke had never been those things. He could never be those things. He wasn't pleasant and he wasn't biddable or friendly. He couldn't charm and he hated manipulation in all forms. He'd been nothing but a disappointment all 'round, but hell, that was his parents' fault, not his.

They'd wanted him to be something he wasn't and that was their problem.

Whatever—the relationship Morgan had with Cal wasn't his business anyway. He was here to look after her. The end.

Morgan blinked. Rapidly. "I see," she murmured.

Zeke glanced around the room again, hoping she'd drop the subject.

Acknowledgments

To my agent, Helen Breitwieser, and my editor, Deb Werksman, for all their time and effort with this book. And to the amazing Sourcebooks cover artists for making Deep River look so beautiful. And lastly, to my family for putting up with me while I was editing!

About the Author

Jackie has been writing fiction since she was eleven years old. Mild-mannered fantasy/SF/pseudo-literary writer by day, obsessive romance writer by night, she used to balance her writing with the more serious job of librarianship until a chance meeting with another romance writer prompted her to throw off the shackles of her day job and devote herself to the true love of her heart—writing romance. She particularly likes to write deeply emotional stories with alpha heroes who've just got the world to their liking only to have it blown wide apart by their kick-ass heroines.

She lives in Auckland, New Zealand, with her husband, the inimitable Dr. Jax, two kids, one cat, and one dog.

You can find Jackie at jackieashenden.com or follow her on Instagram @jackie_ashenden.

WARM NIGHTS IN MAGNOLIA BAY

Welcome to Magnolia Bay, a heartwarming new series
with Southern flair from author Babette de Jongh

Abby Curtis lands on Aunt Reva's doorstep at Bayside Barn with nowhere
to go but up. Learning animal communication from her aunt while taking
care of the motley assortment of rescue animals on the farm is an important part of Abby's healing process. She is eager to begin a new life on her
own, but she isn't prepared for the magnetism between her and her wildly
handsome and distracting new neighbor…

For more info about Sourcebooks's
books and authors, visit:
sourcebooks.com

WELCOME BACK TO RAMBLING, TEXAS

From acclaimed author June Faver: The women of Rambling tackle small-town living in the heart of Texas Hill Country.

Reggie Lee Stafford is a hometown girl living in Rambling, the small Texas town where she was born. As a single mother, her world revolves around her young daughter and her beloved job at the local newspaper. But her peaceful life is turned upside down when Frank Bell—the bane of Reggie's teenage existence—returns to town to claim his vast inheritance.

"June Faver is a must-read author."
—*Harlequin Junkie*